A6

Kristy and her friends love babysitting and when her mum can't find a babysitter for Kristy's little brother one day, Kristy has a great idea. Why doesn't she set up a babysitting club? That way parents can make a single phone call and reach a team of babysitting experts. And if one babysitter is already busy another one can take the job. So together with her friends, Claudia, Mary Anne and Stacey, Kristy starts THE BABYSITTERS CLUB. And although things don't *always* go according to plan, they have a lot of fun on the way!

*Catch up with the very latest adventures
of the Babysitters Club in these great
new stories:*

And coming soon. . .

COLLECTION 8

Book 22
JESSI RAMSEY, PETSITTER

Book 23
DAWN ON THE COAST

Book 24
KRISTY AND THE
MOTHER'S DAY SURPRISE

Ann M. Martin

Scholastic Children's Books,
Commonwealth House, 1–19 New Oxford Street,
London, WC1A 1NU, UK
A division of Scholastic Ltd
London ~ New York ~ Toronto ~ Sydney ~ Auckland ~
Mexico City ~ New Delhi ~ Hong Kong

Jessi Ramsey, Petsitter
Dawn on the Coast
Kristy and the Mother's Day Surprise
First published in the US by Scholastic Inc., 1989
First published in the UK by Scholastic Ltd, 1991

First published in this edition by Scholastic Ltd, 1998

ISBN 0 590 11313 5

Typeset by M Rules
Printed by Cox & Wyman Ltd, Reading, Berks.

1 2 3 4 5 6 7 8 9 10

CONTENTS

JESSI RAMSEY, PETSITTER

This book is for my friends
Nicole, Anna, Rebecca,
Katie and Alison

1st
CHAPTER

"Meow, meow, meow. Purr, purr."

I leaned over the edge of my bed and peered down at the floor.

"Stroke me," said a small voice.

It wasn't a talking animal. It was my sister, Becca, pretending she was a cat.

I patted the top of her head and said, "Becca, I really have to do my homework."

"Then how come you're lying on your bed?" asked Becca, getting to her feet.

"Because this is a comfortable way to work."

"You're supposed to sit at your desk."

This is true. My parents believe that homework magically gets done better if you're sitting up, rather than if you're lying down.

I sighed. Then I changed the subject, which usually distracts Becca. "Why are you a cat tonight?" I asked her.

3

She shrugged. "I'm trying all the animals. It's fun to pretend."

The night before, Becca had been a dog, the night before that, a horse.

"Well, kitty, let me finish my work," I said.

"Meow," replied Becca, who dropped to her hands and knees and crawled into the hallway.

Becca is eight and has a great imagination. If she weren't so shy, she'd probably make a really terrific actress, but she has awful stage fright.

I do not have stage fright, which is lucky since I'm a ballet dancer and have to perform in front of audiences all the time.

I suppose I should stop and introduce myself. I am Jessi Ramsey, and I'm eleven and in sixth grade. "Jessi" is short for "Jessica." (And "Becca" is short for "Rebecca", as if you couldn't have guessed.) Becca and I live with our parents and our baby brother, Squirt. Squirt's real name is John Philip Ramsey, Junior. When he was born, he was so tiny that the nurses in the hospital started calling him Squirt. Now his nickname seems sort of funny. Well, it always has been funny, but it seems especially funny since Squirt, who has just learned to walk, is now the size of most other babies his age.

Anyway, as I said before, I'm a ballet dancer. I've been taking dance classes for years. My ballet school is in Stamford, which isn't too far from Stoneybrook, Connecticut, where my family and I live. We haven't lived here long, though. We moved to Connecticut from New Jersey just a few months ago when my dad was offered a job he couldn't turn down.

Oh, something else about my family – we're black. Actually, that's much more important than I'm making it sound. You know what? It wasn't so important when we were living in Oakley, New Jersey. Our old neighbourhood was mixed black and white, and so was my ballet school and my ordinary school. But believe it or not, we are one of the few black families in the whole of Stoneybrook. In fact, I'm the only black pupil in my whole grade. When we first moved here, some people weren't very nice to us. Some were even unkind. But things have settled down and are getting better. Becca and I are making friends. Actually, I have a lot more friends than Becca does. There are two reasons for this: one, I'm not shy; two, I belong to the Babysitters Club. (More about that later.)

My mother is wonderful and so is my father. We're a very close family. Mama, Daddy, Becca, Squirt and me. No pets. We've never had a pet, although Becca apparently wishes we had one. (Sometimes I do, too, for that matter.)

In case you're wondering what the

Babysitters Club is, let me tell you about it. It's very important to me because that's where I found most of my friends. The club is really a business, a sitting business. It was started by Kristy Thomas, who's the chairman. There are six of us in the club. We sit for kids in our neighbourhoods, and we get lots of jobs and have lots of fun.

My best friend in Stoneybrook is Mallory Pike. Mal and I have a lot of classes together at Stoneybrook Middle School. And Mal is the one who got me into the Babysitters Club. The girls needed another member and ended up taking both of us. We were just getting to be friends then – and now that we've been in the club together for a while, we're best friends. (I have another best friend in Oakley – my cousin Keisha.)

Anyway, the people in the club are Mallory, Kristy, me, plus Claudia Kishi, Mary Anne Spier and Dawn Schafer. Two people who are sort of part of the club but who don't come to our meetings are our associate members, Logan Bruno and Shannon Kilbourne. (I'll tell you more about them later.) It's funny that we six club members work so well together, because we are *so* different. We have different personalities, different tastes, different looks and different kinds of families.

Kristy Thomas, our chairman, is . . .

well, talk about not shy! Kristy is direct and outgoing. Sometimes she can be loud and bossy. But basically she's really nice. And she's always full of ideas. Kristy is thirteen and in eighth grade. (So are all the club members, except Mal and me.) She has long brown hair and is pretty, but doesn't pay much attention to her looks. I mean, she never bothers with make-up, and she always wears jeans, a sweater and trainers. Kristy's family is sort of interesting. Her parents are divorced, and for a long time, Kristy lived with just her mum, her two older brothers, Sam and Charlie (they're in high school), and her little brother, David Michael, who's seven now. But when her mum met this millionaire, Watson Brewer, and got remarried, things really changed for Kristy. For one thing, Watson moved Kristy's family into his mansion, which is on the other side of Stoneybrook. Kristy used to live next door to Mary Anne Spier and across the street from Claudia Kishi. Now she's in a new neighbourhood. For another thing, Kristy acquired a little stepsister and stepbrother – Watson's children from his first marriage. Karen is six and Andrew is four. Although it took Kristy some time to adjust to her new life, she adores Karen and Andrew. They're among her favourite babysitting charges. Kristy's family has two pets – an adorable puppy named

Shannon and a fat old cat named Boo-Boo.

The vice-chairman of the Babysitters Club is Claudia Kishi, and she is really cool. I think she's the coolest person I know. (I mean, except for film stars or people like that.) Claud is just amazing-looking. She's Japanese-American and has gorgeous, *long*, jet-black hair; dark, almond-shaped eyes; and a clear complexion. Really. She could be on TV as the "after" part of an advertisement for spot lotion. Claud loves art, Nancy Drew mysteries, and junk food, and she hates school. She's clever, but she's a terrible pupil. (Unfortunately, her older sister, Janine, is a genius, which makes Claudia's grades look even worse.) Claudia also loves fashion, and you should see her clothes. They are amazing, always outrageous. For instance, she'll wear a miniskirt, black tights, ankle socks, high-top trainers, a shirt she's painted or decorated herself and big earrings she's made. Her hair might be pulled into a ponytail and held in place with not one but six or seven puffy ponytail holders, a row of them cascading down her hair. I'm always fascinated by Claudia. Claud lives with Janine, her parents and her grandmother, Mimi. The Kishis don't have any pets.

Mary Anne Spier is the club secretary. She lives across the street from Claudia. And, until Kristy's family moved, she lived next door to the Thomases. Mary Anne

8

and Kristy are best friends, and have been pretty much for life. (Dawn is Mary Anne's other best friend.) I've always thought this was interesting, since Mary Anne and Kristy are not alike at all. Mary Anne is shy and quiet and, well, kind of romantic. (She's the only club member who has a steady boyfriend. And guess who he is – Logan Bruno, one of our associate members!) Mary Anne is also a good listener and a patient person. Her mum died years ago, so Mary Anne's father brought her up, and for a long time, he was strict with her. Really strict. I didn't know Mary Anne then, but I've heard that Mr Spier made all these rules, and there was practically nothing she was allowed to do. Lately, Mr Spier has relaxed, though. He won't let Mary Anne get her ears pierced, but at least she can go out with Logan sometimes, and she can choose her own clothes. Since she's been allowed to do that, she's started dressing *much* better – not as good as Claudia, but she cares about how she looks, unlike Kristy. Mary Anne's family is just her and her dad and her grey kitten, Tigger.

Dawn Schafer is the treasurer of the Babysitters Club. I like Dawn. She's great. Dawn is neither loud like Kristy nor shy like Mary Anne. She's an individual. She'd never go along with something just because other people were doing it. And she always sticks up for what she believes in. Dawn is basically a California girl. She moved to Connecticut about a year ago, but she still longs for warm weather and she loves health food. She even *looks* like a California girl with her white-blonde hair and her sparkling blue eyes. Although you'd never know it, Dawn has been through some tough times lately. When she moved here, she came with her mother and her younger brother, Jeff – her parents had just got divorced. Mrs Schafer wanted to live in Stoneybrook because she'd grown up here, but that put 1500 kilometres between Dawn's mother and Dawn's father. As if the divorce and the move weren't enough, Jeff finally decided he couldn't handle the East Coast and moved back to California, so now Dawn's family is cracked in two, like a broken plate. But Dawn seems to be handling things okay. Luckily, she has her best friend (Mary Anne), and she and her mother are *extremely* close. Just so you know, the Schafers live in a lovely old farm-house that has a secret passage (honest), and they don't have any pets.

Then there's Mallory. Mallory Pike and I are the club's two junior officers. All that means is that we're too young to babysit at night unless we're sitting for our own brothers and sisters. Speaking of brothers and sisters, Mal has *seven* of them. She comes from the biggest family I know.

Apart from that, and apart from the fact that Mal is white and I'm black, we're probably more alike than any two other club members. We both love to read books, especially horse stories, we both enjoy writing (but Mal enjoys it more than I do), we both wear glasses (mine are only for reading), and we both think our parents treat us like babies. However, there was a recent break-through in which we convinced our parents to let us get our ears pierced! After that, Mal was even allowed to have her hair cut decently, but I'm still working on that. Neither of us is sure what we want to be when we grow up. I *might* want to be a professional dancer and Mal *might* want to be an author or an author/illustrator, but we know we have time to decide these things. Right now, we're just happy being eleven-year-old babysitters.

Oh, one other similarity between Mal and me. Neither of us has a pet. I don't know if Mal wants one – she's never mentioned it – but I bet her brothers and sisters do. Just like Becca.

"Hiss, hiss."

Becca was in my doorway. She was lying on her stomach.

"Now what are you?" I asked.

"I'll give you a hint." Becca flicked her tongue out of her mouth.

"Ew, ew!" I cried. "You're a snake. Slither away from me!"

Giggling, Becca did as she was told.

I went back to my homework, but I couldn't concentrate. Not because of Becca, but because of next week. I was going to have next week off. Well, sort of. Ordinarily, my afternoons are busy. When school finishes, I go either to a ballet class or to my regular sitting job. My regular job is for Matt and Haley Braddock, two really great kids. But next week, my ballet school would be closed and the Braddocks were going on a holiday – even though the school term would not be over. So, except for school and meetings of the Babysitters Club, I would be free, free, free! What would I do with all those spare hours? I wondered. Easy. I could put in extra practice time, I could read. The possibilities were endless!

2nd
CHAPTER

"Hi! Hi, everyone! Sorry I'm late." I rushed breathlessly into the Wednesday meeting of the Babysitters Club.

"You're not late," said Kristy, our chairman. "You're just the last one here."

"As always," I added.

"Well, don't worry about it. But it *is* five-thirty and time to begin." Kristy sounded very businesslike.

Mallory patted the floor next to her, so I shoved aside some of Claudia's art materials and sat down. We always sit on the floor. And Dawn, Mary Anne and Claudia always sit on Claudia's bed. Guess where Kristy sits – in a director's chair, wearing a visor, as if she were the queen or something.

Club meetings are held in Claudia Kishi's room. This is because she's the only one of us who has a phone in her

13

bedroom, and her own personal, private phone number, which makes it easy for our clients to reach us.

Hmmm. . . I think I'd better stop right here, before I get ahead of myself. I'll tell you how the club got started and how it works; then the meeting won't sound so confusing.

The club began with Kristy, as I said before. She got the idea for it over a year ago. That was when she and her mum and brothers were still living across the street from Claudia, and her mother was just starting to go out with Watson Brewer. Usually, when Mrs Thomas wasn't going to be around, Kristy or Sam or Charlie would take care of David Michael. But one day when Mrs Thomas announced that she was going to need a sitter, neither Kristy nor either of her older brothers was free. So Mrs Thomas got on the phone and began calling around for another sitter. Kristy watched her mum make one call after another. And as she watched, that mind of hers was clicking away, thinking that Mrs Thomas could save a lot of time if she could make one call and reach several sitters at once. And that was when Kristy got the idea for the Babysitters Club!

She talked to Mary Anne and Claudia, Claudia talked to Stacey McGill, a new friend of hers, and the four of them formed the club. (I'll tell you more about Stacey in

14

a minute.) The girls decided that they'd meet three times a week in Claudia's room (because of the phone). They'd advertise their club in the local paper and around the neighbourhood, saying that four reliable sitters could be reached every Monday, Wednesday and Friday afternoon from five-thirty until six.

Well, Kristy's great idea worked! Straight away, the girls started getting jobs. People really liked them. In fact, the club was so successful that when Dawn moved to Stoneybrook and wanted to join, the girls needed her. And later, when Stacey McGill had to move back to New York City, they needed to replace her. (Stacey's move, by the way, was unfortunate, because in the short time that the McGills lived in Stoneybrook, she and Claudia became best friends. Now they really miss each other.) Anyway, Mal and I joined the club to help fill the hole left by Stacey, and Shannon Kilbourne and Logan Bruno were made associate members. That means that they don't come to meetings, but if a job is offered that the rest of us can't take, we call one of them to see if they're interested. They're our backups. Believe it or not, we do have to call them every now and then.

Each person in the club holds a special position or office. There are the associate members, Shannon and Logan, and there are the junior officers, Mal and me. The

15

other positions are more important. (I'm not putting the rest of us down or anything. This is just the truth.)

As chairman, Kristy is responsible for running the meetings, getting good ideas, and, well, just being in charge, I suppose. Considering that chairman is the most important office of all, Kristy doesn't do a lot of work. I mean, not compared to what the other girls do. But then, the club *was* her idea, so I think she deserves to be its chairman.

Claudia Kishi, our vice-chairman, doesn't really have a lot to do, either, but the rest of us invade her room three times a week and keep her line busy. Also, a lot of our clients forget when our meetings are held and call at other times with sitting jobs. Claud has to handle those calls. I think she deserves to be vice-chairman.

As secretary, Mary Anne Spier is probably the hardest-working officer. She's in charge of the record book , which is where we keep track of all club information: our clients' addresses and phone numbers, the money in the treasury (well, that's really Dawn's department), and most importantly, the appointment calendar. Poor Mary Anne has to keep track of everybody's schedules (my ballet lessons, Claud's art classes, dentist appointments, etc.) *and* all our babysitting jobs. When a call comes in, it's up to Mary Anne to see who's free. Mary Anne is neat and careful and hasn't made a mistake yet.

This is a miracle.

Dawn, our treasurer, is responsible for collecting subs from us every Monday, and for keeping enough money in the treasury so that we can pay Charlie, Kristy's oldest brother, to drive her to and from meetings, since she lives so far away now. The money is spent on other things, too, but we make sure we always have enough for Charlie. What else is the money spent on? Well, fun things, like food for club parties. Also new materials for Kid-Kits.

I suppose I haven't told you about Kid-Kits yet. They were one of Kristy's ideas. A Kid-Kit is a box (we each have one) that's been decorated and filled with our old toys and books and games, as well as a few new items such as crayons or sticker books. We bring them with us on some of our jobs and kids love them. The kits make us very popular babysitters! Anyway, every now and then we need treasury money to buy new crayons or something for the kits.

The last thing you need to know about is our club notebook. The notebook is like a diary. In it, each of us has to write up every single job she goes on. Then we're supposed to read it once a week to find out what's been going on. Even though most of us don't like writing in the notebook, I have to admit that it's helpful. When I read it, I find out what's happening with the kids our club sits for, and also about babysitting problems and how they were handled. (The club notebook was Kristy's idea, of course.)

"Order, order!" Kristy was saying.

I had just settled myself on the floor.

"Wait a sec," Claudia interrupted. "Doesn't anyone want something to eat?"

Remember I said Claudia likes junk food? Well, that may have been an understatement. Claudia *loves* junk food. She loves it so much that her parents have told her to stop eating so much of it. But Claud can't. She buys it anyway and then hides it in her room. At the moment, she's got a bag of Quavers under her bed, a packet of liquorice sticks in a drawer of her jewellery box, and a bag of M&M's in the pencil case in her notebook. She's very generous with it. She offers it around at the beginning of each meeting since we're starved by this time of day. And we eat it up. (Well, sometimes Dawn doesn't since she's so into health food, but she *will* eat crackers or pretzels.)

"Ahem," said Kristy.

"Oh, come on. You know you'll eat something if I get it out," Claudia told her. Claudia usually stands up to Kristy.

"All right." Kristy sounded as cross as a

bear, but this didn't prevent her from eating a handful of M&M's.

When the sweets had been passed around, Kristy said, "*Now* are we ready?"

(She really can be bossy.)

"Ready, Miss Thomas," Claudia replied in a high, squeaky voice.

Everyone laughed, even Kristy.

We talked about some club business, and then the phone began to ring. The first call was from Mrs Newton. She's the mother of Jamie and Lucy, two of the club's favourite sitting charges. Mary Anne gave Dawn the job. Then the phone rang twice more. Jobs for Mal and Mary Anne. I was sort of relieved that so far, none of the jobs had been for next week. I was still looking forward to my week off.

Ring, ring.

Another call.

Claudia answered the phone. She listened for a moment and then began to look confused. "Mrs Mancusi?" she said.

Kristy glanced up from the notebook, which she'd been reading. "Mrs Mancusi?" she whispered to the rest of us. "She doesn't have any kids."

We listened to Claud's end of the conversation, but all she would say were things like, "Mm-hmm," and "Oh, I see," and "Yes, that's too bad." Then, after a long pause, she said, "Well, this is sort of unusual, but let me talk to the other girls and see what they say. Someone will call you back in about five minutes. . . Yes. . . Okay. . . Okay, 'bye."

Claudia hung up the phone and looked up from some notes she'd been making. She found the rest of us staring at her.

"Well?" said Kristy.

"Well, the Mancusis need a petsitter," Claudia began.

"A *petsitter?*" Kristy practically jumped down Claud's throat.

"Yeah, let me explain," Claud rushed on. "They're going on holiday next week. They've had this nice holiday planned for months now. And you know all those animals they have?"

"Their house is a zoo," Mary Anne spoke up.

"I know," Claud replied. "All I could hear in the background was barking and squawking and chirping."

"What's the point?" asked Kristy rudely.

"Hang on," said Claud. "Give me a minute. The *point* is that the Mancusis had a petsitter all lined up and he just called and cancelled."

"That is *so* irresponsible," commented Mallory.

"I know," agreed Claud. "Now the Mancusis can't take their holiday, not unless they have a petsitter."

"Oh, but Claudia," wailed Kristy, "how

20

could you even *think* about another pet-sitting job?"

"Another one?" I asked.

"Yeah," said Kristy. "The very first job I got when we started the club – my first job offer at our first official meeting – was for two Saint Bernard dogs, and it was a disaster."

I couldn't help giggling. "It was?" I said. "What happened?"

"Oh, you name it. The dogs, Pinky and Buffy, were sweet, but they were big and boisterous and they liked making mischief. What an afternoon that was! Anyway, I swore we would never petsit again."

"But Kristy," protested Claudia, "if the Mancusis can't find a petsitter, they'll have to cancel their dream holiday."

Kristy sighed. "All right. Suppose one of us was crazy enough to *want* to petsit – don't the Mancusis need someone every day?"

"Yes, for a few hours every day next week, plus the weekend before and the weekend after. They're leaving this Saturday and returning on Sunday, a week later."

"Well, that kills it," said Kristy. "I don't want any of my sitters tied up for a week."

At that, I heard Dawn mutter something, that sounded like . . . well, it didn't sound nice. And I saw her poke Mary Anne, who mouthed "bossy" to her. Then

21

Mal whispered to me, "Who does Kristy think she is? The queen?"

All of which gave me the courage to say (nervously), "Um, you know how the Braddocks are going away?"

"Yes?" replied the other club members, turning towards me.

"Well . . . well, um, my ballet school is closed next week, too. Remember? So I'm available. For the whole week. I could take care of the Mancusis' pets. I mean, if they want me to." (So much for my week of freedom.)

"Perfect!" exclaimed Claud. "I'll call them right now."

"Not so fast!" interrupted Kristy. "I haven't given my permission yet."

"Your *permission*?" cried the rest of us.

Kristy must have realized she'd gone too far then. Her face turned bright red.

"Listen, just because *you* had a bad pet-sitting experience—" Dawn began.

"I know, I know. I'm sorry." Kristy turned towards me. "Go ahead," she said. "You may take the job."

"Thank you."

Claud called Mrs Mancusi back, as promised. As you can probably imagine, Mrs Mancusi was delighted to have a sitter. She asked to speak to me. After thanking me several times, she said, "When could you call in? My husband and I will have to show you how to care for the animals.

22

There are quite a lot of them, you know."

After some discussion, we decided on Friday evening, right after supper. It was the only time the Mancusis and I were all free. Since the Mancusis live near my house, I knew that would be okay with my parents.

I hung up the phone. "Gosh, the Mancusis are going to pay me really well."

"They had better," Kristy replied. "I don't think Claud told you exactly how many pets they have. There are three dogs, five cats, some birds and hamsters, two guinea pigs, a snake, lots of fish and a load of rabbits and tortoises."

I gulped. What had I got myself into?

3rd
CHAPTER

As soon as I saw Mr and Mrs Mancusi, I realized I knew them – and they knew me. They're always out walking their dogs, and I'm often out walking Squirt in his pushchair, or babysitting for some little kids. The Mancusis and I wave and smile at each other. Until I met them, I just didn't know their names, or that besides their dogs they owned a small zoo.

This is what I heard when I rang their doorbell: *Yip-yip*, *meow*, *mew*, *chirp*, *cheep*, *squawk*, *squeak*, *woof-woof-woof*.

By the way, I am a pretty good speller and every now and then my teacher gives me a list of really hard words to learn to spell and use in sentences. On the last list was the word *cacophony*. It means a jolting, nonharmonious mixture of sounds. Well, those animal voices at the Mancusis' were not jolting, but they *were* nonharmonious and they *were* a mixture.

The door opened. There was Mrs Mancusi's pleasant face. "Oh! It's *you*!" she exclaimed, just as I said, "Oh! The dog-walker!"

"Come on in." Smiling, Mrs Mancusi held the door open for me.

I stepped inside, and the cacophony grew louder.

"SHH! SHH!" said Mrs Mancusi urgently. "Sit. . . Sit, Cheryl."

A Great Dane sat down obediently. Soon the barking stopped. Then the birds quietened down.

Mrs Mancusi smiled at me. "So you're Jessi," she said. "I've seen you around a lot lately."

"We moved here a few months ago," I told her, not mentioning that, in general, the neighbours hadn't been too . . . talkative.

Mrs Mancusi nodded. "Is that your brother I see you with sometimes?" she asked. (A bird swooped into the room and landed on her shoulder while a white kitten tottered to her ankles and began twining himself around them.)

"Yes," I answered. "That's Squirt. Well, his real name is John Philip Ramsey, Junior. I have a sister, too. Becca. She's eight. But," I added, "we don't have any pets."

Mrs Mancusi looked fondly at her animals. "I suppose that makes us even," she said. "My husband and I don't have any children, but we have plenty of pets. Well, I should start—"

At that moment, Mr Mancusi strode into the front hall. After more introductions, his wife said, "I was just about to let Jessi meet the animals."

Mr Mancusi nodded. "Let's start with the dogs. I suppose you've already seen Cheryl," he said, patting the Great Dane.

"Right," I replied. I pulled a pad of paper and a pencil out of my bag so that I could take notes.

But Mr Mancusi stopped me. "Don't bother," he said. "Everything is written down. We'll show you where in a minute. Just give the animals a chance to get to know you. In fact," he went on, "why don't you talk to each one? That would help them to feel more secure with you."

"Talk to them?" I repeated.

"Yes. Say anything you want. Let them hear the sound of your voice."

I felt a bit silly, but I patted the top of Cheryl's head (which is softer than it looks) and said, "Hi, Cheryl. I'm Jessi. I'm going to walk you and take care of you next week."

Cheryl looked at me with huge eyes – and yawned.

We all laughed. "I suppose I'm not very impressive," I said.

On the floor in the living room lay an apricot-coloured poodle.

"That's Pooh Bear," said Mrs Mancusi. "Believe it or not, she's harder to walk than Cheryl. Cheryl is big but obedient. Pooh Bear is small but devilish."

I knelt down and patted Pooh Bear's curly fur. "Nice girl," I said. (Pooh Bear stared at me.) "Nice girl. . . Um, I'm Jessi. We're going to take walks next week." Then I added in a whisper, "I hope you'll behave."

The Mancusis' third dog is a golden retriever named Jacques. Jacques was sleeping in the kitchen. He tiredly stuck his paw in my lap when I sat down next to him, but he barely opened his eyes.

"Now Jacques," began Mr Mancusi, "is only a year old. Still pretty much a puppy. He tries hard to behave, but if Pooh Bear acts up, he can't help following her lead."

"Right," I said. I tried to think of something creative to say to Jacques, but finally just told him I was looking forward to walking him.

"All right. Cats next," said Mrs Mancusi, picking up the kitten. "This little fluffball is Powder. He's just two and a half months old. But don't worry. He knows how to take care of himself. Also, his mother is here."

"Hi, Powder," I said, putting my face up to his soft fur.

Then Mrs Mancusi set Powder on the ground and we went on a cat-hunt, in search of the other four. Here's who we found: Crosby, an orange tiger cat who can fetch like a dog; Ling-Ling, a Siamese cat with a *very* loud voice; Tom, a patchy grey cat with a wicked temper; and Rosie, Powder's mother.

Next we went into the Mancusis' study, where there were several large bird cages holding parakeets, cockatoos and macaws.

"Awk?" said one bird as we entered the room. "Where's the beef? Where's the beef? Where's the beef?"

Mr Mancusi laughed. "That's Frank," he said. "He used to watch a lot of TV. I mean, before we got him." I must have looked astonished, because he went on, "It's natural for some birds to imitate what they hear. Frank can say other things, too, can't you, Frank?"

Frank blinked his eyes but remained silent.

"See, he isn't really trained," added Mr Mancusi. "He only talks when he feels like it."

Mrs Mancusi removed the bird that had landed on her shoulder earlier and placed him in one of the cages. "Often, we leave the cages open," she told me, "and let the birds fly around the house. I'd suggest it for next week, but most people don't feel comfortable trying to get the birds back in the cages, so maybe that's not such a good idea."

It certainly didn't sound like a good one to me.

I started to leave the study, but Mr Mancusi was looking at me, so I peered into the bird cages and spoke to Frank and his friends.

In the kitchen were a cage full of hamsters and a much bigger cage, almost a pen, that contained two guinea pigs, I looked in at the hamsters first.

"They're nocturnal," said Mrs Mancusi. "They're up all night and asleep all day. You should see them in the daytime. They sleep in a big pile in the middle of the cage."

I smiled. Then I looked at the guinea pigs. They were pretty interesting, too. They were big, bigger than the hamsters, and they were sniffing around their cage. Every so often one of them would let out a whistle.

"The guinea pigs are Lucy and Ricky. You know, from the *I Love Lucy* show," said Mr Mancusi. "They shouldn't be any trouble, and they *love* to be taken out of their cage for exercise."

"Okay," I said, thinking that Lucy and Ricky looked like fun.

We left the kitchen and walked towards a sun porch. The job, I decided, was going to be big but manageable. I could handle it.

Then I met the reptiles.

The aquarium full of terrapins wasn't

too bad. I don't love terrapins, but I don't mind them.

What was bad was Barney.

Barney is a snake. He's very small and he isn't poisonous, but he's still a snake. A wriggling, scaly, tongue-flicking snake.

Thank goodness the Mancusis didn't ask me to touch Barney or take him out of his cage. All they said was I'd have to feed him. Well, I could do that. Even if I did have to feed him the insects and earthworms that the Mancusis had a supply of. I'd just try to wear oven gloves. Or maybe I could stand ten feet away from his cage and throw the worms in.

"Nice Barney. Good Barney," I whispered when the Mancusis stopped and waited for me to talk to him. "You don't hurt me – and I'll stay away from you."

Next the Mancusis showed me their fish (about a million of them), and their rabbits (Fluffer-Nut, Cindy, Toto and Robert). And after *that*, they took me back to the kitchen, where they had pinned up lists of instructions for caring for each type of animal, plus everything I'd need to feed and exercise them – food dishes, food (several kinds), leads, etc. I would be going to their house twice a day. Early in the morning to walk the dogs and feed the dogs and cats, and after school to walk the dogs again and to feed all the animals.

When I said goodnight to the Mancusis

I felt slightly overwhelmed but confident. The job was a big one, but I'd met the animals, and I'd seen the lists of instructions. They were very clear. If the animals would just behave, everything would be fine . . . probably.

Saturday was my test. The Mancusis left late in the morning. By the middle of the afternoon, Cheryl, Pooh Bear and Jacques would be ready for a walk. After that, the entire zoo would need feeding. So at three o'clock I headed for the Mancusis' with the key to their front door. I let myself in (the cacophony began immediately), managed to put leads on the dogs, and took them for a nice, long walk. The walk went fine except for when Pooh Bear spotted a squirrel. For just a moment, the dogs were taking *me* on a walk instead of the other way around. But the squirrel disappeared, the dogs calmed down and we returned to the Mancusis' safely.

When the dogs' leads had been hung up, I played with the cats and guinea pigs. I let the rabbits out for a while. Then it was feeding time. Dog food in the dog dishes, cat food in the cat dishes, fish food in the tank, rabbit food in the hutch, guinea pig food in the guinea pig cage, bird food in the bird cages, terrapin food in the aquarium, hamster food in the hamster cage and finally it was time for . . . Barney.

I looked at his cage. There he was, sort

of twined around a rock. He wasn't moving, but his eyes were open. I think he was looking at me. I found a spatula in the kitchen, used it to slide the lid of Barney's cage back, and then, quick as a wink, I dropped his food inside and shoved the lid closed.

Barney never moved.

Well, that was easy, I thought as I made a final check on all the animals. A lot of them were eating. But the hamsters were sound asleep. They were all sleeping in a pile, just like Mrs Mancusi had said they would do, except for one very fat hamster. He lay curled in a corner by himself. What was wrong? Was he some sort of outcast? I decided not to worry, since the Mancusis hadn't said anything about him.

I found my door key and got ready to go. My first afternoon as a petsitter had been a success, I decided.

4th CHAPTER

Sunday

Oh, my lord waht a day. I babbysat for Jamie newton and he invinted Nina marshal over to play. That was fine but I thoght it would be fun for the kids to see all the amiak over at the ~~Mr. Mar~~ makusses or howover you spell it. So I took them over but Jamie was afriad of the ginny pigs so we took the kids and the dogs on a walk but we ran into Chewey and you now waht that means -- truoble.

Well, it was trouble, as Claudia said, but it wasn't too bad. I mean, I'm sure we've all been in worse trouble.

Anyway, on Sunday afternoon when I was about to head back to the Mancusis', Claudia was babysitting for Jamie Newton. Jamie is four, and one of the club's favourite clients. Kristy, Mary Anne and Claudia were sitting for him long before there even *was* a Babysitters Club. Now Jamie has an eight-month-old sister, Lucy, but Claud was only in charge of Jamie that day. His parents were going visiting, and they were taking Lucy with them.

When Claudia arrived at the Newtons', she found an overexcited Jamie. He was bouncing around, singing songs, making noises, and annoying everybody – which is not like Jamie.

"I don't know where he got all this energy," said Mrs Newton tiredly. "I hope you don't mind, but I told him he could invite Nina Marshall to play. Maybe that'll run off some of Jamie's energy. Anyway, Nina is on her way over."

"Oh, that's fine," said Claud, who has sat for Nina and her little sister Eleanor many times.

The Newtons left then, and Claudia took Jamie outside to wait for Nina.

"Miss Mary Mack, Mack, Mack," sang Jamie, jumping along the front walk in time to his song, "all dressed in black,

34

black, black, with silver buttons, buttons, buttons, all down her back, back, back. She jumped so high, high, high," (Jamie's jumping became even bouncier at that part) "she touched the sky, sky, sky, and didn't come back, back, back, till the Fourth of July, ly, ly!"

Lord, thought Claudia, I have hardly ever seen Jamie so wound up.

Unfortunately, Jamie didn't calm down much when Nina arrived. Claudia suggested a game of ball – and in record time, an argument broke out.

"If you miss the ball, you have to give up your turn," announced Jamie.

"Do not!" cried Nina indignantly.

"Do!"

"Do not!"

"Whoa!" said Claudia, taking the ball from Jamie. "I think that's enough ball. Let's find something else to do today."

"Miss Mary Mack, Mack, Mack—" began Jamie.

Claudia didn't want to listen to the song again. She racked her brain for some kind of diversion – and had an idea. "Hey, you two," she said excitedly, "how would you like to go to a place where you can see lots of animals?"

"The *zoo*?" exclaimed Nina.

"Almost," Claud replied. "Do you want to see some animals?"

"Yes!" cried Jamie and Nina.

"Okay," said Claud. "Nina, I'm just going to call your parents and tell them where we're going. Then we can be on our way."

Fifteen minutes later the Mancusis' doorbell was ringing. I had arrived to do the afternoon feeding and walking. As you can imagine, I was surprised. Who would be ringing their bell? Somebody who didn't know they were on holiday, I decided.

I peeped out the front windows before I went ahead and opened the door. And standing on the doorstep were Claud, Jamie Newton and Nina Marshall! I let them in right away.

"Hi, everyone!" I exclaimed.

"Hi," replied Claud. "I hope we're not bothering you."

"Nope. I just got here. I'm getting ready to walk the dogs."

"Oh," said Claudia. "Well, if it isn't too much trouble, could Jamie and Nina look at the animals? We're sort of on a field trip."

I giggled. "Of course. I'll show you around."

But I didn't have to do much showing at first. Pooh Bear was lolling on the floor in the front hall, and then Rosie wandered in, followed by Powder, who was batting his mother's tail.

Jamie and Nina began patting Pooh Bear and Rosie and trying to cuddle Powder.

When the animals' patience wore out, I took Jamie and Nina by the hand and walked them to the bird cages. Frank very obligingly called out, "Where's the beef? Where's the beef?" and then, "Two, two, two mints in one!"

"Hey," said Jamie, "I know a song you'd like, Frank." He sang Miss Mary Mack to him. "See?" he went on. "Miss Mary Mack, Mack, Mack. It's kind of like 'Two, two, two mints in one!'"

Next I showed the kids the rabbits and then the guinea pigs.

"We can take the guinea pigs out—" I started to say.

But Jamie let loose a shriek. "NO! NO! Don't take them out!"

"Hey," said Claud, wrapping Jamie in her arms, "don't worry. We won't take them out. What's wrong?"

"They're beasties!" Jamie cried. "They come from outer space. I saw them on TV."

"Oh Jamie," Claud said gently. "They aren't beasties. There's no such—"

"*Beasties*?" exclaimed Nina.

"Yes," said Jamie. "They're mean and awful. They bite people and then they take over the world."

"WAHHH!" wailed Nina. "I want to go home!"

I nudged Claudia. "Listen," I said, "I have to walk the dogs now anyway. Why don't you and Jamie and Nina come with me?"

"Good idea," agreed Claudia.

Jamie and Nina calmed down as they watched me put the leads on Pooh Bear, Jacques and Cheryl.

"Can Nina and I walk a dog?" asked Jamie.

"I'd really like to let you," I told him, "But the dogs are my responsibility. The Mancusis think *I'm* caring for them, so I'd better walk them. I'll bet you've never seen one person walk three dogs at the same time."

"No," agreed Jamie, as I locked the front door behind us. He and Nina watched, wide-eyed, as I took the leads in my right hand and the dogs practically pulled me to the pavement.

Claud laughed, I laughed, and Jamie and Nina shrieked with delight.

The beasties were forgotten.

"I'll walk you back to your neighbourhood," I told Claudia.

"You mean *Cheryl* will walk us back to our neighbourhood," said Claud with a grin.

Cheryl was trying hard to be obedient, but she's so big that even when she walked, Jamie and Nina had to run to keep up with her.

"Actually," I told Claudia, "Pooh Bear is the problem. She's the frisky one. And when she gets frisky, Jacques gets frisky."

"Well, so far so good," Claud replied.

And everything was still okay by the time we reached Claudia's house. Just a few more houses and Jamie would be home again.

That was when Chewbacca showed up.

Who is Chewbacca? He's the Perkinses' black Labrador retriever. The Perkinses are the family who moved into Kristy Thomas's old house, across the street from Claudia. We sit for them a lot, since they have three kids – Myriah, Gabbie and Laura. But guess what? It's harder to take care of Chewy by himself than to take care of all three girls together. Chewy isn't naughty; don't get me wrong. He's just mischievous. Like Cheryl, he's big and lovable, but he gets into things. You can almost hear him thinking, Let's see. *Now* what can I do? Chewy finds things, hides things, chases things. And when you walk with him, you never know what might catch his eye – a falling leaf, a butterfly – and cause him to go on a doggie rampage.

"Uh-oh, Chewy's loose!" said Claudia.

"Go home, Chewy! Go on home!" I coaxed him. I pointed to the Perkinses' house (as if Chewy would know what that meant).

Jamie added, "Shoo! Shoo!"

Chewy grinned at us and then pranced right up to the Mancusis' dogs. He just made himself part of the crowd, even though he wasn't on a lead.

"Well, now what?" I said as we walked along. Cheryl and Jacques and Pooh Bear didn't seem the least bit upset – but what would I do with Chewy when we got back to the Mancusis'? . . . And what would happen if Chewy saw something that set him off?

"Turn around," suggested Claudia. "Let's walk Chewy back to his house."

Jamie, Nina, Claudia, Pooh Bear, Jacques, Cheryl and I turned around and headed for the Perkinses'. But Chewy didn't come with us. He sat on the pavement and waited for us to come back to him.

"He is just too clever," remarked Jamie.

I rang the Perkinses' bell, hoping someone would get Chewy, but nobody answered.

"I suppose he'll just have to walk with us," I finally said.

We rejoined Chewy and set off. Chewy bunched up with the dogs again as if he'd been walking with them all his life.

"Oh, no! There's a squirrel!" Claudia cried softly. "Now what?"

Chewy looked at the squirrel. The squirrel looked at Chewy.

Pooh Bear looked at the squirrel. The squirrel looked at Pooh Bear. Then it ran up a tree.

Nothing.

The rest of the walk was like that. A leaf drifted to the ground in front of the dogs. "Uh-oh," said Nina. But nothing happened. A chipmunk darted across the pavement. We all held our breath, sure that Chewy or Pooh Bear or maybe Jacques was going to go off his (or her) rocker. But the dogs were incredibly well-behaved. It was as if they were trying to drive us crazy with their good behaviour.

We circled around Claudia's neighbourhood and finally reached the Perkinses' again. This time they were home and glad to see Chewy. We left him there, and then Claud took Jamie and Nina home, and I returned to the Mancusis' with the dogs. I played with the cats and guinea pigs and rabbits, and I fed the animals. In the hamster cage, the fat one was still curled in a separate corner. I wondered if I should be worried about him. When I stroked him with my finger, he didn't even wake up. I decided to keep my eye on him.

5th
CHAPTER

On Monday afternoon I raced to the Mancusis', gave the dogs a whirlwind walk, played with the animals, fed them and then raced to Claudia's for a club meeting. I just made it.

When I reached Claudia's room, Kristy was already in the director's chair, visor in place, the club notebook in her lap. But it was only 5.28. Two more minutes until the meeting would officially begin. Dawn hadn't arrived yet. (For once I wasn't the last to arrive!) Claudia was frantically trying to read the last two pages of *The Clue of the Velvet Mask*, a Nancy Drew mystery. Mary Anne was examining her hair for split ends, and Mallory was blowing a gigantic bubble with strawberry gum.

I joined Mal on the floor.

"Hi," I said.

Mal just waved, since she was concentrating on her bubble.

"Hi, Jessi," said Claudia and Mary Anne.

But Kristy was engrossed in the notebook and didn't say anything. When Dawn came in, she snapped to attention, though.

"Order, please!" she called. "Come to order."

Reluctantly, Claudia put her book down. "Just one *paragraph* to go," she said.

"Well, nothing ever happens in the last paragraph," remarked Mary Anne. "The author tells you which mystery Nancy's going to solve next."

"That's true."

"ORDER!" shouted Kristy.

Boy, was I glad I was already *in* order.

"Bother!" said Claud.

Kristy ignored her. "Ahem," she said. "Dawn, how's the treasury?"

"It'll be great after I collect subs," replied Dawn.

Groan, groan, groan. Every Monday Dawn collects subs, and every Monday we groan about having to give her money. It's not as if it's any big surprise. But the same thing—

"Please pay attention!" barked Kristy.

My head snapped up. What was this? School?

I glanced at Mallory who mouthed, "Bosslady" to me and nodded towards Kristy. Then I had to try not to laugh.

43

"All right," Kristy went on, "has everyone been reading the notebook?"

"Yes," we chorused. We *always* keep up with it.

"Okay," said Kristy. "If you're really reading it—"

"We are!" Claud exploded. "Gosh, Kristy, what's wrong with you lately? You're bossier than ever."

For a moment Kristy softened. "Sorry," she said. "It's just that Charlie suddenly thinks he's the big shot of the world. Next year he'll be in college, you know. So he bosses Sam and David Michael and me around nonstop." Kristy paused. Then her face hardened into her "I am the chairman" look.

"But," she went on, "I *am* the chairman, which gives me the right to boss you club members around."

"Excuse me," said Claudia in an odd voice, and I wondered what was coming, "but as chairman just what else *do* you do – besides get ideas, which any of us could do."

"Oh, yeah?" said Kristy.

"Yeah."

"Well, what brilliant ideas have you had?"

"I believe," Mary Anne spoke up, "that Claudia was the one who designed the alphabet blocks that say The Babysitters Club. That's our logo and we use it on every leaflet we give out."

"Thank you, Mary Anne," said Claudia. "And I believe that Mary Anne worked out who sent her the bad-luck charm, which was the first step in solving that mystery a while ago."

"And Mallory— I began.

"Okay, okay, okay," said Kristy.

But the other girls weren't finished.

"I," said Dawn, "would like to know, Kristy, just what it is—"

Ring, ring.

We were so engrossed in what Dawn was saying that we didn't all dive for the phone as usual.

Ring, ring.

Finally Mary Anne answered it. She arranged a job for Mallory. Then the phone rang two more times. When *those* jobs had been arranged, we looked expectantly at Dawn. (Well, Kristy didn't. She was glaring at us – all of us.)

Dawn picked up right where she'd left off. "—just what it is you do besides boss us around and get great ideas."

"I run the meetings."

"Big deal," said Claudia.

"Well, what do *you* do, Miss Vice-chairman?" asked Kristy hotly.

"Besides donating my room and my phone to you three times a week," Claudia replied, "I have to take all those calls that come in when we're not meeting. And there are quite a few of them. You know that."

45

"And," spoke up Dawn, "*I* have to keep track of the money, collect subs every week – which isn't always easy – and be in charge of remembering to pay your brother, and of buying things for the Kid-Kits."

"*I*," said Mary Anne, "probably have the most complicated job of anybody." (No one disagreed with her.) "I have to arrange *every single* job any of us goes on. I have to keep track of our schedules, of our clients, their addresses, and how many kids are in their families. It is a huge job."

"And we do these jobs *in addition* to getting ideas," pointed out Dawn.

There was a moment of silence. Then Mary Anne said, "Okay. We have a problem. But I've got an idea. I suggest—"

"We do *not* have a problem," Kristy interrupted her. "Trust me, we don't. All you need to do is calm down and you'll see that things are actually under control." Kristy paused. When none of us said anything, she went on, "Okay, now I have a really important idea. Forget this other stuff. To make sure that each of you is reading the notebook once a week, I'm going to draw up a checklist. Every Monday, in order to show me you've been keeping up with the notebook, you'll initial a box on the chart."

"*What*!"exclaimed Claudia.

Dawn and Mary Anne gasped.

Mallory and I glanced at each other. We hadn't been saying much. We didn't want to get involved in a club fight. Since we're the newest and youngest members, we try to stay out of arguments. It's hard to know whose side to be on. We don't want to step on any toes. And the easiest way to do that is to keep our mouths shut.

But the other girls *wanted* us to take sides.

"Jessi, what do you think?" asked Claudia. "Mallory?"

I hesitated. "About the chart?" I finally said.

"Yes, about the chart."

"Well, um, I – I mean. . ." I looked at Mal.

"See," Mal began, "um, it – I. . ."

Claudia was thoroughly annoyed. "Forget it," she snapped.

"Kristy, there is absolutely no reason to make a checklist for us," said Dawn. "There's not even any reason to *ask* us if we've been reading the notebook. We always keep up with it. Each one of us. Don't we say yes every time you ask us about it?"

The argument was interrupted by several more job calls. But as soon as Mary Anne had made the arrangements, the club members went right back to their discussion.

"There's no need for the checklist," Dawn said again.

"Don't you trust us?" Mary Anne wanted to know.

Kristy sighed. "Of course I trust you. The checklist will just, well, prove to me that I can trust you. Then, I won't have to ask you about reading the notebook any more."

"But can't you *just trust us?*" said Mary Anne.

Kristy opened her mouth to answer the question, but Dawn spoke up instead.

"You know," she said, changing the subject, "personally, I am tired of having to collect subs on Mondays. Everyone groans and complains and makes me feel about *this* big." Dawn held her fingers a couple of inches apart.

"We don't mean to complain—" I started to tell Dawn.

But Claudia cut in with, "Well, *I'm* pretty tired of getting those job calls all the time. You know, some people don't even try to remember when our meetings are. Mrs Barrett hardly ever calls during meetings. She calls at nine o'clock on a Sunday night, or on a Tuesday afternoon, or – worst of all – at eight-thirty on a Saturday morning."

"And I," said Mary Anne, "am especially tired of arranging sitting jobs. I'm tired of keeping track of dentist appointments and ballet lessons—"

"Sorry," I apologized again. (I am really wonderful at apologizing.)

"Oh, it's not your fault, Jessi. Everyone has things that need organizing. In fact, that's the problem. I'm up to my ears in lessons and classes and dental visits. I've been doing this job for over a year now, and I'm just tired of it. That's all there is to it."

"What are you all saying?" Kristy asked her friends.

"That I don't like arranging," Mary Anne replied.

"And I don't like collecting subs," said Dawn.

"And I don't like all the phone calls," added Claudia.

I looked at Mal. Why didn't Kristy speak up? What did she not like about being chairman? Finally it occurred to me — nothing. There was nothing she didn't like because . . . because her job was pretty easy and fun. Conducting meetings, being in charge, getting ideas. Kristy had the easy job. (Mal and I did, too, but we had been *made* junior officers with hardly any club responsibilities. We hadn't had a say in the matter.)

I think we were all relieved when the meeting broke up. Well, I know Mal and I were, but it was hard to tell about the others. They left the meeting absolutely silently. Not a word was spoken.

Mal and I stood around on the pavement in front of the Kishis' until the other girls left. As soon as Mary Anne had disappeared into her house across the street, I said, "Whoa! Some meeting. What do you think, Mal?"

"I think," she replied, "that this is not a good sign. I also think that you and I might be asked to take sides soon."

"Probably," I agreed, "but it's going to be very important that we stay neutral. No taking sides at all."

6th CHAPTER

Tuesday

Oh, wow. I don't have words to describe what happened today. I could write down, awful, disgusting, horrible, shivery, blechh, but even those words don't say it all. I'd better just explain what happened. You see, I was baby-sitting for Myriah and Gabbie Perkins, and I decided to take them over to the Mancusis' to visit the animals. I knew Claudia had done that with Jamie and Nina, and I thought it was a good idea. (How did I know Claudia had done that? Because I read the notebook, Kristy, that's how.) So I walked the girls over to the Mancusis'....

Mary Anne just loves sitting for the Perkinses. Remember them? They're the owners of Chewy; they're the family who moved into Kristy's house after the Thomases left it for Watson's mansion. The three Perkins girls are Myriah, who's five-and-a-half, Gabbie Ann, who's two-and-a-half and Laura, the baby. Laura is so little that we usually don't take care of her, just Myriah and Gabbie. At the moment, Laura usually goes wherever her mother goes.

Myriah and Gabbie are fun and we sitters like them a lot. The girls enjoy adventures and trying new things, which was why Mary Anne thought they'd like the trip to the Mancusis'. And they did like it. The awful-disgusting-terrible-shivery-blechh thing had nothing to do with the girls. In fact, Mary Anne was the one who caused it. Myriah helped to solve it.

I'd better go back a little here. Okay, at about four o' clock on Tuesday afternoon I returned to the Mancusis' after walking the dogs, and found the phone ringing.

"Hello, Mancusi residence," I said breathlessly as I picked up the phone.

"Hi, Jessi, it's Mary Anne."

Mary Anne was calling to find out if she could bring Myriah and Gabbie over. I told her yes, of course, and about twenty minutes later they showed up.

"Oh boy! Aminals !" cried Gabbie. Her

blonde hair was tied in two bunches that bobbed up and down as she made a dash for the Mancusis' kitchen.

"All kinds!" added Myriah. Myriah's hair was pulled back into one long ponytail that reached halfway down her back. She followed her sister.

The girls began exploring the house. The cats and dogs weren't too interesting to them since they've got one of each at their house – Chewy, and their cat, R.C. But the other animals fascinated them.

I showed them Barney. I showed them Lucy and Ricky. I explained everything I could think of to them. We moved on.

"These are—"

"Easter bunnies!" supplied Gabbie, as we looked in at Fluffer-Nut, Robert, Toto and Cindy.

"You can hold them," I said. "The rabbits like to have a chance to get out of their hutch."

So Myriah held Toto, and Gabbie held Fluffer-Nut. For a few minutes, the girls giggled. I looked around for Mary Anne. When I didn't see her, I was relieved instead of worried. I didn't want to talk about Kristy or our club problems with her.

Soon the girls grew tired of the rabbits, so we put them back.

"Now these," I told Gabbie and Myriah, "are hamsters. Since they're sleeping, we

53

won't disturb them. But see how fat that hamster's face is?" I pointed to one on top of the pile of hamsters. It was not the fat hamster. He was still off by himself in that corner of the cage. He seemed to have made a sort of nest. No, I pointed to one of the other hamsters.

'He looks like he has the mumps!" said Myriah.

"He does, doesn't he? But his fat cheeks are really—"

"AUGHHH!"

The scream came from the direction of the sun porch.

"Mary Anne?" I called.

"AUGHHH!" was her reply.

I put the lid back on the hamster cage, took Myriah and Gabbie by their hands, and ran with them to the sun porch.

A truly horrible sight met our eyes. We saw Barney's cage and the lid to Barney's cage – but no Barney.

"Mary Anne, what on earth happened?" I cried.

"Barney's loose!" was her response. "The *snake is loose!*"

Mary Anne and I got the same idea at the same time. We jumped up on one of the big porch chairs, the way people do when they've just seen a mouse.

Myriah and Gabbie looked at us as if we were crazy.

"What are you *doing*?" exclaimed

Myriah. "Barney's just a little snake. He can't hurt you. Besides, he could probably slither right up on to that chair. You can't escape him that way."

"Oh, EW!" shrieked Mary Anne.

"How did Barney get loose?" I asked her

"Well, I'm not sure, but I think he just crawled out of his cage, or slithered out or whatever sn-snakes do. I – I mean, he did it after I forgot to put the lid back on his cage. I took it off so I could get a closer look at him, and then I heard someone saying, "Where's the beef? Where's the beef?" so I left to see who it was. And then I found the birds, and *then* I remembered Barney, and when I came back to replace the lid on his cage, he was gone, I am *so* sorry, Jessi."

"*Oh. . .*" I cried.

"Shouldn't we *find* Barney?" asked Myriah sensibly. "Before he gets too far away?"

"I suppose so." I couldn't believe I was going to have to search for a snake. I couldn't think of anything more stupid than searching for something you didn't want to find – or anything worse than searching for a flicking tongue and a long, scaly body.

But it had to be done, and done fast.

"Let's split up," I suggested. "Barney probably couldn't have got upstairs, so we don't need to search there. Mary Anne, you and Gabbie look in the back rooms on this floor. Myriah and I will look in the front rooms."

"Okay," agreed Mary Anne, and we set off.

The search was a nightmare. Well, it was for Mary Anne and me. For Myriah and Gabbie it was like playing hide-and-seek with an animal. The odd thing was, I was so afraid of Barney that I was *less* worried about *not* finding him and having to tell the Mancusis he was lost than I was that we *would* find him. I went looking gingerly under chairs and tables and couches, always terrified that I'd come face to face with Barney and his flicking tongue.

But after twenty minutes of searching, there was no sign of Barney. And we'd been through every room on the first floor.

"Uh-oh," I said, as the four of us met in the hallway. "Now what? How am I going to tell the Mancusis that Barney is missing?"

"Long distance. It's the next best thing to being there!" called Frank from his cage.

We began to laugh, but then I said, "This is serious. We have to find Barney."

"Yeah," said Mary Anne. "I am *so* sorry, Jessi. If – if you have to tell the Mancusis that . . . you know . . . I'll help you."

"Hey!" said Myriah suddenly. "I just thought of something. We're learning about animals in school, and Barney is a snake and snakes are reptiles and reptiles are cold-blooded. If I had cold blood, I'd want to warm up."

"Could Barney have got outside?" I said nervously. "Maybe he wanted sunshine. We might never find him outdoors, though."

"Well, let's look," said Mary Anne.

So we did. And we hadn't looked for long when Mary Anne let out another shriek.

"Where is he?" I cried, since I knew that was what her scream had meant.

"Here," she yelled. "On the back porch."

I ran around to the porch and there was Barney, peacefully sleeping in a patch of sunshine.

"You were right," I whispered to Myriah. "Thank you." Then I added, "How are we going to get him back in his cage, Mary Anne?"

Mary Anne looked thoughtful. "I have an idea," she said. "Do the Mancusis have a spare aquarium somewhere?"

I wasn't sure. We checked around and found one in the garage. It was empty but clean.

"Okay," said Mary Anne, "what we're going to do is put this aquarium over Barney. I'll – I'll do it, since I was the one who let him loose."

I didn't argue. The four of us returned to

the porch, and Mary Anne crept behind Barney, holding the overturned aquarium. She paused several feet from him. "I hope he doesn't wake up," she said.

I hoped he didn't, either!

Mary Anne tiptoed a few steps closer, then a few more steps closer. When she was about a foot away from him, she lowered the aquarium. Barney woke up – but not until the aquarium was in place.

"Now," said Mary Anne, "we slide a piece of really stiff cardboard under Barney. Then we carry him inside and dump him in his own cage. This is my spider-catching method. You see, I don't like spiders, and I also don't like to squish them, so when I find one in the house, I trap it under a cup or a glass and take it outside."

Well, Mary Anne's suggestion was a good one. I found a piece of cardboard in a pile of newspapers the Mancusis were going to throw away. Mary Anne carefully slid it under Barney, the two of us carried him inside, Myriah opened his cage for us – and we dumped him in. I think Barney was relieved to be at home again.

Believe me, *I* was relieved to have him home. But if I'd known what was going to happen at our club meeting the next day, I would have thought that a snake on the loose was nothing at all.

7th
CHAPTER

The Wednesday club meeting started off like most others, except that I actually arrived early! It was one of the first times ever. My work at the Mancusis' had gone quickly that day, and the dogs had behaved themselves, so I had reached Claudia's fifteen minutes before the meeting was to begin. I had even beaten Kristy.

"Hi, Claud!" I said when I entered her room.

"Hi, Jessi."

Claudia sounded sort of glum, but I didn't ask her about it. Her gloominess probably had something to do with the Kristy problem, and I wanted to stay out of that. So all I said was, "Nice shirt."

Claudia was wearing another of her great outfits. This one consisted of an oversized, short-sleeved cotton shirt with gigantic leaves printed all over it, green leggings – the same green as the leaves on her shirt – bright yellow ankle socks, her purple hightops, and in her hair a headband with a gigantic purple bow attached to one side.

Claud is so, so cool . . . especially compared to me. I was also wearing an oversized shirt – a white sweatshirt with ballet shoes on the front – but with it I was just wearing jeans and ordinary socks and trainers. And honestly, I would have to do something about my hair soon. It looks okay when it's pulled back, I suppose, but I want it to look special.

I sat down on the floor. Since no one else had arrived, I suppose I could have sat on the bed, but Mallory and I just don't feel comfortable doing that. We're the youngest and we belong on the floor. That's all.

I was about to ask Claud if she'd printed the leaves on her shirt herself, when Dawn burst into the room.

"Hi, you two!" she said cheerfully. She tossed her long hair over one shoulder.

"Hi," replied Claudia. "You're in a good mood."

"I'm thinking positive," Dawn informed us. "Maybe it'll help the meeting along . . . I mean, I *know* it will help the meeting. This meeting," she went on, "is going to be wonderful. There aren't going to be any prob. . ."

Dawn's voice trailed off as Kristy strode into club headquarters. Without so much as a word, she crossed the room to Claudia's notice board, pulled out a few drawing pins, and fixed a piece of paper right over a collection of photographs of Claudia and Stacey.

Kristy turned to us and smiled. "There!" she announced proudly, as if she had just achieved world peace.

"There what?" said Claudia darkly.

"There's the checklist. I made it last night. It took forev—"

"And you put it up over my *pictures*!" exclaimed Claudia. "Not on your life. Those are pictures of Stacey and me before she moved away." Claudia marched to the notice board and took the checklist down. She gave it back to Kristy. "Find another place for this, Miss Bossy."

"Gosh, I'm *sorry*, Claud," said Kristy. "I didn't know those pictures were so important to you."

"Well, they are."

Personally, I thought Claud was over-reacting a little. I suppose Kristy thought so, too. The next thing I knew, she was pinning the checklist up over the photos again.

Claudia yanked it off.

Kristy put it back up.

Claudia yanked it off again. This time, the checklist ripped. From one side hung a wrinkled strip.

Mallory and Mary Anne arrived just in

time to hear Kristy let out a shriek and
Claudia yell, "Leave this thing *off*! I don't
want it on my notice board. I don't care
how long it took you to make it!"

"Girls?" The gentle voice of Mimi,
Claudia's grandmother, floated up the
stairs. "Everything is okay?" (Mimi had a
stroke last summer and it affected her
speech. Sometimes her words get mixed up
or come out funny.)

"YES!" Claudia shouted back, and I
knew she didn't mean to sound cross. She
lowered her voice. "Everything's fine,
Mimi. Sorry about the yelling."

"That okay. No problem."

Claudia and Kristy were standing nose-
to-nose by Claud's desk. They were both
holding on to the checklist, and I could tell
that neither planned to give it up. Not
easily, anyway.

The rest of us were just gaping at them –
Mallory and Mary Anne from the doorway,
Dawn from the bed, and I from the floor.

"You," said Claudia to Kristy in a low
voice, "are not the boss of this club."

Kristy looked surprised. Even I felt a
little surprised. I don't think Kristy had
meant to be bossy. She was just overexcited
about her checklist.

But Kristy retorted, "I am the *chairman*
of this club."

"Then," said Claudia, "it's time for new
elections."

"*New* elections?" Kristy and Mallory and I squeaked.

"Yes," said a voice from the doorway. "New elections." It was Mary Anne.

Claudia and Kristy were so taken aback that they both let go of the checklist. It fell to the floor, forgotten.

Everyone turned to look at Mary Anne.

And then Mallory spoke up. Even though she's only a junior officer of the club, she's known for having a cool head in tough situations. So she took charge. "Everybody sit down," she said quietly. "In your usual seats. We have some things to straighten out. And we'd better calm down in case the phone rings."

As if Mal were psychic, the phone did ring then. We managed to arrange a job for the Barrett kids. By the time that was done, we had settled into our places. Kristy, in the director's chair, had even put her visor on.

"Okay," she began, "a motion has been made for . . . for. . ."

"New elections," supplied Claudia.

"All right, I'll consider the idea," said Kristy.

"No way," said Dawn, who, since the checklist, had barely said a word. "You can't just consider the idea. Elections are our right. I *demand* new elections."

"Me too," said Mary Anne.

"Me too," said Claudia.

Mallory and I exchanged a worried glance. We were certain to be asked our opinion soon. And we were still trying to remain neutral.

Sure enough, Kristy looked down at Mal and me. I cringed. I knew she wanted us on her side. If we were, then the club would be divided three against three.

"Mallory, Jessi, what do you think about the elections?" Kristy asked.

It would have been awfully nice to side with Kristy. Siding with the chairman is always nice. But I just couldn't. I didn't want to get involved in a club fight. I knew Mal didn't, either.

Since Mal wasn't speaking, I finally said, "What do we think about the elections?"

"Yes," said Kristy sharply.

"I. . . Well, I. . ." I shrugged. Then I looked helplessly at Mal.

"I— That's how . . . um. . ." was all Mallory managed to say.

"Do you want them?" Mary Anne asked us. "Not that your positions would change, but you'd be voting."

Mallory and I did some more stammering. I think both of us felt that elections were a good idea, but neither of us wanted to admit it. Furthermore, a new worry was already creeping into my worry-laden mind. *How* would Mal and I vote in an election? If we voted to keep Kristy chairman, all the other club members would hate us. If we voted Kristy out, Kristy would hate us, and whether she was the chairman or the secretary, the club was still hers because she had dreamed it up and started it.

"Jessi? Mallory?" said Kristy again. We didn't even bother to answer, and suddenly Kristy threw down the pencil she'd been holding and exclaimed, "Okay, okay; okay. We'll have an election." I suppose she could tell that no one was on her side. Jessi and I might not have been on the *other* side, but we weren't on hers, either.

"Good," said Claudia. "Well, we're ready."

"Not *now*!" cried Kristy as the phone rang.

We arranged three jobs, and then Kristy went on, "I don't want to waste one of our ordinary meetings on elections. Besides, people ring all the time during meetings."

"They ring plenty of other times, too," Claud couldn't resist saying.

"Whatever," said Kristy. "Anyway, I'm calling a special meeting for the elections. Saturday afternoon at four o'clock. *This* meeting is adjourned."

"Whew!" I said to Mallory when we were safely outside. "I don't like the sound of this."

"Me neither," agreed Mallory. "Not at all."

8th
CHAPTER

On Thursday, I had help at the Mancusis'.
Mallory came over so that we could discuss
the election problem, and Becca came over
so that she could play with the animals. The
night before, she'd been so excited about
the trip to the Mancusis' that she practically couldn't sleep. Nevertheless, she was a
big help that afternoon, and so was Mallory.

Becca and I reached the Mancusis'
about fifteen minutes before Mal did. I
wanted to walk the dogs before I began
feeding the animals, so we would have to
wait for Mal to arrive. I used the time to
introduce Becca to the animals.

"Come on," I said to her. "Come and
see the birds. You'll love them."

"Just a sec," replied Becca. She was lying
on the floor, playing with Ling-Ling and
Crosby, who were enjoying every second of
her attention.

66

When Becca finally got to her feet, I led her back to Frank. I was just about to say, "This is Frank. Listen to what he can do," when Frank said, "The quicker picker-upper! The quicker picker-upper!"

Becca began to giggle. "That's great! How did he learn to do that?"

"Watched too much TV, I suppose. Like some people I know," I teased my sister.

"Oh, Jessi," replied Becca, but she was smiling.

"Try saying, 'Where's the beef?'" I suggested.

"Me?"

I nodded.

"Okay." Becca stood directly in front of Frank and said clearly, "Where's the beef? Where's the beef?"

"Long distance," replied Frank.

Becca and I laughed so hard that we didn't hear Mallory ring the doorbell until she was leaning on it for the third time.

"Oh! That's Mal!" I cried. "I'll be right back, Becca."

I dashed to the door and let Mal in.

"What took you so long?" she asked cheerfully. (Mal is usually cheerful.) "I rang three times."

I explained about Frank, and then, of course, I had to show him to her. I led her back to Becca and the birds, and Becca promptly said, "Hi, Mallory. Listen to this.

Hey, Frank, where's the beef? Where's the beef?"

"The quicker picker-upper!" Frank answered.

When we had stopped laughing, I said, "Come on, you two. We've got to walk the dogs. Cheryl looks desperate."

I took the leads from the hooks and before I could even call the dogs, they came bounding into the kitchen.

"Okay, you three. Ready for a walk?" I asked. (Stupid question. They were *dying* for a walk.)

I snapped their leads on and they pulled me to the front door. "Come on!" I called to Becca and Mallory, who were still talking to Frank. "The dogs can't wait!"

Becca and Mallory clattered after me. As we ran through the doorway and down the steps, Mal asked, "Can we help you walk them? We could each take one lead."

"Thanks," I replied, "but I'd better do it myself. Besides, they're used to being walked together. You can hold on to them while I lock the door, though."

So Mallory took the leads from me while I locked the Mancusis' door. Then she handed them back, and we set off down the street – at a fast pace, thanks to Cheryl and her very long legs.

"Keep your eye on Pooh Bear," I told Becca and Mal. "She's the troublemaker."

"The little one?" exclaimed Becca.

"Yup," I said. "For instance, up ahead is . . . Oh, no, it's a cat! For a moment I thought it was just a squirrel, but a cat's worse. Pooh Bear might – OOF!"

Pooh Bear had spotted the cat, who was sunning itself at the end of the driveway. She jerked forward with a little bark, straining at the lead. Jacques spotted the cat next, and then Cheryl, although Cheryl doesn't care about cats. Anyway, the cat heard the barking, woke up, saw the dogs, and fled down the driveway.

"*Hold* it, you three!" I yelled to the dogs. Pooh Bear and Jacques were practically dragging me down the street. Cheryl, too. She always likes a good run.

"We'll help you, Jessi!" I heard my sister cry. A few moments later, she and Mallory grabbed me around the waist. They pulled back so hard that the dogs stopped short, and all of us – dogs, Mal, Becca and I – fell to the ground. When we humans began to laugh, the dogs started licking our faces.

It took several minutes to sort ourselves out and stop laughing, but finally we were on our feet and walking again. Things went smoothly after that.

"I never knew dog-walking was so hard," commented Becca.

"It's only hard when you're walking Pooh Bear, Jacques and Cheryl," I told her. "And when they're in the mood for cat-chasing."

We returned to the Mancusis' and I let

the dogs inside and hung their leads up. "Okay," I said, "feeding time."

"*Please* can I feed some of the animals?" begged Becca. "Even though it's your job? I'll be really good and careful."

"We-ell . . . okay," I said, relenting. "You have to follow instructions exactly, though, okay?"

"Yes, yes, yes! Okay!" Becca was so excited she began jumping up and down.

"All right. You can feed the guinea pigs, the rabbits and the cats. Let me show you what to do."

I gave Becca instructions, and then Mal came with me while I fed the other animals. I started with the dogs because they absolutely cannot wait, and they are gigantic pains when they're hungry.

"Well," said Mallory, as I spooned dog food into Cheryl's dish, "What do you think about the elections?"

I groaned. "Please. Do we have to talk about them?"

"I think we'd better."

"I know. You're right. I was just trying to . . . I don't know what. Oh well. Hey, Mal, you're not thinking of leaving, are you?" The idea had just occurred to me and it was an awful one, but if Mal and I refused to take sides, would we feel forced to leave the club?

"Thinking of leaving?" exclaimed Mal. "No way. No one's going to get rid of me *that* easily. . . But the meetings *are* pretty uncomfortable."

"I'd say so," I agreed.

"And how are we going to vote on Saturday?" wondered Mallory.

"Well, I suppose," I began slowly. "Let me think. Okay, there are four offices – chairman, vice-chairman, secretary, and treasurer. And you and I are going to remain junior officers, so it'll be the same four girls running for the same four offices."

"Right," agreed Mallory.

I finished feeding the dogs, rinsed off the spoon I'd used, changed the water in their bowls, and moved on to the bird cages.

"Yesterday I was thinking," I told Mallory, "that if we vote Kristy out of her office – if we make her secretary or some-thing – she'll be furious with us, which won't be good. I mean, I'll always think of the club as hers, whether she's chairman or not, because it was her idea and she started it. And I don't want her to be angry with us. On the other hand, if we vote for Kristy for chairman, all the other girls will be furious with us, and that won't be good, either. It almost doesn't matter how we vote for Mary Anne and Dawn and Claudia, but where Kristy is concerned, we lose either way."

"Wait a sec," Mal cut in. "Won't the voting be secret?"

"It should be, but even if it is, everyone

71

will work out who voted for whom. People always do."

"Oh, brother," said Mallory. "You're right. *And* I just thought of something even worse. If enough feelings are hurt by the voting, the club could *break up*. It really could. Then what?"

"I don't know," I said, heading for the hamster cage. "I hadn't even thought of that."

Mal and I peered in at the hamsters.

"Do they always sleep in a pile?" asked Mallory.

"Pretty much," I replied. "Except for that one. I pointed to the one in the corner. "He sleeps by himself, and you know, I think he's fatter than he was a few days ago. I'm getting worried about him."

"Well, at least he's eating," said Mal.

"Maybe he's got too fat to move," I joked, but I didn't try to smile at my joke. I was too worried. I was worried about the hamster, and worried about our special Saturday meeting.

Mal and Becca and I finished feeding the animals and changing their water. Becca played with the cats again and then it was time to leave.

"Goodbye, Cheryl! Goodbye, Ling-Ling!" Becca called. "'Bye, Barney! 'Bye, Fluffer-Nut! 'Bye, Frank!"

"Awk!" squawked Frank. "Tiny little tea leaves!"

9th CHAPTER

Thursday

I always look forward to sitting for Jackie Rodowsky, our walking disaster, even though he's more of a challenge than almost any other kid I can think of. Today was a challenge as usual, but it was a different kind of challenge. Jackie's having a tough time -- and I tried to help him with his problem. I'm not sure I did, though. In fact, I think I might have been bossing him around. I mean, I suppose I was bossing him. Have I always done that? Or is it just lately? Well, anyway, Jackie was nice about it.

73

Kristy *might* have been bossing Jackie around? I'll say she bossed him! The good thing is that I think she learned something from Jackie. Let me start back at the beginning of the afternoon, though, when Kristy first arrived at the Rodowskys'.

Ding-dong.

"Rowf! Rowf-rowf." Bo, the Rodowskys' dog, skidded to a halt at the door and waited for someone to come and open it so that he could see who was on the other side. A moment later, the door was opened by Jackie himself.

"Hi, Kristy," he said gloomily.

"Good afternoon, Eeyore," Kristy replied with a smile.

"Huh?" said Jackie.

"You look like Eeyore. You know, the sad donkey from *Winnie-the-Pooh*."

"Oh."

"What's wrong?"

"I'll tell you later. Come on in."

Kristy stepped inside. She took a good look at Jackie's sad face. He's got this shock of red hair and a faceful of freckles. When he grins, you can see that he's missing teeth (he's only seven), so he looks a little like Alfred E. Neuman from *Mad* magazine. You know, "What, me worry?" But not that day. Jackie wasn't smiling.

"My brothers are at their lessons," Jackie informed Kristy, "Dad's at work, and Mum's going to a meeting."

Kristy nodded. That often happens. Jackie doesn't take any lessons because he's too accident-prone. He's our walking disaster. When Jackie's around, things just seem to happen. Vases fall, dishes break, earrings disappear. Things happen to Jackie, too. *He* falls or breaks things or loses things. Which is why he doesn't take lessons anymore. He tried to, but there were too many accidents when he was around.

Mrs Rodowsky came downstairs then, and Kristy greeted her and listened to her instructions for the afternoon. Then Mrs Rodowsky kissed Jackie goodbye and left.

"So," said Kristy, "what's up, Jackie? You look like you have a big problem."

Jackie nodded. "Yeah, I do."

"Do you want to tell me about it? I don't know if I could help, but I might have a couple of suggestions."

"Well," Jackie answered, "I could tell you, I suppose. That won't hurt anything."

"Go on, then," said Kristy.

Jackie heaved a huge sigh.

"Wait, let's make ourselves comfortable." Kristy led Jackie into the games room and they settled themselves on the couch, Bo between them.

"Okay," said Kristy.

"All right. See, in my class," Jackie began, "our teacher said we were going to have elections." (Elections? thought Kristy.)

"There are all kinds of great things you can run for – blackboard washer, messenger, register-taker."

"Sounds like fun," said Kristy.

Jackie nodded. "That's what I thought. I wanted to run for the job of taking care of Snowball. He's our rabbit. That sounded like the most fun of all." Jackie stopped talking and stroked Bo behind his ears.

"But?" Kristy prompted him.

"But there's no way I'm going to win."

"How come?"

"'Cause I'm running against Adrienne Garvey. Adrienne is . . . is. . ." Jackie paused, thinking. "Well, she never rubs holes in her exercise book pages, and she never gets dirty, even in art class. And she always finishes her work on time. And she never forgets her lunch or trips or spills or *anything*!"

"Miss Perfect?" Kristy suggested.

"Yes," said Jackie vehemently. "And all the other kids will vote for her. I just know it. They don't like Adrienne much, but they know she'll do a good job. She'll never forget Snowball, and she'll keep his cage neat and all that."

"What about you?"

"Me?" replied Jackie. "You mean, what kind of job would I do?"

Kristy nodded.

"Just as good as Adrienne!" Jackie cried. "Honest. I take good care of Bo, don't I,

76

Bo?" (Bo whined happily.) "But, see, Bo's not mine. I mean, not just mine. He belongs to my brothers *and* me, so I don't take care of him every day. And Snowball wouldn't be mine, either. He belongs to the whole class. But if I got the job, he would *feel* like mine since I would be the only one taking care of him. And I know I could do a good job. I know it."

"Then prove it to the kids in your class," said Kristy. "Show them that you'll be as neat and as responsible as Adrienne. Maybe even neater."

"And responsibler?"

Kristy smiled. "That, too."

"But how am I going to show them that?" wondered Jackie.

"Well, let's think it over."

"I – I could be neat myself," said Jackie after a few moments, sitting up straighter.

"That's a good start."

"And I could try to keep my exercise book neat. And my desk neat."

"Even better."

Jackie paused, frowning.

"Do you think you can do those things?" asked Kristy.

"'Course I can!" To prove his point Jackie jumped to his feet. "Watch me neaten up," he cried, and then added, "I did this once before for a wedding. . . Okay, buttons first." Jackie's shirt was buttoned wrong, so that on top an extra button stuck up under his chin, and on the bottom one shirt-tail trailed an inch or two below the other.

Jackie unfastened the first button – and it came off in his hands.

"Uh-oh," he said, but his usual cheerfulness was returning. "Um, Kristy, if you could . . . whoops!" Another button came off.

"Here," said Kristy, "let me do that for you."

"No," said Jackie, "I have to learn to—"

Too late. Kristy was already unbuttoning and rebuttoning Jackie's shirt. "There you go," she said. "Now the next thing I think you should do is start a campaign – you know, slogans, speeches, that sort of thing."

"But *I*," Jackie replied, "think I should practise filling Bo's dish neatly. It's almost time to feed him anyway."

"Well," said Kristy reluctantly, "okay." She was thinking that she really wanted to help Jackie win the election for the job of Snowball-Feeder. But she was also thinking that Jackie plus a bag of dog food equals big trouble. However, if Jackie believed that feeding Bo would help him, then Kristy would go along with his idea.

"Where's Bo's food?" Kristy asked.

"It's – Oh, I just remembered. We used up a bag yesterday. We have to start a new one. Mum keeps them in the basement."

Kristy cringed. Jackie was going to carry a bag of dog food from the basement up to the games room and then up to the kitchen? "Be careful," she called after him.

Jackie disappeared into the basement. A moment later, Kristy heard his feet on the stairs. "I'm coming!" Jackie announced. "And I'm being careful!"

Jackie reached the games room safely.

He grinned at Kristy.

He headed up the stairs to the kitchen.

Halfway there, the bottom of the bag gave way. Dog biscuits cascaded down the stairs into the games room.

Jackie looked at Kristy in horror. Then he smacked his forehead with the heel of his hand. "I did it again!" he exclaimed. His face began to crumple.

"Oh, Jackie," said Kristy, eyeing the mess. "Don't cry. It wasn't your fault." She wanted to reach out and give him a hug, but a sea of dog biscuits lay between them.

Jackie stood miserably on the steps. "I *know* it wasn't my fault," he cried.

"It couldn't have been," agreed Kristy. "The glue on the bottom of the bag must have come undone."

"But that's just it!" Jackie replied. "Don't you see? It came undone while I was holding it. Not Mum. Not Dad. Not my brothers. Not the man at the grocery shop. Me. I'm bad luck. Maybe that's why the kids at school don't want me feeding Snowball."

"Then make the kids forget about your bad luck," suggested Kristy.

"How?"

"Campaigning. I'll help you with it as soon as we put this food into another bag."

"All right," said Jackie, but he didn't sound very enthusiastic.

Kristy found a rubbish bag and the two of them swept the dog food crumbs into it. When nothing was left on the stairs, Kristy got out the vacuum cleaner.

"Let me do that," said Jackie.

"No, *I'll* do it." Kristy wasn't about to let Jackie touch an appliance. "Okay," she said a few minutes later, as she switched the vacuum cleaner off, "let's plan your campaign."

Jackie found a pencil and a pad of paper. He and Kristy sat down on the couch again, but Jackie immediately got up.

"Forgot to feed Bo," he said. "See? I am responsible. I remember to take care of animals." He ran upstairs, fed Bo, and returned to the couch without a single accident.

"All right," said Kristy, "now what I think you should do—"

"Kristy?" Jackie interrupted. "Can I tell you something?"

"Of course."

"I like you, but you're an awfully bossy

babysitter. You buttoned my shirt when I wanted to do it myself, you wouldn't let me vacuum up the mess I made, and now you're going to plan my campaign for – Whoops!"

Jackie had dropped his pencil into a heating grate. He and Kristy had to scramble around in order to get it out. In the excitement, Jackie forgot about what he'd said to Kristy. But Kristy didn't. It was all she could think of later as she helped Jackie with his campaign – and tried very hard not to be too bossy.

Was she really such a bossy person?

10th CHAPTER

I was scared to go to the Friday meeting of the Babysitters Club.

Isn't that silly? I really was afraid, though, so while I was at the Mancusis' feeding the animals and worrying about the hamster, I phoned Mal.

"Hi," I said. "It's me."

"Hi, Jessi. Where are you?"

"At the Mancusis'. I'm almost finished, though. Um, I was wondering. Do you want me to call at your house so we can walk to the meeting together?"

"Are you scared too?"

Now this is what I love about Mallory. I suppose it's why we're best friends. We know each other inside out, and we're always honest with each other. Mal knew I was scared. And she admitted that she was scared. She could easily just have said, "Are you scared?" but she said, "Are you scared, *too*?" which is very important.

"Yeah, I am," I told her.

"Well, *please* call. I'd feel much better."

So of course I called. Mallory and I walked to Claudia's with our arms linked, as if we could fend off arguments and yelling and hurt feelings that way.

We had to unlink our arms at the Kishis' front door, though. It was the only way to get inside.

Mimi greeted us in the hallway.

"Who's here?" I asked her.

I must have looked scared because she answered, "All others. But do not worry, Jessi. I know problems will . . . will work out."

I nodded. "Thanks, Mimi."

Mal and I climbed the stairs as slowly and as miserably as if we were going to our own funerals. We walked down the hallway. I heard only silence. I threw a puzzled glance back to Mallory, who shrugged.

A few more seconds and I was standing in Claudia's doorway. Well, there was the reason for the silence. Everyone was present all right, but no one was talking – not to Kristy, not to each other.

Mary Anne was sitting stiffly on the end of Claudia's bed. She was gazing at the ceiling; her eyes looked full of tears.

Claudia, at the other end of the bed, was leafing silently through one of her sketchbooks.

Dawn was seated between Mary Anne and Claudia, and her long hair was falling across her face, almost as if she hoped to hide from everyone by not being able to see them.

And Kristy, well, Kristy looked like she always looks. She was poised in the director's chair, her visor in place, a pencil over one ear. I couldn't read the expression on her face, though.

Oops! I thought, as I paused in the doorway. If I stand here too long, Kristy will say, "What's wrong with you two? Are you going to stand there all day? Come on in so we can get started."

But Kristy didn't say a word. She just glanced at Mal and me and gave us a little smile. So we crept into Claudia's room and settled ourselves on the floor.

Kristy waited another minute until the digital clock on Claud's desk read 5:30. That minute was the longest one of my life. I was dying to whisper something to Mal like, "This room feels like a morgue," or, "Calm down, everybody. You're too cheerful. You're going to get out of control." But I couldn't. For one thing, in all that silence, everyone would have heard what I said. For another, I think the girls sort of *wanted* to feel bad, and I wasn't about to be responsible for cheering them up.

"Order," said Kristy as the numbers on the clock switched from 5:29 to 5:30.

Everyone already was in order.

"Well, um, is there any club business?" asked Kristy.

No one said a word. No one even moved.

Since it wasn't Monday, there were no subs to be collected, and Kristy didn't need to ask if we'd read the notebook. (Not that she'd bring it up. I had a feeling "notebook" was going to be a dirty word for a while.)

Kristy cleared her throat. "Well," she said in this falsely cheerful voice, "any snacks, Claud?"

Silently Claudia reached behind the pillows on her bed and pulled out a bag of crisps and a bag of popcorn. She passed the crisps to Dawn and the popcorn to Kristy. The bags circled the room in opposite directions. No one reached into the bags. No one took so much as a kernel of popcorn, not even Kristy, who had asked about food in the first place.

I suppose that had just been something for Kristy to say, that she wasn't really hungry. And that was when I realized that she – our chairman, our queen – was as uncomfortable as the rest of us were.

Ring, ring.

Thank heavens. A phone call. I had never been more relieved to hear that sound. Like robots, Dawn answered the phone and Mary Anne arranged a job for Claudia with the Marshall girls.

Ring, ring.

Another call came in. Then another and another.

At about 5:50, the phone stopped ringing, and Kristy, looking more uncomfortable than ever, said, "All right. I – I have a few things to say about the elections tomorrow."

"We're still going to have them, aren't we?" asked Claudia.

"Of course. But I wanted to work out a way to avoid ties in the voting. This is what I came up with. First of all, Jessi and Mallory, you'll be voting, as you know."

We nodded.

"There are two reasons for that," Kristy continued. "One, you're club members, so you *should* vote. Two, we need five people voting in order to prevent a lot of ties. I know that sounds confusing, but you'll see what I mean in a few minutes."

"Okay," Mal and I said at the same time.

"Next, the voting will be secret. I'll make up ballots with boxes by our names. All we'll have to do is write X's in the boxes. I don't think we can get much more secret than that."

Stony silence greeted Kristy. I frowned. Wasn't anyone else relieved to hear what she'd just said?

Kristy continued anyway. "The last thing," she said, "is that, you, Mary Anne, you, Claudia, you, Dawn and I – the four of

86

us – will be able to vote in the election for each office except the one we hold. In other words, I can vote in the elections for vice-chairman, secretary, and treasurer, but not chairman. The reason for this is that without me, for instance, five people will be choosing from among four people for chairman. A tie is possible, but not likely. I think we'll avoid a lot of revotes this way."

"Anything else?" asked Dawn from behind her hair.

"No, that about covers it."

"I'll say it does," snapped Claudia.

"What's that supposed to mean?" Kristy replied.

Yeah, I wondered. What *is* that supposed to mean?

"Can I answer?" spoke up Mary Anne. Her voice was wobbling ever so slightly.

"Be my guest," said Claudia.

Mary Anne drew in a deep breath, probably to control her voice. "Kristy," she began, "have you ever heard of a democracy?"

Sensing an argument, Kristy replied sarcastically. "Why, no. I never have. What is a democracy, Mary Anne?"

Mary Anne tried hard to ignore the tone of Kristy's voice. "In a democracy," she said, "everyone has a say—"

"Which is why we're holding elections," Kristy interrupted, "and why we're all voting in them."

"I don't believe it," Dawn muttered. "She did it again."

"Kristy, would you listen to Mary Anne, please?" said Claudia.

Kristy rolled her eyes. Then she turned her gaze on Mary Anne and waited.

"In a democracy," Mary Anne began again, "everyone has a say in running the country. This club should be a democracy, too, Kristy, and the members should have a say in running things. In other words, you should have consulted us about the voting – about the ballots and the way the elections will be run."

Kristy blushed. I really thought she was going to apologize, but Dawn cut her off.

"But *nooooo*," Dawn said sarcastically. "You just barge ahead and do whatever seems right to you. You, you, you. You never think of what other people might want or feel."

It is not a good idea to make absolute statements like that – you *never*, *no one* does, *everybody* does. I have learned this the hard way. If I say to my mother, "But Mama, *everyone* is wearing them," she'll reply, "Everyone? Your grandfather? Squirt?" You know, that sort of thing.

So naturally Kristy pounced on the "you never think" part of what Dawn had said. "I *never* think of other people? What about when Claudia broke her leg and wanted to leave the club. Didn't I help her through

88

that? I even helped her work out what was wrong. And what about—"

"But Kristy," said Mary Anne in a small voice, "so many times you just don't think. You just don't. . ." Mary Anne's wavery voice finally broke and she burst into tears.

Dawn jumped to her feet. "Oh, that is nice, Kristy. That is really nice. Now look what you did."

"Look what *I* did?! I didn't do that! Mary Anne cries all the time. She does it by herself."

Dawn didn't answer. She walked out of Claudia's room in a huff.

"Be back here at four o'clock tomorrow," Kristy shouted after her. She looked at the rest of us. "You, too," she added. "This meeting is adjourned."

Mary Anne didn't move from her place on the bed, and Claud edged toward her, looking sympathetic. Mallory and I waited for Kristy to leave. Then we left, too. We walked slowly down the stairs.

When we were outside, I said, "Well, was the meeting as bad as you thought it might be?"

"Yup," replied Mallory. "How about you?"

"Worse. It was worse. Do you have a good feeling about tomorrow?"

"Not really. Do you?"

"No. Well, 'bye, Mal."

"'Bye, Jessi."

11th CHAPTER

On Saturday morning I woke up with butterflies in my stomach. I felt just like I do on the morning of a dance recital. Nervous, nervous, nervous. What on earth would happen at the special meeting that afternoon? I lay in bed and worried.

It was funny. I'd only been living in Stoneybrook, Connecticut, for a few months, but the Babysitters Club had become extremely important to me. Maybe that was because it was the first place here, besides Mallory's house, where I'd felt completely accepted; where I'd felt it truly didn't matter that I'm black.

If the club were to break up – if the girls were to get so angry with each other that they decided not to continue it – what would happen? I knew I'd still have Mallory, and I knew I'd still be friendly with the other girls, but it wouldn't be the same. Not to mention that I *love* babysitting and I'd miss all the jobs I get through the club.

I heaved a deep sigh, trying to make the butterflies in my stomach calm down. I rolled over. At last I sat up. Maybe, I thought, if I stay in bed I can make time stop, and four o'clock will never arrive. Unfortunately, I'm too old to believe in things like that any more.

I got out of bed, put some clothes on, and went downstairs. But I didn't go into the kitchen for breakfast. Instead, I checked my watch, decided it wasn't too early for a phone call, and dialled Mallory's number.

I sprawled on the couch in the study.

"Hello?" said a small voice on the other end of the phone.

"Hi. . . Claire?" (The voice sounded like Mallory's five-year-old-sister.)

"Yeah. Is that Jessi?"

"Yup. How are you?"

"Fine. I lost a tooth! And guess what – after *I* lost it, the *Tooth Fairy* lost it."

"She did? How do you know?"

"'Cause I found some money under my pillow and I found the tooth on the floor. The Tooth Fairy must have dropped it after she left the money."

I managed not to laugh. "I suppose even the Tooth Fairy makes mistakes," I said to Claire. "Listen, can I talk to Mallory, please?"

"Of course," answered Claire. "Mallory-silly-billy-goo-goo! Phone for you!"

A few moments later, I heard Mallory's voice. "Hello?"

"Hi, it's me."

"Hi, Jessi. How long did you have to talk to Claire?"

"Just for a few minutes."

"That's good. She's in one of her silly moods, in case you couldn't tell."

I laughed. Then, "So," I said, "are you ready for this afternoon?"

"I hope so."

"What do you think is going to happen?"

"You know, I really don't have any idea."

"Do you know who you're going to vote for?" I asked.

"I've been trying not to think about it," Mal told me. "And I tried so hard that I really haven't thought about it, and now I don't know who to vote for."

"Oh. I just don't know who to vote for, full-stop."

Mal sighed.

I sighed.

"Well," I said finally, "I'd better get going. I have a lot to do before the meeting. The Mancusis come home tomorrow, so today I want to make sure everything is perfect at their house. I've got to walk the dogs and feed the animals as usual, but I also want to clean out some of the cages, change the litter in the cats' box, that sort of thing."

"Okay. Will you call for me again this afternoon? It'd be nice to walk to the meeting together," said Mallory.

"Of course," I replied. "I'll see you around a quarter to four."

We said goodbye and hung up, and then I wandered into the kitchen, where I found my mother and Squirt. "Morning," I said.

"Morning, honey."

"Where are Daddy and Becca?"

"Your father went into the office for the morning, and Becca's gone over to Charlotte's house."

I nodded. I sat down in front of Squirt's high chair and made faces at him. "Mama?" I said after a while.

My mother looked up from the recipe card she was reading. "Yes, darling? Aren't you going to eat breakfast this morning? Everyone else has eaten already."

"I'll eat," I replied, "but I have to ask you about something first."

Mama could tell it was important. She sat down next to me at the table. "What is it, darling?"

As best I could, I explained to her what was going on in the Babysitters Club. I told her everything – how Kristy can be bossy sometimes, that the other girls are upset, and what might happen at the elections that afternoon.

"Go-bler?" said Squirt from his high

chair. He was playing with a set of plastic keys and two red rings.

"Jessi," said Mama, "I think you want me to tell you how to vote, don't you?"

"Well, yes," I answered. "I mean, even just a hint or something."

"But I can't give you answers. You have to make up your own mind. I will give you one piece of advice, though."

"Okay."

"Vote for the person you honestly think is best suited for each office. Don't worry about anything else."

"All right. Thanks, Mama."

I ate my breakfast, feeling somewhat let down. My mother always has the answers. Why couldn't she tell me who to vote for? But I knew there was no point in asking her again. I would just have to work things out for myself, and I would have plenty of time to think while I worked at the Mancusis'.

The first thing I did was walk Pooh Bear, Cheryl and Jacques. It was late morning and the dogs were frantic to get outside. I snapped their leads on and led them to the front door. As soon as it was opened a crack, Pooh Bear pushed her way through. The dogs tried to bound across the front lawn while I was still trying to lock the Mancusis' door.

"Hold on!" I yelled.

I locked the door, and the dogs pulled

me to the street. We took a wild walk, racing past people, bicycles and letter boxes. At last the dogs slowed down, and I relaxed a little.

I decided to think about the elections. I would consider one office at a time, starting with treasurer. Dawn, I thought, made a good treasurer. She always collected our subs, she always remembered to pay Charlie, she always let us know when the treasury was getting low. But if she didn't like the job, then . . . well, Claudia certainly couldn't be treasurer. She's terrible at maths. Mary Anne's okay at it, but she was so good as secretary. That left Kristy. Somehow, I just couldn't see her as treasurer of the Babysitters Club.

This isn't getting me anywhere, I thought as I walked the dogs back to the Mancusis'.

I decided to try a different office. Vice-chairman. Claudia really was the perfect vice-chairman, what with her own phone and her own phone number. But, okay, she was tired of the job. So let's see. Kristy could be our vice-chairman, but how was she going to answer all the calls that come in at non-meeting times? She couldn't. Not unless we moved club headquarters to her house. Maybe she could ask her mother and stepfather for her own phone . . . that sounded like an awful lot of trouble to go to, just to switch offices in the club.

I couldn't solve that problem, so I put

the election dilemma aside while I saw to the animals. I let the dogs back in the house and fed them. Then I changed their water. They ate quickly (and messily) and ran off. I cleaned up their area of the kitchen.

Then I moved on to the cats. Since they were in the living room, sleeping, I cleaned up their dishes and placemats first. I set their food out, I cleaned their litter box, found the Mancusis' vacuum-cleaner, and vacuumed up the stray kitty litter that was strewn across the floor.

I worked very hard. I took care of the birds and the bird cage, the rabbits and their hutch, and the fish and aquarium.

Time for the hamsters. I leaned over and peered into their cage. The fat one in the corner suddenly woke up and looked back at me with bright eyes.

"Why are you all alone?" I asked him. I stuck my finger in the cage to stroke the hamster, but he lunged for me. I pulled my hand back just in time. "Whoa! What's wrong with you?" I exclaimed. I paused. I realized what I had just said, "What's wrong with you?" A cold feeling washed over me. Something was wrong with the hamster. Maybe he had broken a bone. Maybe that's why he didn't want to be with the others and why he was bad-tempered.

Whatever was wrong had been wrong

all week. It had been wrong since the Mancusis left, maybe even before that. The Mancusis hadn't noticed for some reason, but I had. I'd noticed straight away. Why hadn't I done anything about it? What would the Mancusis think if they came back and I pointed out the hamster, saying he'd been sick or hurt all week, and then admitted that I hadn't done anything for him? That certainly wasn't very responsible. If I were babysitting and one of the kids got sick or broke a bone, I'd call his parents or his doctor or an ambulance. Well, I certainly wasn't going to call the Mancusis long distance about a maybe-sick hamster . . . but I could take the hamster to the vet.

I grabbed the phone and dialled my number.

My mother answered.

"Mama!" I cried. "One of the hamsters is very sick. He sleeps in the corner by himself, and he's getting fatter and fatter, and just now he almost bit me. I think he might have a broken bone. Anyway, I noticed something was wrong last weekend and I don't know why I didn't do anything, but I didn't, and—"

"Jessi, darling, slow down," Mama broke in. "What do you want to do?"

"Take the hamster to the vet. Can you drive me?"

"Of course. Bring the address of the vet

97

with you. And give me a few minutes to get Squirt ready. Your father's still at work. Oh, and please be careful with the hamster, especially since he's biting."

"Okay," I replied, calming down a little. "Thanks, Mama. You know which house is the Mancusis', don't you?"

Mama said she did, so we got off the phone. I was just about to work out how we were going to take the hamster to the vet, when something occurred to me. I looked at my watch. Two-thirty. The special meeting of the Babysitters Club was supposed to start in an hour and a half.

I would never make it.

12th CHAPTER

I couldn't worry about the meeting, not just then, anyway. I had to get the hamster ready for the trip to the vet. What could I carry him in? I ran into the Mancusis' garage and found a pile of cardboard boxes. Among them was a shoe box. Perfect, I thought.

I filled the shoe box with shavings and carried it inside. Then I had to work out how to get the hamster into the shoe box. I didn't want to touch him in case he was hurting. Finally, I cleaned out an empty dog-food can, made sure there were no rough edges, placed some treats in it, put it in the hamster cage right next to the fat hamster – and he crawled in! Then I moved the can into the box. We were all set.

The hamster crawled back out of the can and quickly settled down in the box. He didn't try to get out. Even so, I punched some holes in the lid of the box, planning to bring it with me. You never know what might happen, so it's always best to be prepared.

Beep, beep.

That must be Mama, I thought.

I grabbed the box and my jacket and went outside, being careful not to jostle the box. The Mancusis' front door key was in my pocket. I remembered to lock their front door.

"Thanks, Mama!" I cried, as I slid into the front seat of her car.

Behind me, Squirt was strapped into his car seat. He was babbling away.

"Let's see this little fellow," said Mama.

I removed the lid and held out the box.

"He seems quiet," commented Mama, "but—"

"He's been just like this all week," I interrupted her.

"Okay, then. We'd better be on our way. Where's the Mancusis' vet?"

I gave her the address. Then I sat back. I felt relieved just to be doing something.

"Broo-broo-broo-broo," sang Squirt as we drove along.

We pulled into the vet's car park, and I put the lid back on the box. No telling what we would find when we got inside. Well, it was a good thing I did. The waiting room was a madhouse. Mama stepped out of the car carrying Squirt and a few of his toys, and I stepped out with the hamster in the box. When I opened the door to the vet's office I was surprised. I'd never been to a vet because we've never had a pet, so I don't know what I thought the waiting room would be like, but. . .

For a start, it was noisy. Most of the people were sitting there with dogs or cats. The cats were safely in carrying cases, except for a Siamese on a lead. And they were fairly quiet, but two cats – the Siamese and a tabby cat – were yowling loudly. And plenty of the dogs were barking; the little ones with high, sharp yips, the big ones with deep rowfs.

Squirt looked around. Taking in the people and animals, and listening to the noise, his lower lip began to tremble.

Mama patted him on the back. It's okay. Mr Squirt," she said, "It's just a lot of—"

Suddenly my mother let out a shriek. She pointed at something across the room. I looked and saw it, too.

It was a snake. And not just a little garter snake like Barney, either. Some great big kind of snake was draped around the neck of a boy who looked as if he were about fourteen years old.

"Oh, my. . ." my mother started to say.

She looked like she might faint, so I tried to work out how to catch both her and Squirt without squashing the hamster, if she did.

But she didn't. Thank goodness.

And from across the room the boy said politely, "Don't worry. He's just a boa constrictor. He's not poisonous or anything. Sorry he scared you."

My mother smiled at him, but headed for seats as far from the boy as possible. She sat Squirt safely in her lap. "All right, darling," she said to me, "you'd better go and tell the receptionist about your hamster and explain why you don't have an appointment."

"Okay." I carried the hamster across the waiting room, skirting around the boy with the snake, and stepped up to the desk. I placed the box on the desk and opened it.

"Yes?" said the receptionist.

"Hi," I began. "My name is Jessi Ramsey. I'm petsitting for the Mancusis this week and one of their hamsters is sick."

"Oh, the Mancusis," said the woman. She seemed to remember the name. I realized that with all their animals, they must have to go to the vet fairly often. "What seems to be the trouble?"

"Well, it's just that he doesn't sleep with the other hamsters and he's very bad-tempered." I edged the box forward and the woman peered in at the hamster.

"Fat, isn't he?" she commented.

"Yes," I replied. "In fact, he's fatter than he was a week ago. I think maybe he's in pain. Something just doesn't seem right."

The woman nodded. "Okay. If you're

worried, it's better to have things checked out. I have to tell you, though, that because you don't have an appointment, and because this isn't an emergency, you might have a long wait. It's hard to tell. There are five vets in today, which is a lot, but there are also a lot of animals waiting."

"That's okay," I told her. "Just as long as he gets checked." I started to stroke the hamster's head before I replaced the lid on the box, but thought better of it. Then I made my way back to Mama.

I was beginning to feel awfully nervous. I checked my watch. Two forty-five. A quarter to three. Our special meeting would start in a little over an hour. Could I possibly make it? Was there any way?

I sat down next to Mama and tried hard not to bite my nails.

Then Squirt leaned over from his place on Mama's lap and said, "Pockita?" which is his way of asking to play patty-cake. We played patty-cake until a girl about Becca's age came into the waiting room with her father. She was holding a kitten, and she headed for the empty seats next to Mama. Her father spoke to the receptionist.

"What an adorable kitten," said my mother as the girl settled herself in a seat.

Immediately the girl stood up again. "Her name is Igga-Bogga," she said. She offered Igga-Bogga to us, and Mama and I took turns holding her, while Squirt patted her.

Igga-Bogga was skinny. And she was pure white, not a patch or a stripe or even a hair of another colour anywhere. If she were my cat, I would have named her Misty or Clouds or Creampuff.

I was about to mention those names to the girl, when she spoke up again. "Guess what. It's so sad. Igga-Bogga is deaf."

"Deaf." I cried.

The girl nodded. "That happens sometimes with white cats."

Her father joined us and he and Mama began talking about white cats being deaf. I looked at my watch. Three-ten. Less than an hour until the special meeting. What could I do? The hamster was my responsibility, my sitting responsibility. If I were babysitting on a week-day afternoon and the parents didn't come home and I had a club meeting to go to – well, I'd just have to miss the meeting, wouldn't I? Sitting responsibilities come first. So right now, a sick hamster came first.

I knew I was right, yet I started tapping my fingers and jiggling my feet. Oh, I *hate* being late and missing events I'm supposed to go to, and I *especially* hate upsetting Kristy.

"Miss Ramsey?" It was the receptionist.

My head snapped up. "Yes," I said. "I'm right here."

I picked up the hamster and his box and got to my feet. Next to me, Mama gathered up Squirt and his toys.

I checked my watch for the umpteenth time. Three-thirty! How did it get to be three-thirty? I would have to call Kristy as soon as I could safely step out of the vet's office.

A nurse led Mama and Squirt and me through a doorway, down a corridor and into an examining room.

"Hi, there. I'm Mr West," said a friendly looking man wearing a white lab coat. He stuck his hand out.

Mama and I shook it, and I introduced us.

"So you've got one of the Mancusi pets here?" said Mr West when the introductions were over. "Let me take a look."

While Mr West examined the hamster, I ducked into the waiting room to use the pay phone I'd seen there. First I called Kristy.

". . . so I'm not going to be able to make the meeting," I finished up after I'd told her the story. "I'm really sorry."

"No problem," Kristy replied easily. "You did the right thing."

"I did?" I said. "Even though it's a hamster?"

"The hamster is your sitting charge," said Kristy. "Pets, kids, it doesn't matter. You're being responsible. That's what matters."

"Listen, I'll phone the others and tell them the meeting has been postponed.

We'll try to arrange it for eleven o'clock tomorrow morning, but phone me tonight to check on the time."

"Okay," I said. "Thanks again, Kristy."

I hung up the phone, then dropped in another coin and called Mal to explain why I wouldn't be calling at her house to pick her up.

When that was done, I returned to Mr West's office. I found him and my mother grinning.

"What?" I said. "Why are you smiling?"

"Because," answered Mama, "your hamster isn't a he, he's a she. And *she* is pregnant!"

"I'd say she's going to have her babies within the next twenty-four hours," added Mr West. "You were lucky you didn't touch her today. A pregnant hamster should not be handled." Mr West instructed me to transfer the other hamsters to a separate cage so the mother could be alone with her babies after giving birth. "And don't handle her at all," he said again. "A pregnant hamster is very delicate. Put her back in her cage by lowering the box inside it and letting her crawl out."

"Okay," I replied. Then I thanked Mr West.

I rode back to the Mancusis' in high spirits. "Just think," I said to Mama. "The hamster is a girl, not a boy, and she's going to have babies! I'll have to give her a name.

106

I want to be able to call her something."

Mama dropped me off and Squirt waved to me from the car window."

"Goodbye!" I called. "'Bye, Squirt. Thank you for helping me, Mama. I'll be home as soon as I walk the dogs again and do the afternoon chores."

Mama beeped the horn as she drove down the street.

I ran to the Mancusis' garage before I did anything else. There I found the aquarium we had used to capture Barney. I poured shavings into it and added some food and a spare water bottle, and gently moved the hamsters into it. Then, even more gently, I set the shoe box in the old cage and let the pregnant hamster crawl out.

"What should I call you?" I asked aloud as she settled into her nest in the corner of the cage. "Maybe Suzanne. I always liked that name. . . No. Suzanne is silly for a hamster. Chipper? No, too cute. And it sounds like a boy's name. Sandy? You are sand-coloured. No, that's boring." After lots of thinking, I decided to call her Misty, which is what I would name a white kitten if I had one. The hamster wasn't anywhere near white, but I decided that didn't matter. Misty was a good name.

I went home feeling excited. When I came back in the morning, Misty would be a mother!

13th
CHAPTER

On Sunday morning I woke up super-early.
I had a lot to do at the Mancusis' before I
left for Claudia's. I had to walk the dogs,
feed the dogs and cats, and finish the
chores I had begun the day before. And of
course I wanted to check on Misty and
her babies.

I ran straight for Misty as soon as I'd
closed the Mancusis' door behind me.
When I reached the kitchen, though, I
slowed down and tiptoed inside. I peeped
into Misty's cage.

Nothing.

Just Misty and her nest and a pile of
shavings.

"Oh, you haven't had them yet," I said,
feeling disappointed. I began to wonder if
Mr West had been wrong. Then what?
Well, the Mancusis would be home in the
afternoon. I would tell them the story and

108

let them decide what to do. At least Misty had been to a vet.

Besides, I told myself, Mr West said the babies would be born in the next twenty-four hours. There were about seven more hours to go until the twenty-four were up.

So I left Misty to herself, walked the dogs, fed them and the cats, finished the cleaning, and then . . . took off for our special club meeting. I dropped by Mallory's house on the way, since we were still planning to arrive at Claudia's together.

Mallory was waiting on her porch steps. "Hi!" she called when she spotted me.

"Hi," I replied.

Mallory ran across her front lawn. "Has the hamster had her babies yet?" she asked breathlessly. (I'd told Mal everything the night before.)

I shook my head. "Not yet. I wish she had. I wanted her to have them before the Mancusis get back."

"Maybe we could check on her after the meeting," suggested Mal.

"Oh! That's a good idea. We could *all* come."

Mal made a face at the thought, but the only thing she said was, "Do you know who you're going to vote for?"

I nodded my head slowly. "I think so. I probably won't know for sure until I'm actually voting, but right now I *think* I know."

"Funny," said Mal. "I feel the same way. . . Should we say who we're going to vote for?"

"No," I replied. "Better not. We should go ahead with what we've planned. If we say anything, we might change each other's minds."

"Okay."

A few more minutes and Mal and I had reached the Kishis' house. We looked at each other.

"Dum da-dum dum," sang Mal ominously.

I laughed – or tried to.

Mal opened the door. We went inside and straight up to Claud's room. Kristy was already there, busily sorting through some slips of paper.

"Hi, you two," Claud greeted us.

"Hi," we replied, settling into our places on the floor.

"What—" Claud started to say, but she was interrupted by the arrival of Mary Anne and Dawn, both looking a little sleepy.

When everyone was sitting in her usual spot, Kristy surprised us by beginning the meeting with, "Tell us about the hamster, Jessi."

I jumped to attention. I'd been preparing for the voting. Now I had to switch gears. "Well," I said, "this is good news. The hamster isn't sick—"

"Oh, that's wonderful!" cried Dawn. "So it was a false alarm?"

"Not exactly," I answered. "The hamster turns out to be a she. By the way, I'm calling her Misty for the time being. And Misty is. . ." (I looked at Mal, dragging out the suspense.)

"Yes?" shrieked Mary Anne.

". . . going to have babies!" I exclaimed. "Probably lots of them. Mr West said hamsters usually give birth to six to twelve young. Those were his exact words. And it should happen any minute now, because yesterday afternoon he said it would happen within the next twenty-four hours."

"That is so exciting!" squealed Dawn.

"Babies!" exclaimed Mary Anne.

"Lots of them!" added Claudia.

"The Mancusis will be thrilled!" cried Kristy.

For a moment, I felt as if I were in an ordinary club meeting, back before we had started fighting all the time. Then Kristy said, "When the meeting is over, maybe we could go to the Mancusis' and see how Misty is doing." (Mal elbowed me.) "But right now," she went on, "we have a job to do."

I watched the faces of the other club members turn from happy and expectant to worried and uncertain.

Kristy organized the pile of papers before her into a neat stack. "Now," she said, "I've made those special ballot papers, just like I said I would. Each piece of paper is headed with the name of one of the offices. Below that are the names of the four officers. All you have to do is make an X in the box by the name of the person you'd like to see in the office. Okay?"

The rest of us nodded our heads.

"Great," said Kristy. "Let's start with treasurer." She handed blank ballots to Mary Anne, Claudia, Mal and me, and then gave one to herself.

"Everyone votes except Dawn," she reminded us.

Mary Anne raised her hand. "Uh, Kristy," she said timidly, "I'm – I'm really sorry, but I have to say something about that."

"Yeah?" replied Kristy.

"Well, it's just – it's just that, for instance, Dawn might not want to be the treasurer any more, but maybe she's got a good idea about who the new treasurer should be. Who would know that better than Dawn? I understand what you said about ties, but I think we should *all* get a vote. If there's a tie, we'll have to revote. If we have to have too many revotes, then we'll think about letting only five people vote. But we should vote with six first."

I have to hand it to both Kristy and Mary Anne. Kristy listened to Mary Anne's suggestion and took it seriously, and Mary Anne didn't cry.

"Okay," said Kristy, "let's vote on what Mary Anne said. Nothing fancy, just a show of hands. All those in favour of letting everyone vote in the elections, raise your hand."

Five hands went up. (Guess which one didn't?)

"Great. I suppose we're all voting," said Kristy. "Luckily, I made extra ballot papers, in case of mistakes, so we're ready."

Kristy handed a ballot paper to Dawn. Then she gave each of us a blue ballpoint pen.

I looked at my ballot, my heart pounding. TREASURER was written across the top. Below it were the names Kristy, Claudia, Mary Anne and Dawn. A box had been drawn to the left of each name.

I paused for a moment, but I knew what I was going to do. I picked up the pen and made an X next to Dawn's name. She was the best treasurer I could think of. But I was pretty sure she was going to kill me when she found out what I'd done (*if* she found out). The business of elections had started because the girls were tired of their old jobs and wanted a change. Well, too bad. I couldn't help that. Dawn was my choice for treasurer.

I glanced around Claudia's room and tried to measure the tension in the air. Funny, but there didn't seem to be much of it. The club members were busy voting, that was true, but more than that, no one was arguing. I think we were relieved that election day had finally come, no matter what it would bring.

When everyone had voted, we folded our papers in quarters and gave them back to Kristy, who carefully put them in a pile. Then she handed out the ballots for secretary, a few minutes later the ones for vice-chairman, and last of all, the ones for chairman. Each time, I voted quickly, knowing just what I had to do.

After the ballots for the office of chairman had been collected, Kristy said, "Let me just take a quick look through the ballot papers. If I see a lot of problems, I'll ask you to help me count."

Kristy picked up the ballot papers for treasurer and glanced at them.

"Hmm," she said.

She looked at the ballot papers for secretary.

"Huh," she said.

She looked at the ballot papers for vice-chairman.

"Well," she said.

And then she looked at the ballot papers for chairman.

She burst out laughing.

"What *is* it?" cried Claudia.

"You will not believe this," Kristy told us. "I hardly believe it myself."

"But?" Dawn prompted her.

"But we unanimously voted ourselves back into our old offices! We all voted for Dawn for treasurer – even Dawn did. We all voted for Mary Anne for secretary – even Mary Anne did. And so on. You even voted for me for chairman."

There was a moment of silence. Then every single one of us began to laugh. Dawn laughed so hard she cried. Kristy laughed so hard I thought she was going to fall out of the director's chair. And all the time we were laughing I was thinking. Now I understand what Mama meant when I asked her to tell me how to vote. She meant (but wanted me to work out for myself) that we shouldn't worry about who thought what or who would be angry or who would laugh about our choices. The purpose of an election is to vote the best person into an office. That's all. And we realized that. We realized that the best people were already in the offices and we wanted to keep them there.

The laughter was fading, and Kristy straightened up in her chair. "What happened?" she asked us.

I raised my hand, heart pounding. I usually don't speak up much in meetings, but I was pretty sure I had the right answer this time. "I think," I began, "that we realized the best people had already been elected to the offices. I mean, Dawn is organized, but Mary Anne is even more organized, and Dawn is better at keeping figures straight, so Dawn's the perfect treasurer and Mary Anne's the perfect secretary. It would be difficult to name anyone but Claudia as vice-chairman, and Kristy, you really deserve to be chairman since the club *was* your idea."

Everyone was looking at me and nodding. I added one more thing. "Can you live with the results of the election?" I asked the four officers. "You were pretty fed up with your jobs a little while ago."

"I can do it," said Dawn quickly, and the others agreed. "There are parts of my job I don't like, but I suppose I know I'm best at this job. And it would really mess up the club to start switching things around."

My friends were smiling again. Then Kristy's smile faded. "I have something to say," she began. "Okay, we realized we were in the right offices. But I have to admit that right office or not, I have been too bossy. Maybe I do come up with good ideas, but I shouldn't force them on you. It's – it's just this thing with Charlie, I suppose. Do you know something? I don't think he's acting like a big shot because he'll be at college. I think he's worried that he won't get into college, and he's taking his worries out by bossing me around. Then I take things out by bossing everyone else around. Jackie Rodowsky pointed that out to me. I mean, he pointed out that I was bossing him around. So I'm going to try to be better. No more forcing rules on you. When I get a new idea we'll vote on it, okay?"

"All *right!*" cried Claudia.

So the meeting ended happily. And when Kristy suggested again that we go over to the Mancusis', everyone wanted to see Misty. And Mal didn't mind. She was glad our club was a club again.

So was I.

14th
CHAPTER

We arrived at the Mancusis' just before twelve-thirty. Mr and Mrs Mancusi wouldn't be home until later in the afternoon.

I unlocked the front door, feeling like a nervous grandmother. How was Misty doing? Had she had her babies yet? How long did a hamster take to have babies anyway?

"Follow me," I said. "Misty's in the kitchen." (For some reason I was whispering.)

I tiptoed into the kitchen, and Mal, Kristy, Claudia, Dawn and Mary Anne tiptoed after me. I paused in the doorway, listening for unusual sounds, although what sounds a baby hamster might make I cannot imagine.

At last I looked into Misty's cage. There she was, a golden brown body. . . And there were four tiny pink bodies! They looked like jelly beans. They had no hair at all and their eyes were closed.

I gasped. "She's had them!" I whispered. "Misty had four babies!"

Everyone crowded around the cage.

"Make that five," said Kristy softly.

"Oh, EW!" exclaimed Mary Anne, backing away. "That is disgusting."

"No, it isn't. It's beautiful," said Dawn.

"Five babies. I wonder what the Mancusis will name them," said Mal. "I wonder if there will be more than five."

"I wonder if they'll keep them," said Claudia. "Do you think they will, Jessi?"

I shrugged. "I don't think another cageful of hamsters would be much extra work."

"Is there anything we're supposed to be doing for Misty or her babies?" asked Mary Anne, even though she wouldn't look in the cage any more.

"I don't think so," I replied. "Mr West said to be sure not to touch the babies, even if I think one is dead. He said Misty will know what to do. He said the babies – actually he called them pups – will get scattered all around the cage, but that Misty will take care of them."

We watched her for a few more minutes. Finally I said, "Maybe we should leave Misty alone. If I were in a cage giving birth to hamsters, I wouldn't want six faces staring at me."

"If you were in a cage giving birth to

hamsters," said Mal, "you'd be a miracle of science."

"No, she'd be in a zoo!" said Kristy.

We left the kitchen and wandered into the living room.

"Aah," said Claudia, "who's this?"

"That's Powder. Hey, do you want to meet the rest of the Mancusis' animals? I mean, do all of you want to meet them?"

"Thanks, but I've already met Barney," Mary Anne replied drily.

"There are other animals here, though, and Kristy and Dawn haven't been here before. Also—"

"Where's the beef? Where's the beef?"

"Aughh!" shrieked Kristy. "Someone's in the house! We're not alone!"

Dawn began to laugh. "It's a bird, isn't it?"

I nodded.

"We used to have one," Dawn told us. "A long time ago. I think it was a parakeet. His name was Buzz. He could say a few words. But the funniest thing he ever did was fly into a bowl of mashed potatoes."

"Dawn!" I exclaimed. "Is that true?"

"Cross my heart," she replied.

It must have been true.

We were all laughing hysterically and couldn't calm down for a while. When we finally did, we checked on Misty (six babies) and then I let Kristy and Dawn meet the animals.

"Hey, Mary Anne!" called Kristy as we

were leaving the sun porch. "Where's the lid of Barney's cage?"

Mary Anne began screaming without even turning around to look at the cage. If she had turned around, she would have seen that the lid was on tightly. Kristy had to confess her joke in order to keep Mary Anne from running home.

At last I suggested that we take Cheryl, Jacques and Pooh Bear on their afternoon walk. I thought my friends might enjoy that.

So we took the dogs on a long walk. When we returned I said, "Well I hate to kick you out, but I have to feed the animals. And I should probably be the only one here when the Mancusis come home."

"Okay," Kristy answered. "We understand."

My friends left. I was alone in the house, although not for long. The Mancusis would return soon. Even so, I phoned my parents to tell them where I was and why I'd be late. Then I looked in on Misty. *Ten* pups! And they were all gathered around their mother in a big jumbly pile of legs and feet and ears. I suppose Misty had finished giving birth. Now she could tend to her babies.

While I waited for the Mancusis, I found a roll of crêpe paper (out in the garage, with all the boxes) and tied a big red bow to each of the dogs' collars.

"You three look lovely," I told them. "You're doggie fashion plates."

"Rowf?" asked Jacques, cocking his head.

"Yes, you're very handsome."

I was about to make bows for the cats when I heard a car pull into the driveway. "Guess who's home!" I called to the dogs.

Of course, they had no idea, but when I ran to the front door, they followed me. I opened the inside door and waved to Mr and Mrs Mancusi as they unloaded their luggage from the car. They were surprised to see me, but they smiled and waved back. Then, their arms weighed down with suitcases, they walked to the front door, while I tried to open it for them and hold the dogs back at the same time. It wasn't easy, but we managed.

As soon as the Mancusis were safely inside, I cried, "Guess what! One of the hamsters had babies! . . . Oh, I hope you had a nice holiday."

"My heavens!" exclaimed Mrs Mancusi. "One of the hamsters had babies? How could we have missed a pregnancy? Are the babies okay? Which hamster is it?"

"Everything's fine. Honest," I told them. "I knew something was wrong, well, I knew something was *unusual*, so my mum drove the hamster and me to your vet yesterday. Mr West looked at her and he told me what to do."

"Oh. . ." The Mancusis let out a sigh of relief.

"Do you want to see the babies?" I asked.

"Of course," said Mr Mancusi. He and his wife put down their suitcases and followed me into the kitchen, the dogs bounding joyfully at our sides.

"It's this one," I said. "I moved the other hamsters to the aquarium on the table." I stood back so the Mancusis could look in at Misty.

"Ah, Snicklefritz." Mrs Mancusi scratched her head. "How did we miss this? I really apologize, Jessi. But I have to congratulate you. You did a terrific job in a difficult situation. We're very grateful to you."

"I suppose," added Mr Mancusi, "that in the excitement when we were trying to get away – our petsitter cancelling and all – we just didn't notice that Snicklefritz was pregnant.

"Well, everything worked out fine," I spoke up. "Mis – I mean, Snicklefritz has ten babies."

The Mancusis watched them for a few moments. Then they turned to me. "Thank you again, Jessi," said Mr Mancusi. "You've been very responsible." He handed me some money – much more than I've got paid for any other job.

"Wow!" I cried. "Thanks. . . Are you sure this isn't too much?"

"Not at all."

"By the way," said Mrs Mancusi, "do

you have any friends who would like a hamster? We'll let the babies go to anyone who will give them good homes – in about three weeks, that is. After the pups are weaned."

"*Anyone*?" I repeated. "Gosh, we've never had a pet. I'm sure my sister Becca would like one. *I'd* like one. And, well, I'll spread the word. I bet I can help you find lots of homes!"

I couldn't believe it. A pet! Would Mama and Daddy let us have one? I had no idea. Neither Becca nor I had ever asked for a pet.

I headed for the front door. The dogs followed me.

"Goodbye, Cheryl. Goodbye, Jacques. Goodbye, Pooh Bear," I said.

The Mancusis were right behind the dogs. "They really like you," Mr Mancusi said. "Oh, and we like their bows. Very nice."

I smiled. "Well, thanks again. If you ever need another petsitter, let me know. And I'll find out about homes for the baby hamsters. I promise."

The Mancusis and I called goodbye to each other and then I ran to my house. I was just about bursting with my news – Snicklefritz's babies and homes for them. Maybe one would become our first pet.

"Mama! Daddy!" I shouted as I burst through our front door.

15th
CHAPTER

The Braddocks were back. Ballet school had started again. My life had returned to normal.

I missed the Mancusi animals, but I could probably visit them any time I wanted to. I'm sure I'd be allowed to walk the dogs from time to time.

Anyway, since my life was back to normal, I babysat for the Braddocks the next day, Monday, and then tore over to Claudia's house. I reached it a full five minutes before the meeting was about to start. I even beat Kristy, but of course she's at the mercy of Charlie, so she doesn't have a lot of control over when she arrives.

Claudia and Dawn were there, though.

"Hi, you two!" I said as I entered Claud's room.

"Hello," they replied, smiling, and Dawn added, "You sound awfully happy."

"Glad to be back at the Braddocks'?" asked Claudia.

"Yes," I answered, "but it's more than that. I'll tell you all about it when everybody's here."

"Okay," said Claud. "Crisps, anyone?"

"Oh, I'm starving!" I exclaimed, even though I sort of watch my diet because I have to stay in good shape for dance class.

"Um, can you help me find them?" asked Claud, looking puzzled. "They might be under the bed, but who knows?"

Claudia and Dawn and I dropped to our stomachs and crawled halfway under Claud's bed. A load of junk had been stashed away there – boxes of art supplies, folders of drawings and sketches, magazines for making collages, that sort of thing. And because Claudia is such a poor speller, they were labelled SKECHES or PANTINGS or BURSHES.

I found the crisps in a box marked CALAGE SUPPLIES.

"Here they are!" I announced.

The three of us crawled out from under the bed, stood up, turned around, and found Kristy, Mallory and Mary Anne staring at us. We began to laugh – all six of us.

"That was so attractive!" said Kristy. "I hope I always come to a meeting just in time to see the three of you backing out from under a bed."

126

"My backside is my best side," replied Dawn, looking serious.

There was more laughter as the members of the Babysitters Club settled in their usual places. Kristy climbed into the director's chair She put the visor on. She stuck a pencil over one ear.

And then she pulled a new checklist out of her pocket, smoothed the creases, and with big, showy sweeps of her arms, pinned it up on the notice board over the photos of Claudia and Stacey.

"There," she said with satisfaction.

Claudia, Mary Anne, Dawn, Mallory and I just stared at her. I suppose my mouth was hanging open. Everybody else's was.

"I don't believe it," muttered Claudia, but just when it looked like she might jump to her feet and strangle Kristy, Kristy jumped to *her* feet and ripped the checklist off the bulletin board.

"Now watch this, everyone," she announced. She scrunched up the checklist and threw it in the waste-paper basket. "Bye-bye, checklist. That's the last of it. You won't see it or hear about it again."

At first the rest of us didn't know what to do. Then we began to smile.

"You mean that was a joke?" exclaimed Claudia. "Oh, my lord! *Kristy. . .*"

Kristy grinned at us. She looked like the Cheshire Cat reclining in his tree.

127

Dawn threw a crisp at her. I think a crisp war might have started if the phone hadn't rung.

"Oh, no! We haven't done any of our opening business!" cried Kristy. "Dawn hasn't collected subs, I haven't—"

Ring, ring.

Kristy stopped ranting and raving and answered the phone. "Hello, Babysitters Club."

We arranged a Saturday afternoon job for me with the Arnold twins. Then Kristy got down to business.

"Dawn?" she said. "Miss Treasurer?"

"I need your subs," announced Dawn.

Dawn collected the subs while we groaned and complained. "I'll walk out with you after the meeting and pay Charlie," she told Kristy.

"Okay. Thanks. That'll be fine. Maybe that will improve Charlie's mood." Kristy paused. "All right," she continued, "any club business?"

"I have something to ask everyone," I said, "but it can wait until after the real club business is over."

Kristy nodded. "Anything else?"

The rest of the girls shook their heads.

"Okay," said Kristy. "I'm done. Over to you, Jessi. Oh, by the way, did you all notice that I didn't ask whether you'd read the notebook?"

"Uh, yes," replied Dawn.

"Good. I'm not going to ask any more. I'll trust you to read it. No questions, no checklists—"

"You'll actually trust us?" exclaimed Mary Anne.

"I'll actually trust you."

The phone rang again, and we arranged another job. When that was taken care of, I said, "Well, guess what. Misty's name turns out to be Snicklefritz and she had *ten* pups yesterday." (Mallory knew this already, since we tell each other everything. But the others hadn't heard.)

"Ten pups!" cried Mary Anne. "What will the Mancusis do with them?"

"Well, that's the rest of my news. The Mancusis are giving them away – to anyone who'll promise the babies a good home. *And* Mama and Daddy said Becca and I can have one! Our first pet! We decided to name our hamster Misty no matter what colour it is, and whether it's a boy or girl."

"Oh, that's great!" cried Mary Anne and Kristy at the same time. (They both have pets.)

"And," I went on, "I'm asking around, finding out if anyone else would like a hamster. How about one of you?"

Claudia shook her head. "They're sweet, but I hate cleaning cages."

Mary Anne shook her head. "A hamster wouldn't last a second with Tigger."

Kristy shook her head. "We've got enough pets at our house already."

Dawn shook her head. "I like hamsters, but if get a pet, I'd like a bigger one. A cat or a dog."

I looked at Mallory. She seemed thoughtful. "We've got ten people in our family," she said slowly, "but no pets. I don't see why we couldn't get one little pet. The younger kids would like a hamster. So would the boys. Well, so would all of us." Mallory dived for the phone. "Mum! Mum!" she cried.

(I could just imagine Mrs Pike saying, "What on earth is the matter?")

"Mum, the Mancusis are going to give the hamster babies away. In about three weeks, I think." (I nodded.) "Could we have one? It would be a good experience for Claire and Margo. And I think Nicky would like a pet. . . Yeah?. . . I know. . . Okay. . . Okay, thanks! This is great! 'Bye, Mum." Mallory hung up. "We can have one!" she announced. "We'll be getting our first pet, too!"

I have never seen so much excitement.

Then the phone rang and we arranged three jobs.

When the phone rang a fourth time, Mary Anne opened the record book again, and we sat up eagerly. I picked up the receiver. "Hello, Babysitters Club," I said.

"Hi," answered a very small voice. "I—

This is Jackie Rodowsky. Is Kristy there, please?"

"Of course, Jackie. Hold on," I told him. I handed the phone to Kristy, whispering, "It's Jackie Rodowsky."

Kristy raised her eyebrows. "Hi, Jackie."

That was all she said, and Jackie burst into tears.

"What's wrong?" she asked him. "What happened? Is your mum at home?"

"She's here," Jackie told her. "And I'm okay. I mean, I'm not hurt. But we had our class elections today."

"Oh," said Kristy. "Right. And what happened?"

"I lost. Adrienne beat me. I tried and tried to show the kids that I could take care of Snowball. But I don't think they believed me." Jackie paused. When he started speaking again, his voice was trembling. "I just – just wanted a pet to take care of by myself. That's all."

"Jackie," said Kristy gently, "I'm sorry you lost. I'm sorry the kids wouldn't pay attention to you. Really I am. Sometimes things work out that way. But listen, could I talk to your mum for a sec, please?" There was a pause while Kristy waited for Mrs Rodowsky to get to the phone. Then she said, "Hi, Mrs Rodowsky. This is Kristy Thomas. Jackie told me about the elections today and I was wondering – could he have a pet of his own? I think he

131

wants one, and I know where he could get a free hamster. . .

Yes. . . Really? Oh, terrific! Could I talk to Jackie again, please?"

So Kristy gave Jackie the good news about his hamster.

"My own? My own hamster?" Jackie shrieked. "Amazing! What will I name it? Is it a boy or a girl? What colour is it?"

Kristy couldn't answer his questions, so we arranged for me to take him over to the Mancusis' in a couple of weeks. The hamsters wouldn't be ready to leave their mother yet, but Jackie could look at them and stroke them and play with them in order to choose the one that would become his very own. Jackie liked the idea a lot. So he thanked Kristy eleven times and then they got off the phone.

"Well, all's well that ends well," said Kristy.

"Huh?" said Claudia.

"I mean, happy endings everywhere you look. We got our club problems straightened out. The sick hamster turned out to be pregnant, and then she had her babies and they were born without any trouble, and now Jessi and Mallory's families will have their first pets, and Jackie lost the election but he got a hamster. Happy endings."

"Yeah," I said, smiling.

The numbers on Claudia's digital clock turned from 5:59 to 6:00.

132

"Meeting adjourned," announced our chairman.

I walked out with Mal. "I wonder," I said, "if I could talk Becca into changing Misty's name to Mancusi."

"Darn!" said Mallory. "That's what I wanted to name our hamster."

"Really?"

"No."

We giggled.

"Call you tonight!" I shouted to Mal as we separated.

Best friends have to talk a lot.

DAWN ON THE COAST

The author
would like to thank
Jan Carr
for her help
in writing this book

1st
CHAPTER

Dear Sunshine,

The countdown is on. Only a few days left until you get on that plane and land in beautiful, ~~sunny~~ California. I can't wait to see you, sweetie. And Jeff is so excited, you'd think it was Christmas morning. California, here you come! See you Sunday night at the airport.

Love and a big hug,
Dad.

A trip to the West Coast. It was the highlight of my spring, that's for sure. When I got to California, I had an absolutely fantastic time. So how come I ended up feeling so confused? Believe me, there's a lot to tell. And I might as well start at the beginning.

First of all, you're probably wondering who Sunshine is. Well, that's me. Of course nobody around here calls me Sunshine. Here in Connecticut they call me by my ordinary name, Dawn Schafer. But not my dad. He started calling me Sunshine when I was little and, unfortunately, it stuck. Maybe he gave me the name because of my long blonde hair. My hair is so light it's almost the colour of cornsilk, and it reaches all the way past my waist. Or maybe Dad gave me the name because I love the sun so much. I really do. I love warm weather and the beach.

I suppose I'm just a California girl at heart. After all, that's where I came from. And that Sunday, I was going back for a visit!

I got the postcard from Dad when I came home from school that Thursday afternoon. I still had so much to do, so much to get ready. I dragged my suitcase out of the cupboard, threw it on the bed, and started to lay out my clothes. I decided to bring my white cotton skirt – I could wear that with anything. And, of course, my bathing suit (a bikini) and my jeans and trainers. I wasn't sure about my yellow cotton dungarees. And would I really need *three* sundresses?

Maybe you're wondering why my dad lives in California and I live in Connecticut Well, sometimes I wonder, too, Believe me, it's not the way I would have arranged it. But even so, things are working out okay. You see, about a year-and-a-half ago, Mum and Dad got divorced. Dad stayed in our house in California and Mum moved me and my brother, Jeff, here to Stoneybrook, Connecticut. I think Mum wanted to come here because my grandparents live here and it's the town where she grew up. To tell the truth, at first I wasn't the happiest, but then I adjusted. I found myself a best friend, Mary Anne Spier, and I got invited to join the Babysitters Club, which is just about the most fun club in the whole world.

My brother, Jeff, didn't adjust so easily, though. In fact, he didn't adjust at all. He started getting sort of nasty with me and Mum, and he even started to get into fights at school. It was pretty bad. His teacher kept calling Mum in and I don't think Mum knew what to do. Finally we decided to let Jeff go back to California for a while. He really just wanted to be back with his friends and live with Dad. I don't think Mum was thrilled with the idea, but she decided that she had to let Jeff try it for six months.

I didn't like the idea at all. It was bad enough that Mum and Dad had to get divorced. Already our family was split. But when Jeff left Mum and me, too, it felt like he was deserting us. And then another part of me thought, hey, why couldn't *I* be the one to get to move back to California?

Now I'm sort of used to the idea. In my head I understand all the reasons why things are the way they are. But sometimes it does seem strange the way the family has divided up. Boys against the girls. Or West Coast against the East Coast. I love Mum, and she and I get to stay together, but of course I love Dad and Jeff, and I miss them sometimes. And I know they miss us, too.

But Mum is great. She and I have got a lot closer through all of this and we've made a whole new life for ourselves. We live in an old, old farmhouse that was built in 1795. No kidding. The rooms are really small and the doorways are so short that tall people have to stoop to get through them. Mum says people used to be shorter in the 1700s.

The best thing about our house, though, is that it has a secret trapdoor in our barn that leads into a long, dark tunnel. You need a torch to walk through. The tunnel leads up into our house and comes out . . . right at the wall to my bedroom! The wall has a special latch that springs open when you touch it. Talk about exciting. You should've seen the faces on my friends in the Babysitters Club when I showed them.

Maybe I should tell you a little bit about the club. There're six of us in it now, and we also have two associate members. What it is is just what it says, a club for babysitters. It was Kristy Thomas's great idea. She's our chairman. She thought that it would be great if there was a club that all the parents in the neighbourhood could use whenever they needed a sitter. That way, they'd be pretty sure of getting someone for the job and they'd only have to make one call. Great for them, and great for us, too, since we're all super sitters and we love the work. Leave it to Kristy to come up with a good business idea. And leave it to Kristy to organize the whole thing.

What we do is this: Three times a week we have meetings in the afternoon. We meet at Claudia's house because she has a phone in her room . . . with her very own number! Claudia is Claudia Kishi and she's our vice-chairman. Claudia is about as different from Kristy as you can get. Kristy is kind of small for her age and is a real tomboy. She always wears the same thing – jeans, a sweater and trainers. But not Claudia. You can always count on Claudia to be wearing some really unusual outfit, like a white jumpsuit with a wide purple belt and purple trainers. Claudia is Japanese-American and she's got beautiful, long, shiny black hair that she arranges differently practically every day. She loves art, too, so she has a really interesting sense of style.

After those two, there's Mary Anne Spier, our club secretary, and, as I said, she's my best friend in Stoneybrook. Mary Anne lives alone with her father because her mother died when she was a baby. Her father's been sort of strict with her and a lot of people think Mary Anne's quiet. It's true, she can be shy sometimes. But wouldn't you know it, she was the first one of us to get a boyfriend!

Speaking of boyfriends, when I first moved to Stoneybrook and became friends with Mary Anne, we found out something really exciting – my mum and Mary Anne's dad used to go out together in high school! Then, for a while, they even started going out together again! Imagine. My mum going with my best friend's dad. Mary Anne and I were in seventh heaven. We were hoping our parents might even get *married* to each other. That would've made Mary Anne and me sisters! Now things have cooled off a little, but as Mary Anne says, you never know. . .

So that's part of the club. Kristy, Claudia, Mary Anne and I are all in eighth grade, so we are *very* experienced sitters. We used to have another eighth-grade member, Stacey, but she moved back to

New York City, which was really sad, so we had to get someone to fill Stacey's place in the club. That's where Mallory and Jessi come in. Mallory and Jessi are our sixth-grade members. They can't sit at nighttime, except for their own brothers and sisters, but both of them are really good. We know Mallory really well because we babysit for her family, the Pikes. The Pikes have eight kids, and since Mallory is the oldest, she used to help us out.

Jessi is Mallory's friend and she's a new-comer to Stoneybrook. Her family is one of the first black families in the neighbour-hood, so I think that in the beginning, Jessi felt a little strange. When she first moved here, she wasn't even sure she wanted to continue with her ballet lessons, and she is a really talented ballet dancer – long-legged and graceful.

Wow! When I think about it, I do have a nice bunch of friends in Stoneybrook. As I was packing that day, I also started thinking about my friends in California. Clover and Daffodil (those are the kids I used to babysit for) and, of course, Sunny, who had been my best friend in California since second grade. That reminded me – I'd better stick suntan lotion in my suitcase. Sunny and I would probably want to go to the beach one day. Then I started making a list of all the other bits and pieces I would need.

Just then my mum came home. She

usually doesn't get home from work until 5:45 or so, but that day she was early.

"Hi, Dawn!" she called up the stairs.

I could hear her kick off her shoes in the living room, drop her bag on the couch and her keys on the kitchen table. That's my mum, all right. I love her, but she is a little on the disorganized side. Mum padded up the stairs and plonked herself down on the one corner of my bed that wasn't covered with stuff.

"What's this?" she said, picking up my list. When she saw what it was, she laughed. "I suppose you didn't learn that from your old mother," she said.

It's true. If Mum ever bothered to make a list, she'd probably lose it.

"How was work today?" I asked her.

Mum sighed and looked vaguely across the bed at all my things.

"You're going to have such a good time," she said.

I suddenly realized that when I went off to California, Mum was going to be left all alone in Stoneybrook.

"Mum, are you going to be all right?" I asked. "I mean, all alone?"

She tucked her legs under her, like she had so many times lately when we found ourselves sitting in my room talking.

"Of course I am, darling," she said. "What? Are you worried about me? Don't worry. I've got Granny and Grandad while you're gone. And Trip's already asked me out to dinner. . ."

"The Trip-Man!" I groaned. Trip is a man who was dating my mother. I call him the Trip-Man. He's a really conservative type. Tortoiseshell glasses, you know what I mean. How could I leave Mum alone with *him*?

"Mum," I said, "I feel kind of funny going off to be with Dad and Jeff, and you having to stay here."

"It's only for your spring holiday," she said. "Besides, think of what an adventure I'm going to have without you. I'll probably misplace my keys and not find them the whole time you're away. And when I go out with Trip, I'll probably end up wearing one brown shoe and one red."

I threw my arms around Mum and gave her a quick kiss.

"Oh, Mum," I said. "I'm so glad that you and I stuck together. What if you were here and I was there? What if the family was even more split up than it is now? I'll never leave you. Never."

Mum didn't answer me, she just stared across my bed at the suitcase and all my clothes. Her eyes got a little misty, but immediately she turned to me and said, "You didn't start anything for dinner yet, did you?"

Weekday dinners are usually my job.

"Not yet," I said. "I was thinking maybe barley casserole. . ."

"Let's go out," Mum said suddenly. "What do you say? We'll go to Cabbages and Kings and have one of those wonderful tofu dinners."

"Or the avocado salad," I said.

"Aaaah, avocado. . ." My mother closed her eyes at the thought. "Think of all those wonderful California avocados you're going to be gobbling down soon. Come on. Let's go and celebrate. Avocados, here we come."

I grabbed my jumper and Mum stood up, puzzled, and glanced around the floor.

"Where are my shoes?" she said.

"Living room," I answered.

Mum fumbled in her pockets for her keys.

"Your keys are on the kitchen table," I said. "And your bag is on the couch."

Mum looked a little sheepish.

"What am I going to do without you?" she laughed. "You have to admit. We make a good team."

We walked down the stairs, gathered up Mum's things, and headed out the door. When I got home that night I would have to finish packing my things. But, for then, I left them strewn across my bed. It wasn't every night that Mum and I could decide to drop everything and go to Cabbages and Kings for a close, warm mother-daughter meal. And besides, on Sunday I'd be leaving Stoneybrook for two whole weeks.

2nd CHAPTER

Friday

Dear Dad and Jeff,
   Only two more days to C-Day!
That's what I'm calling my trip
to California now, and I can't,
can't, CAN'T WAIT to see you.
This'll have to be short and
sweet because I'm rushing off
to a slumber party at Kristy's
house. All my Babysitters
Club friends will be there, and
I can't be late, since the whole
thing is a goodbye party for...
                    Yours truly,
                       Dawn

What a party! I was the first one to get to Kristy's that night and, when I arrived, things were still a little quiet and calm. Kristy lives in a mansion. I'm not joking. But you practically need a mansion to hold all her family. There's Kristy and her mum and three brothers, and then there's Watson Brewer, Kristy's stepdad. He and Kristy's mum got married last summer and he has two kids of his own. (They come to stay every other weekend.). That would be plenty, but there's also Boo-Boo, the cat, and Shannon, the puppy.

I knocked on the big wooden door and Kristy let me in. She was wearing her usual – jeans, trainers, a sweater. (What did I tell you?) She shut the door quickly behind me, so that Shannon wouldn't escape. Shanon jumped up on me and licked my arms. She really is a great puppy. She's still young, so her paws are too big for her body.

"Hi, Shann," I said. I petted her soft head and scratched behind her ears.

The doorbell rang again.

"Move it, Shannon," said Kristy. "It's probably Mary Anne."

The madness had started. When Kristy opened the door, it wasn't Mary Anne at all. It was Karen and Andrew, Kristy's stepsister and stepbrother.

"We're here!" Karen shouted into the house. She dropped her overnight bag on the hallway floor. "Daddy! Everybody! Here we are!"

Karen is only six years old, but she's got lots of confidence and is never at a loss for words. Andrew looked up at me and smiled.

"Hi, Dawn," he said. "Are you babysitting us?"

Andrew's only four and sometimes I have babysat for him, although, of course, Kristy takes all the jobs in her own house if she can.

"Not this time, Andrew," I said. "But I think you are going to see lots of babysitters tonight."

"Hi, Karen. Hi, Andrew. Oh, hello, Dawn." Kristy's mother bustled into the room and gave Andrew and Karen each a warm hug and kiss. "Take your stuff up and put it in your rooms," she said. "It's going to be a full house tonight. Kristy's expecting a few guests."

Karen bounded up the stairs with her suitcase and Andrew stumbled after her, trying to keep up.

Kristy put her hands over her ears. "Aughhh!" she cried. "It sounds like wild horses!"

The doorbell rang again. This time it *was* Mary Anne, and Claudia was right behind her.

"Come in, come in." Kristy opened the door a crack, then hustled them in, but

Shannon was too quick for her. The frisky puppy darted between Claudia's legs and scampered right outside.

"Shannon!" Kristy called, and ran out to catch her.

While Kristy was chasing after Shannon, Mallory and Jessi arrived. Jessi saw what was happening and took a ballet leap into the yard, just as Shannon was about to run into the bushes.

"Gotcha!" she said as she grabbed Shannon's collar. We all started clapping and Jessi took a deep bow. "*Grand jeté*," she smiled. "You just never know when one is going to come in handy."

Well, one crisis down, but another was on the way. While Kristy led Shannon back into the house, Karen came screaming down the stairs.

"Ben Brewer!" she shouted. "Ben Brewer! He's clanking his chains!"

For a six-year-old girl, Karen has an amazing intelligence. She's convinced there's a ghost in the house named Ben Brewer, and she tells stories about him all the time. As I looked up, Sam and Charlie were sneaking around the bend at the top of the steps. They're Kristy's older brothers. Sam is fifteen and Charlie's seventeen.

"Shhh," Sam whispered to Charlie. He slipped down the stairs after Karen, grabbed her up from behind, and lifted her over his head.

"Aughhh!" screamed Karen.

Mrs Brewer stuck her head back into the room to see what was going on. David Michael, Kristy's brother who's seven, was right behind her.

"No horseplay on the stairs," said David Michael. (It was obviously a rule he had heard many times.)

"That's right," said Mrs Brewer.

Just then, the front door opened behind us and bumped Claudia and Mary Anne on their backsides.

"Excuse me. Excuse me." Someone was pushing his way through the crowd. It was Watson Brewer, home from work. "Well," he said, as he took a look at the chaos that greeted him. "Five more daughters, huh? Where did I get them all? Hello, girls."

"Hi, Mr Brewer," we chorused.

"All right. All right. That's enough," Kristy said suddenly. "Babysitters upstairs."

I'm surprised she didn't say, "Forward, march!" or "Single file!" (she did sound like General Kristy), but we all trooped up the stairs after her. We left Watson and Kristy's mum kissing hello in the hallway, with their kids and their animals chasing all around them.

"Phew!" Kristy said. She shut the door behind us. Mary Anne, Claudia and I collapsed on the bed. Jessi and Mallory sat cross-legged on the floor. Kristy pulled up a chair. It looked just like a normal meeting of the Babysitters Club, only we were in Kristy's room, not Claudia's. Kristy picked up a clip-board and pencil and tapped on the arm of her chair.

"The meeting will now come to order," she said.

"Meeting!" Claudia cried. "Kristy, this isn't a meeting. It's a party."

I smiled at Mary Anne. Mary Anne is a good friend of Kristy's, but she knows how Kristy loves to be bossy.

"True," said Kristy. "It's not exactly a meeting. But we do have a few things to decide. Pizza, for instance. Do we want some? And, if so, what kind?"

"Pizza would be good," said Mary Anne. Mary Anne is always agreeable. "Does anyone else want pizza?"

"P I I I I Z-Z-A-A!" said Claudia in a deep, rumbling voice. She sounded like Cookie Monster demanding cookies.

"That's three," said Kristy. "Dawn?"

"Do they have broccoli pizza?" I asked.

"Ew!" Kristy made a gagging face.

"It *is* Dawn's party," said Mary Anne. "I think we should do what she wants."

Claudia crinkled up her nose.

"If they do have broccoli, maybe they could put it on only *part* of the pizza," she said.

Claudia was more polite about it, but I think the idea of broccoli pizza was as weird-sounding to Claudia as it was to Kristy. I'm the only member of the club who really likes health food. Everybody else is happier with beefburgers and chips. Especially Claudia. Claudia takes junk food to the extreme. She keeps her bedroom stocked with Quavers and Skittles. In fact, right then she reached into the knapsack she had brought and pulled out . . . a handful of lollipops.

"Lollipops all round," she said, passing them out, "and a fruit roll for Dawn."

We all sucked on our treats while Kristy finished the pizza order. Half a pie with broccoli (if they had it), half plain, and one whole pie with the works – sausage, mushrooms, onions, peppers and pepperoni.

"No anchovies!" everyone voted. For once we were all in agreement.

The rest of the party was just as crazy as the start. When the pizza was delivered, Sam brought it up to Kristy's room. He knocked on the door. "Pizza man," he called in. Kristy let him in and tore open the boxes.

"What'd they give us? What'd they give us?" she said excitedly. "EW!!!!" Kristy jumped away from the boxes in disgust. We all crowded around to see. There, all over the tops of both pizzas, were worms! . . . Rubber worms. Sam's shoulders were shaking with laughter.

"SA-AM!" Kristy said hotly. We should've known Sam would try something like that. Sam is one of the world's champion practical jokers. (By the way, underneath all the worms, the pizza place *had* sent my broccoli.)

After pizza we wheeled out the television and set up a film on Kristy's video recorder.

Kristy had picked out the spookiest film she could find at the store, *Fright Night at Spook Lake*. It was all about a ghost who haunts an old lakeside resort house. When Karen heard the video on, she knocked on the door and asked if she could join us.

"Only if you don't get scared," said Kristy.

"Okay," Karen agreed. She climbed into Kristy's lap.

But when the ghost first came on the screen, Karen shrieked. "That's Ben!" she cried. "That's exactly what Ben Brewer looks like!"

"Karen!" Kristy said firmly. "There is *nothing* to be afraid of. Look at me. Am *I* afraid? Of course not. There's *nothing* to be afraid of."

Just then, in the film, the resort house got strangely quiet. An eerie light filled the inn's reception room and a breeze rustled the curtains. A phone rang loudly – Riiiiing! – and at that moment the real phone right outside Kristy's room rang, too! We all screamed and jumped a mile. Kristy gulped and looked at us. You could tell her heart was racing, and I think she didn't know whether to answer the phone or not, but she did.

"Oh," she said. "Hi, Nannie." She heaved a big sigh. "It's only my grandmother," she whispered to us. "Phew."

When the film was finished, Kristy's mum came in to collect Karen and take her off to bed. We stayed up a long time after that. We pushed Kristy's bed out of the way and put our sleeping bags and bedding in a circle, so that all our heads met in the centre. We just talked and laughed about school and about boys. Claudia got some pieces of paper from Kristy's desk and drew little caricatures of us all. When Jessi posed for hers, she sat on the floor, her legs stretched out on either side of her and her torso folded all the way over so her stomach was flat on the ground.

"Wow!" said Mary Anne.

I think by then we were all getting tired, but nobody wanted to admit it. We talked on, but one by one we started to drift off. Only Mary Anne lay wide awake beside me.

"In two days you'll be in California," she whispered to me.

"Yeah," I said. I didn't sound as excited as I thought I would. All of a sudden I was a little nervous about going. I looked around the room. Here I was, with all my best friends – especially Mary Anne.

It felt so cosy and homely. It felt like . . . like a family.

"You'll be gone for so *long*," Mary Anne whispered. "And you'll have so much fun that you won't even *think* of us."

"Of course I will," I said. "You're my *friends*. Anyway, I'll be home before you know it."

"Well, phone whenever you want," Mary Anne said. "And send me a postcard." She took my hand and squeezed it.

"I'll send you a zillion." I squeezed her hand back.

My thoughts were all jumbled as we lay there in the dark. But the thoughts tumbled into dreams, and soon I was asleep.

3rd
CHAPTER

sunday

Dear Mary Anne,

Well, I told you I'd send a postcard, but bet you never thought it'd be so soon. Here I am on the aeroplane and we've only been "in flight" for fifteen minutes. Not much to report, but I can tell you anything you want to know about oxygen masks, life-jackets, or exit doors. (The airhostess who did the safety demonstration reminds me of a Barbie doll.) It's going to be a _long_ flight.

Love,
Dawn

157

Long flight was right. Long morning, too. That morning I woke up really early, half an hour before my alarm. My brain was racing with all the things I needed for my trip: toothbrush, toothpaste, swimsuit, aeroplane ticket. I even wondered if maybe I had got the ticket wrong. Maybe I was supposed to fly out tomorrow, not today. It surprised me that I was so jittery. I've flown plenty of times before. But that morning, when my alarm went off, believe me, I was wide awake.

I could hear Mum in the shower, so I went down to make myself a quick breakfast. There was cereal in the cupboard, but no milk in the refrigerator. I poured myself a bowl and wondered if maybe I could substitute orange juice for milk. I decided to eat it plain.

Getting Mum to an airport in time is no small task. She thinks you don't have to get there until five minutes before flight time.

"They're always late," she says. "We'll just have to sit there."

I like to count on an extra forty-five minutes to an hour. What if there's a traffic jam? And airlines overbook all the time. I could hear Mum singing away in the shower. I decided to knock on the door.

"In a minute, darling," she said.

It seemed like forever to me, but finally we were both showered, dressed and out of the house. Mum had had her coffee and we had found her keys and I double-checked the things I had stuck in my flight bag: a favourite collection of ghost stories (*Spirits, Spooks and Ghostly Tales*), some magazines and some cards to write to my friends. Since this wasn't a night flight, and since I would be on the plane for practically six whole hours, I decided that I'd better come aboard with a few things to do.

On the way to the airport, Mum let me listen to my radio station and didn't even ask me to turn it down. She didn't say an awful lot during the drive. Every once in a while, she'd pop in with, "You remembered your underwear?" or, "Now don't forget your manners. 'Please, thank you' . . . What am I saying? You know how to behave."

I think Mum was just nervous. I noticed that as she drove, her fingers kept twisting around the steering wheel.

When we got to the airport, Mum found a place in the short-term car park. Then we went in, checked my suitcase, got a seat (No Smoking/Window), and went to wait at the gate. I started to feel as choked up as Mum looked. I glanced at her, and she gave a half smile, and then her eyes welled up and over.

"Are you going to be okay, Mum?" I asked. Now I was beginning to cry.

"Oh, Dawn," she said. "I'm all right.

I'm fine. You'd think I was sending you to Egypt or something."

When it was time for me to board, Mum walked me to the door and gave me a big hug.

"See you soon," I said.

She kissed my cheek. "Right," she said, very quickly.

I got on the plane and distracted myself with settling in. I wanted to make sure to get myself a pillow and a blanket. I wanted to check out the magazines that were on board – *Forbes, Business Week* . . . nothing for me. I suppose I was starting to feel a little better because when the Barbie doll air hostess gave her safety demonstration, I even found myself giggling. But when the plane started to taxi down the runway, I suddenly thought of Mum. I pictured her back in the car park trying to remember where she had parked the car.

"Row C," I thought, trying to send her the message. "Row C."

The plane took off and tears spilled down my cheeks. I was going to California. And Mum was going to be all alone.

Well, if it weren't for that air hostess, I might've cried the whole way out. I certainly wouldn't have had half as much to think about. You see, this air hostess was really strange. First of all, she looked strange. Something about her hair . . . or her makeup. Her cheeks had a cakey look, and when she had put on her lipstick, she had drawn it above the natural line of her lips. Also, she painted on her eyelashes. You know, dark little lines painted on her eyelids. The whole effect was pretty weird. Even when you get made up at the Washington Mall, you don't come out looking *that* strange.

But worst of all, she was a total airhead. Now most of the air hostesses I've met have been pretty down-to-earth. If you want a Coke, they give you a Coke. But this one I had to practically flag down anytime I wanted anything. The main trouble was, sitting next to me, in the aisle seat, was a very attractive guy. He was sandy-haired, good-looking, and had on a crisp white polo shirt with the sleeves rolled up. Well, this air hostess practically drooled every time she walked by him.

"Can I get you anything, sir?" she asked.

When they came around with the drinks trolley, he got an orange juice, and then she wheeled the trolley right on! What about me?

"Excuse me," I said. "Excuse me."

"Excuse me," the man said. "This young girl didn't get a drink."

"Oh, didn't she?" said the air hostess. She would've been blinking her eyelashes, only she couldn't. They were painted on.

"Tomato juice, please," I said. That was that.

Then she came around selling head-phones for the music channels and the film. Once again, the air hostess sold one to Mr Handsome and ignored me. Once again, Mr Handsome came to my rescue. When I finally got my headphones, he winked at me.

"Now you know why I always get an aisle seat," he said.

Mr Handsome's name was actually Tom and he turned out to be not a bad seatmate at all. He was a theatre director, he said, and he was flying out to California to audition some actors. Wow! I thought. A theatre director! I couldn't wait to tell Stacey. He and I had a little conversation about *Paris Magic* (which I hadn't even *seen*, just heard about from Stacey), and he wrote down the names of some other shows he thought I might enjoy.

"Thanks a lot," I said.

I tucked the slip of paper into the pocket of my cotton travelling jacket.

Well, Mr Handsome (I mean Tom) had some scripts with him that he had to read, so I listened to the music on the head-phones and flicked through my book and magazines. But I was getting much too excited to do any real reading.

When it was time for lunch, Tom turned to me and said, "Do you think we'll have to go to battle for you again?" But lunch, I thought, would be no problem. I had ordered a vegetarian lunch ahead of time. You can do that on airlines if you don't want to eat the normal food they give you. I'm not a strict vegetarian, but the vegetarian meals on the planes are always much better.

Anyway, our air hostess had about half the plane to serve before she got to our row.

"Here you go," she smiled at Tom.

"And for the young lady?" he said.

"I get a vegetarian meal," I said.

"No you don't," she said flatly.

"Yes," I said. "I ordered it when I got my ticket."

"Name?" she asked briskly.

"Dawn Schafer."

The air hostess disappeared to the back of the plane and came back with a computer printout. She ran her finger down a list.

"Schafer, Schafer, Schafer. . ." she said. 'Oh. Here you are. Oh, dear."

"Is there a problem?" asked Tom.

"Well," said the air hostess. "I did have a meal for you, but I gave it away. To that gentleman three rows up. He asked for one and I thought it was his."

She handed me a tray with a normal meal. No apology. No question about whether or not I was a strict vegetarian. What if I *couldn't* eat meat?

"Oh, well," she said. "There's certainly no way we can get another meal *in flight*."

Tom was looking faintly amused. I peeled back the tinfoil of my aeroplane lunch. Ew! It looked like the Friday lunch at Stoneybrook Middle School. There was some kind of meat with some kind of sauce on it. Mystery meat, I thought, and there was some messy coleslaw and this disgusting rubbery jelly with lumpy things inside. There was also a salad (okay, I could eat that). And there was a piece of cornbread that *did* look more edible than the rest. What a lunch – cornbread and salad. I turned the meat over with my fork and thought about how Kristy would react if this were really a cafeteria lunch.

"Ew," she'd probably say. "Fried monkey brains." (Or something even worse.)

Tom offered me his cornbread to help fill me up.

The rest of the flight was, well . . . long. Think of it – how often do you have to sit in a cramped seat for six hours at a stretch? The film was a Western, which filled the time, but not much else.

The air hostess, though, had one last opportunity to bungle things. After lunch, when she came around with coffee and tea, I asked if I could have a little real milk to put in my tea. (All she had on the tray was packets of that white chemical stuff.)

"Sure thing," she smiled, with that too-red smile of hers.

Minutes passed, many minutes, and again I had to flag her down.

"My milk, please?" I said.

"Oh, right."

She disappeared, came back, and tossed two of the chemical packets on my tray.

"There you go," she said, and she was gone.

"Do you get the feeling we're characters in some play?" Tom smiled. "A comedy?"

But, really, what did I care about "coffee whitener" or mystery meat or even irritating air hostesses? When the flight was over, I'd never see her again. When the flight was over, I'd be landing in my favourite place in the whole world . . . California!

The pilot's voice came over the intercom.

"We're preparing to land at the John Wayne/Orange County Airport," he said. (That's really what the airport's called. Honest.)

The wheels of the plane hit the runway, I felt the power of the plane pulling back, and there I was!

When I walked off the plane and into the waiting room, my heart was pounding. There were Dad and Jeff on the other side of the guide rope, waiting and waving, both of them with big smiles. Behind Jeff another face squeezed through. Sunny! When I got through the crowd, Jeff took my flight bag, and Dad grabbed me up and swung me around.

"Sunshine!" he said.

"Oh, Daddy," I blushed. (I would have to tell him not to call me Sunshine when Sunny was around. It wasn't just embarrassing, it'd be *confusing*.)

While we waited for my suitcase, everyone chattered at once. I told them all about the air hostess. Jeff told me about all the fun they had planned. Dad kept beaming and ruffling my hair. He even started snapping his fingers and singing that old song, "California Girls". He really was acting crazy.

"That's what fathers are for," he laughed.

It hit me how much I'd missed him.

Before we left, we picked up some postcards of the big John Wayne statue that towers over the airport. (I was now in California, all right.) In the car on the way home, Sunny grinned at me and hinted that she had something to tell me.

"It's sort of a surprise," she said, but she wouldn't tell me any more than that. "Just come over to my house tomorrow night," she said. "Five o'clock."

Sunny always did love surprises. It sounded pretty mysterious to me. I wondered what she had up her sleeve.

4th
CHAPTER

Dear Dawn,
     I'm writing this before you leave
so you get it when you arrive. And
anyway, I miss you already. As
you read this, you're probably getting
ready to go to the beach or to
Disneyland, or you're probably
lunching with film stars. (Do
they have film stars in Anaheim?)
Are the boys cute? Is everyone tanned?
Write back!
                    Your (best) friend,
                    Mary Anne

When I woke up that Monday, my first morning back in California, at first I wasn't sure where I was. The sun was streaming in through the flowered curtains – the same curtains I had had when I lived here before. Maybe I had never left? From down the hall I heard cutlery clinking and I also smelled something wonderful. Breakfast! I threw on my bathrobe and padded down the long, cool, tiled hall to the kitchen. There was Mrs Bruen, the housekeeper Dad had hired. I'd never met her before, but we introduced ourselves.

Mrs Bruen was busy organizing breakfast, so I sat at the table and took in the room. Everything seemed so spacious to me, compared to our little house in Connecticut. The rooms were so big, and the windows . . . Everything was wide open.

Our California house really is cool. It's all on one floor, but that one floor is long and wide and snakes around on two sides. The house is really shaped like a square, with only the top side missing. The floors are all tiled with terracotta and there are slanted skylights in almost all the rooms. Now that Mrs Bruen was taking care of it, the place was bright and sparkling.

Pretty soon Dad and Jeff stumbled into the kitchen. I'd forgotten that I'd be up earlier than they would, with the time change and all. Since it was Monday, usually Dad would be going to work, but he'd arranged to take off the first week of my visit, and that day he was taking Jeff and me . . . to Disneyland.

"All right!" said Jeff.

Jeff and I have been to Disneyland lots of times before, since it's right in Anaheim and that's where our house is, but believe me, Disneyland is always a treat.

Mrs Bruen brought our breakfast over to the table. She'd made fresh melon slices, cheese-and-egg puffs, freshly-squeezed orange juice and wheat crisps. Yum!

"Beats a bowl of dry cereal," I said, thinking of my last meal in Connecticut. My mouth was full.

"What?" asked Dad.

"Not important," I smiled.

"So what do you kids want to see today at Disneyland?" Dad asked. "It'd be nice to have some idea before we hit those queues and crowds."

That's Dad. Mr Organization.

"Star Tours!" cried Jeff. "Big Thunder Mountain Railroad! Jungle Cruise! Space Mountain!" He kept going. "Matterhorn! Pirates of the Caribbean! Davy Crockett's Explorer Canoes! Penny Arcade!"

"Whoa! Slow down," laughed Dad.

Disneyland is made up of seven theme areas, and Jeff had managed to name exhibits and rides in every single one. Dad grabbed a pad and a pen.

"I knew it would be a good idea to talk

about this beforehand," he said. "Okay, let's narrow down what areas of the park we're going to."

Jeff named three choices (Tomorrowland, Bear Country, and Frontierland) and I named mine (Fantasyland, New Orleans Square, and Jungleland). You'll notice that none of our choices overlapped.

"Of course you don't agree," said Dad. "That would be too easy. How about if you each pick two? We could probably manage to squeeze in four altogether."

"Does that count Main Street?" I asked. (Main Street, USA, is the area leading into the park.)

"I suppose not," Dad smiled. "Four, plus Main Street."

"All right!" Jeff said loudly. Jeff was already starting to get what Dad calls "Disneyland Wild".

"So what'll it be?" Dad asked. "Two each."

"Tomorrowland and Frontierland!" said Jeff. "No, Tomorrowland and Bear Country! No! I mean, Tomorrowland and Frontierland! Yeah, that's my vote."

My choices were Fantasyland and New Orleans Square.

Then Dad asked us what rides we wanted to go on and what things we wanted to see. By the time we got out of the house and on the motorway, we had the whole trip planned.

Disneyland is really great. I'd forgotten

170

how much I love it. Dad bought our "Passports" at the front gate. Those are the tickets that let you go all through the park and on all the rides. (Of course, you can't buy things, like food or souvenirs, with them, but I'd brought along plenty of babysitting money for extras.) Jeff had brought his camera with him and took my picture by the Mickey Mouse face as we walked in.

"Dawn! Dawn! Stand over here!" he called to me.

It's things like that that let me know just how much Jeff really likes me. That was only the first picture of many. He must have taken two whole rolls of me that day.

We entered the park and walked up Main Street, USA, which is made up to look like a small American town at the turn of the last century. It has horse-drawn carriages and an old-fashioned fire engine, and because our visit was in the spring, there were tulips blooming everywhere. All the shops that line the street look like old shops, but you can buy really cool things in them.

I dragged Dad and Jeff into three shops. One for postcards (I was going to have a lot of *those* to write), one for Mickey Mouse ears (I bought a pair for each member of the Babysitters Club), and in the last store I got a special present just for Mary Anne (a cuddly Minnie Mouse doll for her bed).

"What do you say, think we've had enough?" teased Dad.

"No!" cried Jeff.

We had just begun.

At the end of Main Street is Sleeping Beauty's Castle, and that's the entrance to Fantasyland. When I was a little kid, I thought that castle was the most beautiful thing I'd ever seen. I could picture myself moving right into it. It really is fantastic. When I walk over the moat and through the castle, I really feel as though I'm in Disneyland.

In Fantasyland, Jeff and I went on the Mad Tea Party ride (you sit inside these oversized teacups and spin all around) and on the Matterhorn Bobsleds. (Dad let Jeff pick one roller coaster ride and that one was it.)

From there we went on to Tomorrowland (with Jeff running ahead all the way). Of course, Jeff wanted to go on Star Tours, which has a really cool flight simulator.

"Too bad, Dawn," Jeff teased as we waited in line. "'Children under three not allowed'."

Believe it or not, that's exactly the kind of talk you miss when you don't have a brother around.

After Star Tours, we headed to Captain Eo, which is a 3-D Michael Jackson video. When we came out, Jeff started moon-walking. Brothers! They drive you crazy, but I have to admit, they can be pretty funny.

"Onwards!" said Dad.

We caught the train that circles the park and rode it all the way to Frontierland. That's where Jeff wanted to go on the Mark Twain Steamboat. "Ah, here we go," said Dad. "A ride for old fogies like me."

The steamboat circles an island and I like to pretend that I'm Mark Twain, navigating the Mississippi, thinking up the stories I'm going to write.

"So. We're finished," Dad said as we got off the boat. "We've done everything on our list."

There was a teasing twinkle in his eye.

"No way!" cried Jeff. "You forgot New Orleans Square!"

Jeff was still more than a little "Disneyland Wild".

Everybody was getting hungry, so we decided to stop in one of the New Orleans "buffeterias" . . . after one more ride.

"Pirates of the Caribbean!" shouted Jeff.

"No," I said. "Haunted Mansion. That was my whole reason for picking New Orleans Square."

"You could split up," Dad suggested.

That's exactly what we did.

Haunted Mansion is right up my (spooky, ghost-ridden) alley. On the outside it's an old New Orleans house. You know the kind. It has those wrought-iron, curlicue trellises bordering all the porches. Inside, though, it's a real spook house. To go through, you get in a Doom Buggy. Sound creepy? That's the least of it. Ghost shadows are cast on all the walls, and eerie music plays in the background. Upstairs, in the attic, there's about a *centimetre* of dust on everything. I'm telling you, one trip through Haunted Mansion equals about *ten* good ghost stories. And I ought to know.

Jeff and I met Dad at the French Market restaurant, where he had already snared a table for us.

"Yum!" I said, as I looked at the menu. It was hard to decide between Cajun-seasoned trout or spinach quiche.

"Want to split them?" Dad asked. It was the perfect solution.

Now that we were sitting down and eating, Jeff began to wind down. Well, a little bit. We finished our meals and watched the Mark Twain steamboat glide by beyond the restaurant porch.

"Hey, Dawn," Jeff said. "Watch this."

Jeff made one of his silly monkey faces.

"Glad to see your sister, huh?" Dad laughed.

"Yeah," Jeff said sheepishly. He smiled at me, an awkward, self-conscious smile. "Sometimes I miss you, Dawn," he said.

Dad ruffled my hair, as if I were a puppy or something.

"We *both* miss you," he said. "That much is for sure."

There I was, back in Disneyland, sitting

with my dad and my brother, and both of them being gushy. It felt really good.

Dad looked at his watch.

"What time do you have to be at Sunny's, Dawn?" he asked.

"Five o'clock," I said. "Whatever her surprise was, I'd better be on time."

"I think we have time to do one last thing," said Dad.

"Jungle Cruise!" shouted Jeff. He was never at a loss for ideas.

"No, this one's for your old man," said Dad. "I spotted it right as we came in the park. Back to Main Street. Let's go."

"Where are we going?" asked Jeff.

"You'll see," said Dad.

He had that glint in his eye.

When we got back to Main Street, Dad led us straight to the Main Street Cinema, an old film house that plays silent cartoon classics, ones like *Steamboat Willie* and *Mickey's Polo Team*. It was really fun to see them.

"They don't really look like the cartoons we have today," I said.

"They're better," said Dad.

"No way!" said Jeff.

All in all, it had been a perfect day in Disneyland. And the day wasn't over yet, either. I couldn't wait to get home to see Sunny. I couldn't imagine what she might have for a surprise.

5th CHAPTER

Monday

Dear Everybody,
Well, I just can't seem to get babysitting off the brain. I'm mailing this to Claudia's so you can all read it at your meeting and I've just came from a meeting of my own. No kidding! There's a California branch of the Babysitters Club. It's called the We ♥ Kids Club and my friend Sunny started it. Some of the things about the club are the same, but it's _very_ California. I'll tell all when I return.

Love,
Dawn

No wonder Sunny wanted to surprise me. When I got back from Disneyland, I ran over to her house. (She lives only a few houses down the block. I used to be there so often I could find it in my sleep.) I got there at five o'clock on the dot. Sunny's mum opened the door.

"Dawn," she smiled. "Look at you! Look how you've grown! Oh, I know I'm not supposed to say that. Come in. Come in."

Sunny clambered down the stairs. She was grinning from ear to ear. She had a scarf in her hands. Sunny and her surprises. . .

"Hold still," she said to me, "and close your eyes."

She tied the scarf on me like a blindfold.

"What. . .?" I said.

"I told you," she insisted. "It's a *surprise!*"

Sunny took my arm and led me up the stairs to her room. She swung open the door and undid my blindfold.

"Ta-da!" she said.

There, in the room, sat two other girls, Maggie Blume and Jill Henderson. I remembered them because I used to be in their class at school. Was this the surprise? I smiled faintly. I knew these girls, but I hadn't ever really been great friends with them.

"Sit down," said Sunny. "Make yourself at home. What are you waiting for?

Haven't you ever been to a meeting of a babysitters club before?"

Sunny still had that wide, teasing grin stretched across her face.

"Babysitting club?" I said.

"Yes," said Sunny, proudly, "the We ♥ Kids Club." And she told me all about it.

"Remember all those letters you sent me?" asked Sunny. "With all the news about your club?"

"Yes," I said. (I must have sent her about a hundred.)

"Well," she said. "It sounded like a good idea. I'd been babysitting a lot around the neighbourhood, and so had Maggie and Jill—"

"It sounded like a *great* idea," Jill broke in. "Before, we were all sitting, but we were just out there on our own."

"So we got the club together," said Maggie.

"And we named it the We ♥ Kids Club," said Jill.

"And it was all I could do to keep it a secret!" Sunny laughed.

To tell you the truth, I was shocked she'd been able to carry it off. Well, if there was a surprise involved, Sunny could do almost anything.

"How long have you been meeting?" I asked.

"Six months," Sunny grinned. "Six long, *silent* months."

Of course, I had lots of questions. I wanted to know exactly how they ran their club. Some things were the same as ours – Sunny had got a lot of ideas from my letters.

"Like advertising," she said. "When we first started, we made up leaflets and stuck them in every letterbox for ten blocks."

"And of course we collect subs," said Jill.

"For Kid-Kits!" Sunny cried out. She was practically exploding from the excitement of finally getting to tell her secret.

"You have Kid-Kits, too?" I asked.

Kid-Kits are a great idea that Kristy thought up. They're boxes that we fill with all kinds of things for kids to play with – books, games, crayons, puzzles. We bring them to the houses we babysit at and, of course, the kids just love them. They're also good for business. They show we really are concerned and involved sitters.

Sunny pulled out her own Kid-Kit, and I took a look through. Play-Doh, biscuit cutters, watercolours . . . and a cookbook!

"'*Kids Can Cook . . . Naturally*,'" I read.

"It's a great book," said Sunny. "All the recipes are easy for kids – none of them involve the oven or stove. And they all use natural foods."

"Wow," I said. Imagine if I tried to introduce that book to my club.

"Oh yeah," said Sunny, "and we've got an appointment book."

She pulled out a thin notebook and opened it to the day's page.

Well, it certainly did look as if the clubs were very alike, but believe me, there were lots of differences, too.

After Sunny had told me about the club, I thought she would call the meeting to order, I almost expected her to pull out a director's chair, just like Kristy sits in, and call for order. Instead we just sort of sat around and talked some more. They told me all about Mr Roberts, their science teacher, and asked me if Connecticut schools make you dissect a worm.

Then the phone rang. Maggie reached for it and took the call. She put her hand over the receiver and said, "Mrs Peters. Thursday. Anybody take it?"

"I will," said Jill.

It was as simple as that.

"Don't you take the information and phone them back?" I asked. That's the way we did it.

"Why?" said Maggie.

I just shrugged my shoulders. Somehow it seemed too complicated to explain.

After the call, Sunny wandered off to the kitchen and brought us back a snack – apple slices with natural peanut butter.

It's true, I thought. I really am back in California. This was a far cry from Claudia's junk-food.

"So who are your officers?" I asked.

180

"Officers?" asked Sunny.

"You know, chairman, vice-chairman, secretary. . ."

"We don't have anything like that," said Sunny. "Everybody just does what they do."

"Oh," I said.

Another call came in. This time Sunny took the job.

Jill pulled a bottle of nail varnish out of her bag and started working on her nails. I could just see Kristy if one of us tried that back in Stoneybrook.

I got up and looked at Sunny's bookshelves – two whole shelves of ghost stories. Sunny and I had fallen in love with ghost stories back in fourth grade, at just about the same time. When our class went to the school library, we used to race each other because we both wanted to get there first, to get whatever ghost books were in that week. (I can still hear Mrs Wright, our teacher, now. "Girls! No running in the halls!") Sunny had a lot of new books on her shelves now, a lot of books I hadn't ever heard of, like *Ghost in Whitcomb's Briar* and *Seven Gothic Ghosts*.

"Have you read *Spirits, Spooks and Ghostly Tales*?" asked Maggie.

"Maggie loves ghost stories, too," Sunny explained. "I got her into them."

"Phew, I have to sit down," I said. What had happened? Had I died and gone to

Dawn heaven? It really felt like it. I was in California, where the weather was warm and beautiful. I was staying with my wonderful, crazy dad and I had my good old brother back, too. Next, I found out that my best friend in California had started up a babysitting club. Where they served *apple slices* for snacks. And to top it all, my old friends liked ghost stories, too! Sunny was piling up books in my arms to take back to Dad's with me.

"Holiday reading," she said.

Just then, the third and last call came in. It was Mrs Austin, Dad's next-door neighbour. She needed someone on Saturday during the day to sit for Clover and Daffodil. I'd been their sitter many times before when I'd lived in California.

"Do you want it?" Sunny smiled at me.

"Definitely!" I said.

Jill handed me the notebook and I pencilled myself in.

We still had a few minutes of the meeting to go, so Jill painted all our fingernails and we sat around, waving our hands back and forth to dry the shimmering gloss.

"I've got one more surprise for you," said Sunny, blowing on her nails.

Another surprise? Sunny's eyes were twinkling. She blurted out the news.

"Our school's on holiday these two weeks, too!"

"Perfect!" I squealed. It was.

When it was time to go home, I grabbed my stack of books, popped in to say good-bye to Sunny's mum, and practically skipped the whole way home. It was 5:30, but the sun was still bright. It warmed my shoulders and toasted my hair.

The We ♥ Kids Club might not be as busy or have as big a business as the Babysitters Club, but it really was fun. I loved the way everything in California was so easy, so free. I swung my hair from side to side as I skipped into the house.

"Hey," said Dad. "You look happy. Anything special?"

I stumbled to the table and dropped my books all over its top.

"Everything!" I laughed.

6th
CHAPTER

Dear Dawn,

Having a wonderful time. Wish you were here. Wait! That's what you're supposed to write to us. Actually, we do wish you were here. We could've used you the other night at the Newtons. The two of us sat for the Newtons, the Feldmans, and the Perkinses. That's eight kids! (Count 'em.) We worked out a plan ahead of time -- we were going to get the kids out of the house -- but guess what? It rained. Help! But rain wasn't the only surprise. Tell you all about it when we see you.

Love,
Mary Anne and Claudia

The Newtons, the Feldmans and the Perkinses. That's one big group, all right. And that group is a handful and a half.

Mrs Newton had arranged everything ahead of time with Mary Anne and Claudia. All the parents were going out together for dinner and a concert, so it seemed natural to put the kids all together and get two sitters. The plan was that everyone would stay at the Newtons'. Jamie Newton is four and his little sister Lucy is just a baby. They're great kids. By themselves they're a pleasure. Then there are the Perkins girls, Myriah, who's five-and-a-half, Gabbie, who's two-and-a-half, and Laura, the baby. (I hope you're counting babies. That makes *two.*) Babysitting for Myriah and Gabbie is usually as easy as babysitting for Jamie. Myriah's really bright and Gabbie is really sweet. She calls everybody by their full names. "Hello Dawn Schafer", she always says to me.

So far, so good. But when you put those kids together with the Feldmans, well, then you might have a problem. The Feldman kids are Jamie and Lucy's cousins. There's Rob Feldman (he's ten), Brenda Feldman (she's six) and Rosie Feldman (she's four). Hmm, what can I say about the Feldmans? Well, for a start, Rob is a girl-hater. He's got it in his head that girls are no good, and that goes double for girl babysitters. His sister Brenda is just a fusspot. It's hard to get her to enjoy anything. And the little one, Rosie, well, she's a one-girl noise machine. (But the thing is, unlike a machine, you can't just turn her off. And she can really give a babysitter a headache.)

When I got to talk to Mary Anne about it, she told me that she and Claudia had tried to plan the whole thing out ahead of time. They were going to give the kids an early dinner, and then, while it was still light, they were going to put the babies in their prams and march the whole group over to the school playground. Outside, Rosie could make as much noise as she wanted. Rob could even hate girls. He could show off on the climbing frame and feel as superior as he wanted. The other kids, of course, would be perfectly happy on the swings or in the sandpit. And when they'd tired themselves out? Home to the Newtons' house and into pyjamas.

Well, it sounded like a good plan. Mary Anne and Claudia were very pleased with themselves for having so much foresight. Except, of course, it rained. Early that evening, when the two of them arrived at the Newtons', the sky had turned a dark shade of purple and a few big, splotchy raindrops had already splattered the front walk.

Mary Anne looked at Claudia. Claudia looked at Mary Anne. Jamie answered the door.

"Hi-hi!" he said.

Gabbie was right behind.

"Hello, Mary Anne Spier. Hello, Claudia Kishi," she said.

Jamie and Gabbie, both with their characteristic welcomes. Mrs Newton was right behind.

"Hi, girls. Great. You're a few minutes early. Everybody's here. The kids are in the playroom. I made a big pot of chilli for dinner. The babies, of course, get their own food. Come in to the kitchen, let me show you."

Mrs Newton had organized everything as well as she could. Dinner was on the stove, cots and sleeping bags had been set out in the living room (this was going to be a *long* evening), and she had settled the kids in the playroom with colouring books and toys. (Rob was watching television.)

Mary Anne and Claudia went to the playroom and sat themselves among the group. Mrs Perkins was there with the babies, who were playing on the floor with soft toys.

"They'll go to bed by seven, seven-thirty," she said.

The parents all gathered around their broods to say goodbye, then they were off. The crowd looked smaller after the six adults had left but, somehow, it did not look quite small enough. Big drops of rain were now pelting the windows. (It kept up the whole night long.)

"How about one of us taking the babies, and the other the kids?" Claudia suggested.

Two little babies or six growing (active) kids. Somehow, it didn't seem balanced. Mary Anne looked sceptical.

"Okay, what if we do it that way, then swap?" Claudia suggested.

Mary Anne took baby duty first and Claudia took the kids.

Now, when you're babysitting for a gang, you'd better place yourself so that you can keep an eye on everybody at the same time. That's one thing we learned when we ran a playgroup last summer. You can't afford to get so involved with any one kid that the whole group falls apart. Claudia pulled a chair up to the play table. Jamie and Gabbie were working at one end and Myriah, Brenda and Rosie were working at the other. All the kids had fresh sheets of white paper and their own little box of crayons. (Thank you, Mrs Newton.) Except for Rob's television blaring in the background, the room was surprisingly peaceful.

Brenda pressed hard on her crayon to colour in the giraffe she was drawing. *Snap!* It broke in half.

"My brown!" she said. "My brown broke!"

She grabbed the brown crayon out of her sister's box.

"Gimme!" Rosie shouted back.

"It's mine!" shouted Brenda.

Rosie began banging the table. She had probably been waiting for just such an opportunity to make a lot of noise.

Now, Claudia is really the one sitter who has a lot of experience with the Feldman kids. A lot of experience, in this case, really means only twice. The first time she encountered this kind of problem, she ignored it and, when they didn't get any attention, the Feldman kids calmed down. The second time she sat for them, Kristy was with her. Kristy had let out a sharp, shrill whistle and called the whole scene to a halt. Claudia didn't know how to whistle like Kristy, so she quietly took the brown crayon out of Brenda's hand and gave it back to Rosie.

"You know that's Rosie's crayon," she said gently.

Just then Mary Anne stepped in and took Brenda's hand. That's babysitting teamwork. "I need some help with the babies," she said. "Brenda, you're a good helper. You come over and work with me."

Surprisingly, Brenda got up from the table and went to join Mary Anne. Claudia quietened Rosie and got her interested in her picture again. Rob looked over from the sidelines.

"I'm the oldest," he muttered. "And I know most about babies."

Mary Anne looked at him curiously.

"Would you like to join us, too?" she asked.

Rob eyed the babies.

"I'm watching television," he said. He turned his attention back to the screen.

Mary Anne and Brenda started a little rolling game for the babies with a cloth ball, but when Brenda rolled it, the ball rolled over towards Rob and bumped his knee.

"Here you go, babies," he said. He rolled the ball gently back.

Mary Anne shot Claudia a look as if to say, "Did you just see what I saw? Is that really Rob Feldman, girl-hater, sitting over there?"

Claudia shrugged her shoulders in reply. Maybe Rob didn't consider babies to be girls yet. Or maybe he had just grown out of his nasty phase. (After all, it had been almost a full year since Claudia had sat for him.)

"Blast off!" he said suddenly, his eyes fixed on the screen. "Babies into space!" Since he was watching a cowboy movie, no one knew quite what he meant.

The kids coloured for a while. At one point, Rosie started up her noise, banging her fists on the table, her feet on the floor, and loudly chanting a song she knew, but she was silenced by, of all people, Gabbie. When Rosie started her tirade, Gabbie put her hands over her ears and stared Rosie straight in the eye.

"You be quiet, Rosie Feldman," she said, very precisely. "You are really hurting my ears."

Rosie was so surprised at getting a telling off from Gabbie that she screwed up her face and went back to her picture.

When it was time for dinner, Mary Anne volunteered to take Brenda and Myriah (the two oldest girls) to the kitchen to serve up the plates.

"What about the babies?" Claudia asked.

"Hmmm," said Mary Anne. "Maybe I could take them up and get them set up in their high chairs and the girls could serve the chilli."

Rob swung around from the television.

"Little babies can't coordinate their hands with their eyes," he said. Then he looked at his cousin. "But you can, can't you, Lucy?"

Mary Anne shot Claudia another look. Well, it was worth a try, she thought.

"Rob," she asked, "why don't you come and help me with the babies in the kitchen. Can you carry Lucy?"

Rob picked Lucy up and followed Mary Anne and the kitchen crowd out of the playroom. He set Lucy into her high chair and strapped her in.

"How do you know so much about babies?" Mary Anne asked as she set the other baby down.

"*Babies in Space*," Rob said tersely.

"Is that a TV show?" Mary Anne asked.

"No," he said, as if everyone knew. "A book."

"Oh," said Mary Anne.

As it turned out, the book was a science fiction story about some scientists who send babies in a rocket to another planet. First, of course, they have to know everything about babies that they can, so the book is filled with little bits and snatches of scientific information about babies and how they develop.

Mary Anne opened a jar of strained pears, stuck a spoon in it, and set it down on Lucy's highchair tray. Rob picked up the jar and started to feed her.

"When babies are nursing, they get immunities from their mothers," he said. He spooned some of the strained pear and aimed it high at Lucy's little mouth. "Ready! Aim! Fire!" He made rocket noises as he dipped the spoon into Lucy's waiting mouth.

Mary Anne told me later that she thought, well, you just never know. Rob Feldman, girl-hater/baby-lover. Now he seemed more like future babysitter material. Who could have thought it? Babysitting is always a surprise.

Dinner went fairly smoothly. Claudia manoeuvred the seating so Brenda wasn't sitting next to Rosie. (Those two were just a *bad* combination.) And after dinner, Rob helped Claudia to get the babies off to bed.

When the parents got home, all the kids were in their pyjamas and *most* were asleep. (Brenda kept waking up confused. "Where am I?") The Perkinses and the Feldmans picked up their pyjama-ed and sleepy-eyed kids, covered them with raincoats, and ran them out to their cars.

"Oh," said Mrs Newton, as she shook out her umbrella. "What a refreshing evening. And how did it go for you girls?"

Mary Anne grinned at Claudia.

"*Surprisingly* well," said Mary Anne.

7th CHAPTER

Thursday

Dear Kristy,
   As I'm writing this I'm wiggling my toes in the hot sand and I just finished slathering sun lotion all over my legs. Oops! Got some on the postcard. Too bad this isn't a letter. I'd stick some sand in the envelope for you. As you can see, I'm happy as a sand crab.

See you (too!) soon,
Dawn

194

Well, Thursday was what I would call a perfect day. (Perfect except for the strange feelings brewing inside me.) Dad volunteered to take me and Jeff, plus the members of the We ♥ Kids Club, *plus* a friend of Jeff's . . . to the beach! (Brave Dad.) Everyone gathered at our house after breakfast in the morning, and it did take us a while to get going.

I had to run back into the house to slip a cover-up over my bikini so I'd feel okay for the car ride. (What if we stopped at a shop for drinks or something?) Sunny, Jill and Maggie arrived in their bikinis and the sight was just too much for Jeff and his friend Luke. "Underwear!" they screamed. "The girls are going to the beach in their *underwear*!" (Ten-year-old boys will be ten-year-old boys, all right.)

There we were, all dragging beach bags with suntan lotion and beach towels, and all wearing flip-flops. No question about where we were heading. I took a look at us as we gathered in the driveway and noticed that we were all blond. Jeff and I are white-blond, but everyone there was some kind of blond or other. Well, this really was a stereotypical California group.

We waited for Jeff to run back into the house (twice) for more comics. I checked to see that I had stuck my Walkman in my bag and, finally, we were off.

In the car, Jeff and Luke insisted on

singing "99 Green Bottles Hanging on the Wall."

"Dad," I said. "Make them stop."

"I think it would take a power greater than I," he said.

Luckily, the boys got bored after about 82 bottles.

When we got to the beach it really was not very crowded. People in California wait until it's really summer to go to the beach, and also, it was the middle of the week. Actually, it was beautiful beach weather. Not a cloud in that whole wide blue sky, and the sun was beating down, warming the sand, the ocean and us!

I ran ahead and found us a big stretch of sand. (We *needed* a big space.) "Blonds over here!" I shouted and everyone ran to the spot and spread out their towels.

"You're right about blonds," said Dad. "We look like the Swedish delegation to the blond convention."

And the whole rest of the day, that's what he called us, "The Blond Convention." Of course, it didn't help when Jill and Maggie pulled out their Sun-Light and combed it through their hair.

"Blond and want to be blonder?" Dad teased. He was using a deep announcer's voice, like a TV commercial. "Try our products. That's Products for Blonds. In the pale yellow packaging."

We arranged the beach towels so that

Dad was on one side of me, and Sunny and the girls were on the other. Jeff and Luke spread their towels a little way away. I think they were looking for a place that would give them the best aim – at us – because, as we lay there in the sun, all covered in oil, Jeff and Luke tossed little bits of dried seaweed and tiny pieces of shells onto our oiled backs and bellies.

"Bull's-eye!" Jeff yelled, when he got a shell right on Dad's bellybutton.

"Why don't you lot go and collect some shells?" Dad suggested. He handed them the red plastic beach bucket we had brought along.

"BO-RING," said Jeff.

"How about digging for clams?" Dad suggested.

"Yeah!" said Luke and Jeff at the same time. They were off and running.

Sunny, Maggie and Jill decided to head down to the edge of the sea and wade in. I wasn't really warm enough yet, so I decided to stay put and let the sun do its work.

"So here you are, Sunshine," Dad said when we found ourselves alone. "Sunshine in the sunshine."

Dad can be really silly sometimes. He grinned at me, then squinted out at the sea.

"I'm glad you could come for a visit," he said.

"Me too."

Somebody walked by us with a radio. I could tell Dad was going to start up a serious talk, and I wasn't sure if I was ready for it. Well, ready or not, a father-daughter chat was in the air. I waited for Dad to start.

"So how's it going in Connecticut?" he asked.

"It's okay," I said.

"School?"

"Fine."

"Friends?"

"Friends? Friends are great," I said. I sat up on my towel and started to push my fingers through the sand.

"How does Jeff seem to you?" Dad continued.

Jeff seemed fine, and I told Dad so. I told him again how unhappy Jeff had been in Connecticut and how much trouble he'd got into at school and all.

"I suppose Jeff's the type who just needs to be at home in California," Dad mused.

"Lucky him," I said, half under my breath. I was surprised at how sullen I sounded all of a sudden. Usually I'm about as even-tempered as they come.

Dad glanced at me and then stared out at the surf where my friends were playing.

"So how's your mother?" Dad asked after a while.

"Oh, you know Mum," I said. "I have to check her every time she goes out of the house for—" I almost said, "for a date with the Trip-Man," but I caught myself just in time. I really didn't want to get into a discussion about the Trip-Man with Dad. I paused awkwardly, then said quickly, "—for work. Out of the house for work."

It felt silly to have something I couldn't talk to Dad about. Somehow, the whole conversation was feeling awkward to me. I didn't know what was the matter. I dug my fingers deeper into the sand.

"Is she, uh . . . doing okay?" Dad asked.

"Pretty good," I said. The truth was, Mum *was* fine. She might be scattered, but that was just Mum. She might be a little weepy every now and then, but that was natural – her family had been split up. "She likes Connecticut," I said. "She sees Granny and Grandad. She loves the farmhouse. . ."

"I hear you have a secret passage," Dad smiled. "Something right out of one of your ghost stories, huh?"

I told him all about the passage, about how we had found it, and how Mallory's brother Nicky had discovered it before any of us.

"He still hides out in there sometimes," I said. "Sometimes when he just needs some solitude."

"In a family with eight kids?" Dad said. "I can see why."

"Well," I said glumly, "I don't have that

problem." Again, the tone of my voice surprised me. What was the matter with me? I was in California, at the beach. . . The *last* thing I should have been doing was complaining.

Dad knew right away that something was up. He waited a while before he said anything. Dad's good that way. He gives you whatever time you need to think things through.

"A little lonely, are you?" he said.

I hadn't thought of it that way before, exactly. Maybe I was. I wasn't sure what I was feeling.

Just then Jeff and Luke ran up and dropped a little sand crab in my lap.

"Ew!" I screamed.

"Jeff. Luke," Dad said sternly.

All of a sudden I felt like running, moving, getting up, doing something. I popped up, brushed the sand crab back on to the sand, and took off for the sea. Sunny and the others were now waist-deep in the water.

"Aughhh!" I cried as I ran towards them, into the surf. The water was cold and shocked my skin, but I plunged in, ducked under, and came up wet and dripping. I bounded out to where my friends stood. The waves crashed against us and we jumped them and laughed. I waved to Dad back on shore. Suddenly I thought how happy, how *ecstatic*, I was to be home.

When my friends and I came back in, we were blue-lipped and shivering. Dad bundled us up in towels and we let the sun do the rest.

I sat at the edge of my towel and built a little sandcastle.

"Want to help?" I asked my friends. They didn't.

I stuck some shells in the castle for turrets. My emotions were beginning to calm. I thought, in passing, of Claudia. The sandcastle looked like something she might make. If Claudia were with us, I thought with a smile, she'd probably be building castles all up and down the shore.

After a while we had a wonderful lunch that Mrs Bruen had packed for us – avocado salad with shrimp and sprouts and an unusual potato salad made with fresh parsley and herbs.

Yum! My friends and I gobbled it up.

When the sun started to fade, we gathered up our things and straggled back to the car.

"Blond Convention, ho!" Dad called, leading the way.

That night, much later, Dad suggested that I call Mum, just to say hi.

I wasn't sure, but I think she sounded a little shaky-voiced when she answered the phone.

"Dawn!" she said. Her voice was

surprised. "So how are you?" she asked. "Are you having a good time?"

I babbled on about the beach, the weather, the housekeeper, my friends.

"We've already been to Disneyland, then today we went to the beach – And, Mum, I don't even have to miss the Babysitters Club. On Saturday I babysit for Clover and Daffodil, and Sunny runs her club just like ours, except it's much more relaxed. . . I'm having a great time. Jeff is really happy, and Dad is just super. . ."

I think I must've babbled on for quite a while. Out of nervousness? Something about it felt wrong.

"I'm so glad, darling," Mum said, when I had finished. Jeff was calling me in the background, so I put Dad on the phone.

There we were in our busy, active household, a family, and there was Mum in the farmhouse all alone. I suppose, at the time, I didn't think of it that way. I certainly didn't realize how much I was really missing Mum. I suppose I wasn't sure *what* I was thinking.

8th CHAPTER

Saturday

Dear Claudia,
   Sorry about that rain you and Mary Anne had when you babysat the other night Here? It never rains. This afternoon I babysat for Clover and Daffodil -- you remember I told you -- they're my old neighbours? Well, it was one of my all-time great babysitting days. Let me put it this way -- I came home with a better tan than I started with. Ah, California. You know how I love the warm outdoors...
                              Dawn

My first job for the We ♥ Kids Club really was a great success. When I got to their house, Clover and Daffodil practically knocked each other over trying to say hello to me. Daffodil was a little more subdued – she's nine years old and more grown-up than Clover, who's only six. Clover was pulling at my sundress before I could even get through the door.

"Whoa!" I said. "It's only me."

"Dawn!" cried Clover. "My favourite babysitter in the whole wide world!"

I must admit, when one of the kids gives you a compliment like that, it's not very hard to love your job.

Mrs Austin gave me a big hug hello. It was as though I was a long-lost friend, returning from a great war or something.

"The kids have been so excited," she said. She drew me into the room.

I always loved the Austins' house, especially the living room. Mrs Austin is a weaver. Dad said when they were young, she and her husband used to be "flower children". (I think he means hippies.) That's why Clover and Daffodil have such odd names. Now, though, Mrs Austin weaves professionally for a few stores that carry expensive hand-crafted goods, and she has three different-sized looms in her living room. The looms sit on the polished wood floor underneath the big bay window. I love to take a look at what she's working on. She mostly makes pieces with deep, rich natural colours. Beautiful warm browns and earthy reds. And there's always something different on the looms.

"I never have to redecorate," she laughs. "Whenever I change projects, I change the whole visual effect of the room."

That day, Clover and Daffodil were each wearing hand-woven cotton waistcoats that their mother had made for them. Clover pulled a small purse out of her vest pocket and shook the money into her hand.

"Pieces of eight!" she cried. "I'm rich!"

I had forgotten about Clover's wild imagination.

"I gave each of the kids some money," Mrs Austin explained. "There's a small carnival that's set up over in the field behind the mall. Since it's such a beautiful day, I thought you might want to walk the girls over and spend the afternoon there."

"Great," I said. The afternoon couldn't be shaping up better.

Mrs Austin grabbed her shawl (hand-woven, of course) and headed out of the door. She was going to a Craft Council meeting, so she'd be gone all afternoon.

Before we could go off to the fair, Clover and Daffodil had to drag me all over the house and show me everything that was new. It had been a long time since we'd seen each other.

"This is the kitchen and this is the

refrigerator," said Clover in her excitement. "She knows *that*, silly," said Daffodil. "Come on. Let me show you my science project."

We went all through Clover's and Daffodil's rooms. They showed me new clothes, new toys, new books, new school projects, report cards, you name it.

As they were winding down, I sat on Clover's bed and she got out her comb to comb through my long hair. (She always did love to do that.)

"I think somebody spun your head into gold," she said. "Did you ever meet a little guy named Rumpelstiltskin?"

Of course I told her no, but I think Clover secretly went on believing her own imaginative version. Daffodil sat quietly by. Sometimes, even though she's older, she gets overshadowed by Clover's more outgoing nature. She's also at that gangly stage – her legs and arms seem a little too long for her body.

"Well," I said, standing up. "Shall we head for the carnival?"

Clover popped up beside me. "To see the gypsies!" she cried. She was down the stairs and out of the door, with Daffodil and I trailing behind her.

The day was warm and dry and the bright blue sky was streaked with thin, wispy clouds. We had only a short walk to get to the fairgrounds. Just as Mrs Austin had said, the fair was set up behind the mall. There were a couple of rides – a ferris wheel and an octopus ride with cages that looped up and over.

"A space creature!" shouted Clover.

There were also lots of sideshows, plenty of food booths (Hmmm. Hot dogs and candyfloss. Not my idea of a healthy treat.) And a fenced-off ring with pony rides.

Clover had me by one hand and I had Daffodil by the other. Clover dragged us from one booth to the next, trying to decide where we should start.

"How about the hoopla?" Daffodil asked in a smallish voice.

"Hoopla!" Clover boomed in echo.

No sooner had she spotted it than we were there. The girls put down their money and got their handful of hoops. As you can imagine, Clover was an enthusiastic player. Enthusiastic, but not very skilled. Out of six hoops she got . . . six misses.

"Oh, well," she shrugged. It was Daffodil's turn.

Clover had thrown her hoops quickly, but Daffodil took her time. She eyed the hook that was the target. She scrunched her eyebrows in concentration. One hit! Two! Three! A miss. Four hits! Another miss.

"Wow!" I said. "Four out of six. That's not bad at all."

Daffodil smiled shyly. Something about

her reminded me of Shannon – she was like a puppy who had not yet grown into its paws.

"Can I try again?" she asked quietly.

"Of course," I said.

Daffodil bought another round of hoops. Again she scrunched up her eyebrows in concentration before she started. One hit. Two. Three. Four. A miss. Another miss.

"Oh," I groaned. "So close!"

Daffodil smiled and said nothing. Clover was already dragging us over to the pony ring.

"Want to ride?" I asked Daffodil.

Daffodil emptied her purse into her hand and counted her quarters.

"Nah," she said. "I think I'll wait."

Clover ran through the gate and hopped on the pony.

"Giddy-up!" she cried. She nudged the pony's ribs with her heels, but the pony stood still. It was waiting for a command from the young woman in jeans and cowboy boots who would lead it around the ring.

"Charge!" cried Clover.

I looked at Daffodil and grinned.

"Who do you think Clover thinks she is?" I asked. "Teddy Roosevelt?"

"Annie Oakley, I betcha," said Daffodil.

As it turned out, Clover was thinking of herself more as an Indian brave. She explained that to us after the pony ride and before the ferris wheel. Then, after the ferris wheel, of course, she had to go on the octopus ride. When she was finished, we were all ready for a little refreshment.

"Candyfloss!" yelled Clover.

Well, what could I do? Clover bought her candyfloss, and Daffodil and I got some fruit juice and vegetable fritters. We found a patch of grass to sit on at the edge of the carnival and let the sights and sounds play around us as we ate our snack.

Daffodil counted her change again.

"I could play two more times," she said.

"Hoopla?" I asked.

She nodded her head. We waited for Clover to finish her candyfloss (of course it got all over her face. She looked like some sort of sticky, pink elf), then we headed back to the booth. Daffodil looked determined. She may be a quiet one, I thought, but she's got a lot of resolve.

Her first game was worse than the others. Only three hits and three misses. Daffodil licked her lips as she bought the rings for her fourth and last game. One hit! Two! Three! Four! Five! . . . We all held our breath. . . Six!

"Yippee!" yelled Clover. She jumped up and down and shook her sister by the arm.

Daffodil's face broke into a wide, bright smile.

"I knew it," she said. "I knew I could do it."

In the back of the booth was a shelf of stuffed animals, which were the prizes.

"The pink elephant, please," Daffodil said to the man running the booth.

It certainly was pink. It was as pink as the candyfloss that still stuck to Clover's cheeks.

"Come on," I said. "Let's go home while we're winners. And let's get you cleaned up." I ruffled Clover's hair. "Miss Teddy Roosevelt-Annie Oakley-Spotted Deer, or whoever you are."

When Mrs Austin got home, she had the same reaction I did to the stuffed elephant.

"It certainly is pink," she laughed. "Congratulations, sweetie."

I don't think Mrs Austin was going to pick that colour for her next weaving project.

The day had been so pleasant, so easy. I was thinking how I couldn't wait to tell Sunny and the others all about it. There was a knock on the door. It was Jeff.

"Mum's on the phone," he said. "Come on."

Mrs Austin slipped me my pay and I ran home after Jeff.

"'Bye, Dawn-Best-Babysitter," Clover called after me.

As I was running I found myself thinking not of Mum, but of the day, of Clover and Daffodil, of Mrs Austin, the We ♥

Kids Club. . . I got on the phone and Mum started talking right away. She told me about Granny and Grandad and then she said she'd run into Kristy and her mother at the supermarket. "Oh," she said, "and Mary Anne called."

Wow! Mum, Granny and Grandad, Kristy, even Mary Anne. I hadn't thought of any of them all day long. What did that mean, I wondered. I suddenly felt wrenched out of one world and yanked into another.

9th
CHAPTER

Dear Dawn,
  Thought you might want to know that nothing has changed in Stoneybrook. Saturday I baby-sat at the Brewers, and you'll be interested to know that Ben Brewer, the old ghost, is alive and well and living on the third floor. At least that's what Karen says. Me, I think Sam has something to do with it. This time, anyway.
          See ya,
            Jessi

Well, some things never change. When you babysit for Karen Brewer, there's bound to be ghosts involved, or witches with magic spells, or some such spookiness. Jessi had taken a job at the Brewers' for Saturday afternoon. Kristy was going shopping with her mother, and Sam, Charlie and Watson were out who knows where. That left the younger ones – David Michael, Karen and Andrew – in need of a sitter, so Jessi filled the job.

Kristy's mum walked Jessi around the house, giving her all the usual information – showing her where the emergency numbers were, the snacks, etc. Of course, Kristy followed right behind. Sometimes you'd think Kristy was the Babysitting Police, not just the chairman of our club.

"Aren't you going to ask about the first-aid kit?" she prompted Jessi.

"Uh, yeah," Jessi stumbled.

"It's right in the medicine cabinet," Kristy's mum said, smiling.

Mrs Brewer could hardly get Kristy away from Jessi and out of the door.

"Shannon and Boo-Boo have been fed," Kristy called from the doorway, "and the plants have been watered, and the dishwasher's run through."

"And the lawn has been mowed," Kristy's mum teased, "and the house has been painted, and the telephone bill's been paid."

Kristy blushed furiously.

"Okay, 'bye," she called to Jessi.

Jessi picked up Andrew and together they waved goodbye.

"Well," Jessi said, when the door had closed. "Now it's just the four of us."

"Oh, no," Karen said firmly. "Five. Ben Brewer."

"Right," Jessi smiled.

"Come on," Karen said, grabbing Jessi's hand. "Time to play Let's All Come In."

"Oh, no," groaned David Michael.

Let's All Come In is a favourite game of Karen's, if you can call it a game. She gets everyone to pretend that they're different characters in a hotel lobby, checking in. What it really is, is an excuse to play dressing-up. Karen dresses up in a long black dress and a hat, and the boys wear sailor caps. I think David Michael has played this game one time too many.

"Andrew and I were in the middle of building a Lego city," he said. "Weren't we, Andrew?"

"Yup," Andrew agreed.

"Looks like it's just you and me," Karen said to Jessi.

"You, me and Ben Brewer," Jessi smiled.

Jessi got the boys settled back in David Michael's bedroom, where there really was a Lego city in progress.

"I'm the architect," David Michael said importantly, "and Andrew is the construction boss. Right, Andrew?"

"Right," Andrew smiled. Construction boss sounded pretty good to him.

Karen took Jessi to her room and began to root through the trunk she kept her dressing-up clothes in.

"Hmm," she said, looking Jessi up and down. "Do you want to be a cocktail waitress or do you want to be coming from the society ball?"

"Society ball, of course," Jessi replied.

"I don't think I have anything here to fit you," Karen said slowly. "You know what that means?"

"What?" asked Jessi.

"That means" – there was an ominous tone in Karen's voice – "we have to go to the other clothes trunk. And it's on *the third floor*."

If this had been a film, right at that moment scary music would have sounded. The third floor was, after all, where Karen believed Ben Brewer lived. As it was, the only sound was the nervous tapping of Karen's little foot. She twisted her fingers and bit her lip.

"I don't know," she said.

"We don't *have* to play Let's All Come In," said Jessi.

Well, that decided it for Karen.

"Oh, yes we do," she said with great conviction. "We can't let a *ghost* rule our lives."

Karen took Jessi's hand and squeezed it firmly but bravely.

"Come on," she said.

For her, I think, being scared is half the fun.

Karen led Jessi up the narrow staircase that leads to the third floor of the Brewer mansion. The third floor is seldom used. The house is so big that the first and second floors can comfortably house the whole family, large as it is. The third floor is really only used for storage. It's like one big attic, even though it's divided into rooms.

As they neared the top of the staircase, Karen began to creep.

"Aughhh!" she screamed suddenly.

"What is it?" Jessi asked.

Karen's eyes, big as saucers, focused on the top of the banister. She didn't say anything, she just pointed.

There, in the dust that covered the wooden banister, someone had etched the words "Turn Back!"

"Maybe we should," said Jessi. She didn't believe in the ghost, and yet. . .

"There's no turning back now," Karen said dramatically. She pressed ahead.

Karen crept down the hall to the room where the other trunk was stored. The door was closed, but not completely. It was open a small crack. Karen pushed the door slowly. *CRASH*! A can clattered on the floor in front of them and water splattered from the can all over their shoes and legs.

Of course, Karen screamed again. At this point, though, Jessi began to be sceptical. The door had obviously been booby-trapped. Why would a ghost booby-trap a door with a can full of water? It seemed to Jessi that the tricks a ghost would play would be, somehow, more ghostly. This seemed more like a practical joke. And if she had to name a practical joker in the house, she was pretty sure she knew who that might be.

Karen swung the door open wide and stamped loudly into the room.

"Ben Brewer!" she called out. "We're coming in. You can't stop us. We've made up our minds."

Karen marched over to the large dusty trunk, unlatched it, and opened its lid. The smell of mothballs flooded the room. Karen lifted up a dark blue crushed velvet dress that lay across the top of the pile.

"How about this dre—" she started to say, but her eye caught a note that had been tucked underneath the gown. The note was written in a thick, dark red ink.

"Blood-red," Karen whispered.

She picked up the note and read it.

"Death to all who enter here," it said.

Karen stood frozen, fixed in one spot. Her face paled.

"I think we'd better go back downstairs," she said to Jessi. Her voice was small and shaking. She dropped the note. It fluttered to the floor. She walked out of the room, gliding, like a sleepwalker or a zombie.

Jessi picked up the note and looked it over. The paper had been torn off a notepad. On the other side was a printed logo.

"SHS," it said.

SHS. Stoneybrook High School.

Jessi folded the note and put it in her pocket. She followed Karen back downstairs.

When Kristy and her mum got home, Karen ran down to the front hallway, frantic to tell them all the latest evidence.

"It *proves*," she said, "that Ben Brewer is living right up there on the third floor. How do we know he won't come down?" she asked. "How do we know he doesn't want to take over the second floor, too?"

As it happened, Sam and Charlie pulled in the driveway right after Kristy and their mum. When Sam came in, Karen was going on about the ghost.

"The note was written in blood," she said, then shuddered. "I wonder whose."

Sam smirked and nudged Charlie. Mrs Brewer shot a look at Sam. He shrugged innocently.

"I wonder how another child would fit into all this," Mrs Brewer wondered aloud.

"Another child?" Kristy asked. "What do you mean?" Mrs Brewer shrugged distractedly. Kristy shook her head and allowed her mum into the kitchen with Karen trailing behind. Jessi pulled the note out of her pocket and handed it to Sam.

"Lose something?" Jessi asked.

Sam grinned sheepishly and shoved the note quickly into his pocket.

Kristy came out of the kitchen.

"Of course this ghost incident will have to be written up in the club notebook," she said. "You realize that all the other club members should be aware of anything this important."

Jessi told me later she just smiled and nodded. Ben Brewer was living in the mansion, all right. It was Sam Brewer who'd made sure of that.

10th CHAPTER

Monday

Dear Stacey,
    There you are in New York City and here I am in California. Whatever happened to good ol' Stoneybrook, Connecticut? I'm having the time of my life. It almost seems as if I never left in the first place. The We ♥ Kids Club is keeping me very busy. It's a babysitters club with a difference.-- NO HULA HOOPS ALLOWED!

                    Dawn

All that weekend I looked forward to the next meeting of the We ♥ Kids Club. I had had such a good time with Clover and Daffodil, and couldn't wait to tell Sunny and the other members of the club.

When I arrived that Monday afternoon, Sunny was sitting on the floor of her room, with newspapers spread out all around her. She had a bag of potting soil, a couple of small clay pots and a few jars in which she had rooted some babies from her spider plant.

"Hi. Come in," she said. "If you can find a place. I'm just potting these."

I sprawled out on an empty stretch of Sunny's green rug. It was the usual relaxed, California atmosphere of the We ♥ Kids Club.

While we waited for Jill and Maggie, I told Sunny all about my afternoon at the Austins, about Clover's wild imagination and about Daffodil's tries at the hoopla.

"I think Clover's going to be an actress," said Sunny. "Or a writer or something like that."

"And Daffodil is the real surprise," I said. "You think because she's quiet she's going to be shy, but she has a real determination in her."

"Did you notice how she's suddenly all leg?" Sunny asked. "She's like a colt or a baby deer. . ."

"Exactly," I laughed.

As we were talking, a warm, homely feeling spread through me. It occurred to me that what we were doing was sharing the exact same kind of information that Kristy has the members of the Babysitters Club write up in the official Club notebook. And here we were just talking. Simple as that. You see, I thought, you *can* accomplish things informally.

Jill and Maggie arrived together, talking about some kids at school. Sunny finished her potting.

"Do you remember Joe Luhan?" Jill asked me.

"Of course." He had been one of the boys in my class.

"Well, he and Tom Swanson are having a party on Sunday. Will you still be here or are you leaving before then?"

"The day before," I said. "I'm leaving on Saturday."

Too bad. That sounded like fun. A party with Joe Luhan and Tom Swanson. I'd grown up with those boys. I knew them better than I knew most of the boys in Stoneybrook.

Sunny's mum poked her head in the door.

"Am I allowed in here?" she asked.

"Mu-um," Sunny moaned. "Of course. What do you think?"

Her mum looked over at me and smiled.

"It just occurred to me," she said.

"Dawn, would you and the girls like to stay for dinner? We won't get many more chances to see you this visit. You're just here for another week, aren't you?"

I looked at Sunny. Sunny looked at me.

"Oh. Stay, stay, stay," Sunny pleaded.

"I'll have to check with Dad," I said. He was back at work that week and wouldn't be home for another half hour. "Can I let you know at the end of the meeting?" I asked Sunny's mum.

"Of course," she said. "If your dad says yes, we'd love to have you." She winked at me. "Spinach lasagna," she said, and she disappeared out of the door.

"Yum," said Sunny. "That reminds me. I'm hungry."

"Me too," said Maggie. "Starving."

"Should I get us our snack?" Sunny asked.

"Yeah!" we all agreed.

Sunny stood up and dusted the potting soil off her hands.

"Yuck! Wash your hands first," Maggie teased.

Sunny wiggled her muddy fingers in Maggie's face.

"No way!" she laughed, then bounded down the stairs.

Since no phone calls were coming in, we just sat around chatting. Jill and Maggie talked some more about the kids I remembered in our class. Right then an idea began taking seed in my mind. I started to picture myself back in the class, and how easy it would be to slip right back in.

Sunny came back up with the food – guacamole dip and cut-up raw vegetables that she had made earlier in the afternoon.

"All *right*," Jill said, grabbing a carrot stick.

"No calls yet?" Sunny asked.

We shook our heads. The phone hadn't rung once.

"Maybe we should work on the recipe file," Sunny suggested.

This was a project I hadn't heard about yet. Sunny pulled a yellow plastic file box off the top of her desk. On the front she had pasted a picture of a bright red apple. Inside were cards with recipes that kids could make and that they liked to eat.

"Healthy recipes," said Sunny. "It's an extension of that cookbook I showed you."

"Wow!" I said. "What a great idea."

Maggie and Jill fished into their bags and each pulled out a recipe she had found over the weekend. Jill's homemade lemonade was from a magazine. Maggie's "Raisin Surprise" was from the back of a raisin box. They set about copying the recipes on to the small yellow index cards.

Sunny munched a celery stick and looked at me. "It'd be great if you could stay for dinner," she said.

I thought back to all the times in the past that I had had dinner over at Sunny's house. How many times had it been? Probably a thousand. Well, at least a hundred. Sunny's mum and dad were great. When we were younger they always let us be excused from the table as soon as we had finished eating, just so we would have a longer time to play.

"I hope you can stay," Sunny said again, and suddenly something popped into my head.

Maybe I *could* stay. Maybe I could *really* stay. Maybe I didn't have to go back to Connecticut at all, or just go back to get my things. Maybe I could move back in with Dad and Jeff, have my old room back, my old friends, my old school.

It was a strange thought, scary and exciting at the same time. Until then, I had just been having a great time, a *fabulous* time, but it had never occurred to me that I could think about making it last forever (or at least for longer). Now that the thought occurred to me, what was I supposed to do?

I was still sitting in the same room, but it felt as though I was in another world. Around me, I could hear Sunny and Jill and Maggie chattering away. Jill rummaged around in her bag for her bottle of nail polish, a different colour this time. The phone rang, a call came in. I think it was one of the neighbours down the street, and Maggie took the job.

"Earth to Dawn. Earth to Dawn," said Sunny. She had her hands cupped over her mouth like a loudspeaker.

"Oh, yeah," I said. "I'm here." (Just barely.)

"So what do you think?"

"About what?"

"About the *nail* polish."

"What about it?"

"Do you think Berry Pink is better on Jill or Luscious Blush?"

Hmm, I suppose I had missed a part of the conversation. I took a look. Jill had half of the old nail varnish on and half of the new.

"Which is which?" I asked.

"Forget it," Jill giggled. "They'll *discontinue* the colours before you decide."

"What time is it?" I asked suddenly.

"Five-thirty," said Sunny. "Hey, you can call your dad now."

Five-thirty. Time to leave.

"I don't think I can stay for dinner," I said abruptly. "I have to do something. I mean, I have to talk to Dad about something."

"But. . ." Sunny started.

The phone rang again.

"It's Mrs Austin," she said. "She needs someone for Clover and Daffodil. Do you want it?" she asked me.

226

"Yeah," I said. "Of course. Thanks. Sign me up. But I've got to run."

Sunny and the others stared after me. I grabbed my bag and ran out of the door. It must have all looked very strange. Well, what can I say? It felt strange for me, too. Suddenly it seemed as though my whole world was changing.

11th CHAPTER

Monday

Dear Mum,
~~I'm writing to~~ talk about
I just ~~want to~~ say that
This is a very difficult
thing ~~for me~~ to

Well, that was a card I never finished writing. How do you tell your mother that you want to move away from her? That you want, in fact, to move to the other side of the country?

When I came back from the We ♥ Kids meeting I ran right to my room. I thought it might help if I wrote a draft of a letter to Mum and worked out how I might approach this very delicate subject. As you see, I didn't get very far.

I decided really, that it was too early to think about Mum. The first step was just to talk to Dad.

Jeff knocked on my door to call me to dinner.

"Hey, Sis," he said. "Get your bod to the table."

How could I get through life without my dopey brother, I wondered. I didn't *want* to leave Jeff. I didn't *want* to leave Dad.

Mrs Bruen had made her usual terrific dinner (fish fillets baked with tomatoes and covered with cheese sauce), and we ate it in the beautiful, clean dining room at a table with a tablecloth and flowers. Everything was arranged nicely, everything was organized. No misplaced bags, no lost keys.

I poured myself some juice from the frosty cold jug.

"Broccoli?" Dad asked me.

"Yes, please."

How would I start?

"Dad," I began.

"Yes?"

"I was thinking. . ."

"Yes?"

"Um. . . Um. . . Hmm. I forgot what I was going to say."

Call me a chicken if you want. It was very difficult for me to bring up the subject. We ate for a while, and I let Jeff and Dad talk.

"Aw, come on," Jeff was saying. "All my friends get to watch more television than *that*."

"Not on school nights," Dad said firmly. "Enjoy your holidays while you can."

"But, Dad. . ."

"You heard me," said Dad. "Subject closed."

That quietened Jeff. It also gave me space to try again.

"Dad," I said.

"Yeah?"

"I was thinking. . ."

"Sounds familiar," Dad grinned.

"Yeah, well, I was thinking. . . I mean, it's just an idea, but I was wondering if . . . well, what I'm thinking is, maybe I want to consider, well, maybe, I want to consider staying in California, moving here like Jeff did."

I paused. Nobody said anything.

230

"It's just that I like it so much here," I continued. "Everything is just my style. The weather, the kids. I mean, I just got this idea today, but actually maybe it's been brewing all along. I'm not even sure that it's what I want. But I'm thinking about it, so I want to bring it up."

Dad was watching me closely. Jeff was watching Dad.

Dad let out a big breath. You'd have thought he was the one doing all the talking.

"Well," he said slowly. "It's certainly a possibility."

Jeff tossed his napkin in the air. He'd been waiting for Dad's response.

"Yippee!" he cried.

"Well," Dad sighed again. "There's a lot to think about here."

It suddenly occurred to me that Dad didn't want me. He didn't seem too enthusiastic. But then he burst into a grin, the kind of grin that's unmistakably his.

"Oh, Sunshine," he said. "You know how happy I would be if you were out here?"

"Yippee!" Jeff yelled again.

"Of course," Dad added quickly, "there's a lot of things we have to consider here. There's your mother. . ." There was a long pause. "And the custody and your school. And, of course, what you really want."

"But it's possible?" I asked.

"Well, from a practical standpoint, yes,"

Dad said. "You've got your own room here. Mrs Bruen is already here and working. . . But from a legal standpoint, I don't know. Your mother has custody, but then, she still has custody of Jeff and here he is. I'd have to talk to her and see, uh, see what we could arrange. Do you want me to call her tonight, just to talk?"

"No!" I was surprised at the strength of my answer.

"Do *you* want to call her?" Dad asked.

"Not yet," I said. I wasn't ready for that at all. "The first thing is I have to work things out, decide what I want."

"You're the only one who *can* decide that, Sunshine," said Dad. "Your mother and I have the legal proceedings to work out, but we've got to know that it's what you want."

"Right," I said.

Dad and I ate the rest of our dinner in relative silence. You wouldn't have noticed the quiet, though. Jeff did a good job of filling that in.

"If you stay here we can go to the beach all the time," he said enthusiastically. "You can come to my school if I'm in an assembly. I can borrow your Walkman, you can borrow my camera. . ."

Jeff went on like that for the rest of the meal, but I hardly heard him. All the things I had to think about were swimming through my head.

When I finished dinner I went back to my room and closed the door. California, Connecticut. California, Connecticut. I couldn't keep my thoughts straight. I decided to write them down.

I tore a piece of paper off my notepad and drew a line down the middle. At the top of the left half I wrote PROS: CALIFORNIA. At the top of the right I wrote PROS: STONEYBROOK. When I finished my list, this is what I had:

PROS: CALIFORNIA	PROS: STONEYBROOK
Dad	Mum
Jeff	
the sun!	
We ♥ Kids Club	Baby sitters Club
Sunny (and others)	Mary Anne (and others)
healthy foods	
the beach	
an organized household	
Clover and Daffodil	the kids in Stoneybrook

I thought about adding "Disneyland" under "California" but decided against it. It didn't seem like enough of a reason to move from one coast to the other, and besides, the California side already had plenty of entries.

Well then, it seemed pretty clear. California. I suppose that's what I wanted.

233

Somehow, though, it didn't seem resolved in my head. I needed to talk about it some more. I couldn't talk about it with Mum, and I'd already talked about it a bit with Dad. Maybe I should call Sunny? I decided against it. She'd just persuade me to stay. Maybe Mary Anne. . . Of course. She'd *said* to call.

I wandered out of my room.

"Dad," I called. "Can I call Mary Anne in Connecticut?"

"It's ten o'clock there," he said.

It was late, but it was holiday time, so she should be awake.

"Can I?" I asked again.

"Of course," he said.

The kitchen was now empty, so I set myself up in there. I opened my address book to the "S" page and ran my finger across. Mary Anne's name was the first. She had, after all, been my first Stoneybrook friend.

As I dialled her number, I could almost hear her voice answering the phone. She'd probably squeal when she heard it was me. Mary Anne was a good choice, I thought. She'd be perfect to talk to in a situation like this. She's the kind of friend who would help me work out what I wanted. I mean, of course, she'd be sad if I wanted to stay in California, but she'd understand.

On the other end, the phone was ringing. Three rings. Four. No one answered.

Maybe they're just pulling into the driveway, I thought. I let it ring again. No one answered. I laid the phone back in its cradle and dropped down in a kitchen chair.

Around me the light was getting softer. The kitchen took on a rosy hue. Ten o'clock in Connecticut. I pictured Mary Anne and her father coming home from wherever they were, turning the lights on in their darkened house. Then I pictured Mum. I wondered what she was doing. Probably she was reading in bed. Or maybe she was out with the Trip-Man. (Horrors!) I wondered what she would say when I told her what I was thinking about. What would she do in that funny old farmhouse all by herself? If only *she* could move back to California, too.

Of course, I knew that was impossible.

The hard thing was, I found myself realizing that the person I really wanted to be talking to about all this *was* Mum. I wanted the two of us to be sitting on my bed, having one of our heart-to-hearts. I wanted her to ask me questions, say wise things. I wanted her to help lead me through all this tangle I seemed to be tied up in.

I started to feel closed in from all the things I had to think about. I went out to the back patio and watched the golden sun fade.

12th CHAPTER

Dear Dawn,

It's business as usual at the Pikes. The other morning I sat there with Mallory, and wouldn't you know it, the triplets were on Nicky's back. Nicky ran off to you-know-where and eventually I had to go and get him. Sound familiar?

Love,
Kristy

P.S. Nicky talked a lot about you, actually. I think he really misses you. Well, he doesn't have long to wait now.

I got the postcard from Kristy that Tuesday, when I still hadn't made up my mind what to do. I didn't find out the details until later, but I could picture the scene at the Pike household, where things are always a little crazy.

The Pikes, you may remember, have eight kids. And that's just one family, not two combined or anything like that. Because it's such a crowd, Mrs Pike always gets two sitters whenever she goes out. Now that Mallory, the oldest Pike, is eleven and in the Babysitters Club, Mrs Pike usually uses Mallory plus one other sitter. That day it was Kristy.

Claire, the youngest Pike (she's all of five years old), let Kristy in. She was still in her pyjamas.

"Moozie!" she cried. ("Moozie" is what she sometimes calls her mum.) "Moozie! Kristy's here."

Moozie didn't appear, but Mallory did.

"Mum'll be down in a minute," she said.

"Where's everybody else?" asked Kristy. (The house seemed strangely quiet.)

"The triplets and Nicky are in the backyard, and Vanessa and Margo are upstairs."

"Well," said Kristy. "Where should we start? How about with you, Claire? Let's get you out of those pyjamas and into your play clothes."

"These *are* my play clothes, Kristy silly-billy-goo-goo," said Claire. "Today I'm wearing my pyjamas *all day long*."

Kristy looked at Mallory. Mallory shrugged. That's another thing about the Pikes. Mr and Mrs Pike hardly have any rules. If Claire were going to school that day, of course she'd have to get dressed. But for staying at home? If pyjamas were what she wanted, pyjamas it was.

Claire streaked up the stairs, waggling her head and crying "Moo!" Was she calling her mother or making cow sounds? Did it matter? This was definitely going to be one of Claire's sillier days.

The back door swung open and the triplets appeared. They each grabbed a cookie from the jar on the kitchen counter and then raced back outside. The door swung open again. It was Nicky. He'd come for *his* cookie. (The triplets are ten and Nicky is eight. He sometimes has a hard time keeping up.) *BANG!* Nicky was back out the door, following his brothers.

"Kristy, hi!" It was Mrs Pike. In her hurry, she grabbed a jumper out of the cupboard. "Oops, that's Vanessa's," she said. She grabbed another. "I should be back early afternoon. More library business. And if the meeting gets out on time, I'm going to squeeze in a haircut."

She gave the sitters last-minute instructions and reminded Mallory that there was canned ravioli and homemade coleslaw for lunch.

Ravioli and *coleslaw*? Well, I suppose when you're getting meals together for eight kids every day, you come up with some pretty unusual combinations.

Mrs Pike called goodbye over her shoulder and hurried out the door.

"I'll go and let Vanessa and Margo know I'm here," Kristy said to Mallory.

To keep all fronts covered, Mallory headed out to the yard.

Vanessa and Margo are two of the middle kids. Vanessa is nine and Margo is seven. You can pretty much trust them to play well by themselves, but you always have to check to see what they're up to. In this case that was a good idea. Claire had joined them and Vanessa was showing her sisters how to write a letter in "invisible ink." She had dragged a carton of milk upstairs and the three of them were dipping paintbrushes into the milk and using it as ink to write messages on white paper.

"Kristy!" Vanessa said when she walked in. "Read my message. Can you, please? It's invisible, like the seas." (Vanessa is a budding poet. She loves to rhyme and doesn't always care so much about making sense.)

Kristy looked at the blank sheet of paper.

"A polar bear in a snowstorm?" she guessed.

"Silly-billy-goo-goo!" cried Claire.

"No, it's a message," said Vanessa. She

239

held the paper flat and blew on it so that the milk would dry. "You can't see it now," she said, "but watch this."

She strode out of the bedroom and into her parents' room, where there was an iron and an ironing board standing up in the corner.

"Heat," she said. "We'll iron the messages and the heat will make the milk letters turn brown."

"Wait a minute. Wait a minute," said Kristy. "I'll be the one to do the ironing."

"But I iron all the time," said Vanessa. "For Mum. I do practically a basket a week."

Kristy considered.

"Well," she said. "You can iron, but I'll supervise. Claire and Margo, you sit over here and watch."

Kristy sat on the edge of the bed and patted places next to her for the two younger girls.

Vanessa waited for the iron to heat up and then ran it lightly over the sheets of paper. As she predicted, the white letters darkened and the messages came clear.

Vanessa's message read:

"Ships on the ocean,
Ships at shore,
Wipe your feet,
And close the door."

Margo's said, "My teacher is a big baboon."

Claire's just said, 'CAT HAT RAT FAT CLAIRE." (Well when you're first learning to write, you don't have a lot of words to choose from.)

"Let's write some for the boys!" Vanessa cried suddenly. She started out the door.

"Hey! Iron off," Kristy reminded her. (When you're a babysitter you *do* have to be thinking about safety all the time.)

Vanessa ran back and unplugged the iron, and the girls ran back to their room to write more secret messages.

By the time lunch rolled around, the girls had a stack of paper a few inches high. Each of the pieces had a secret milk-message written on it. It had been a busy morning.

Mallory was in the kitchen heating up the ravioli. (She had opened a giant-sized can. It looked like it was meant for an army platoon.) Kristy started dishing up the coleslaw.

"Nicky's in a bad mood," Mallory said, filling Kristy in on the backyard crew. "The triplets wouldn't let him play with them."

"Again?" said Kristy. This was an on-going problem.

"Well, they were playing Frisbee and all they'd let him do was fetch it when it went out of the yard."

Nicky banged through the door and into

241

the kitchen. He slumped into a chair and began to kick his feet back and forth.

"Hi, Nicky," said Kristy.

"Hi," Nicky said glumly.

The triplets trooped in behind him.

"Ravioli?" said Byron. "Coleslaw? Ugh!" But he sat right down at the table, and Kristy noticed that when she put his plate in front of him, he gobbled the food right up.

"We've got secret messages for you," Margo said to the boys. She handed Jordan the stack of papers.

"Who cares?" he said. He pushed the papers aside.

"Look at them," Vanessa said. "They've got secret messages on them. Bet you can't read them."

"Don't want to," said Jordan.

Margo grabbed the papers up.

"Well, don't then," she said. "We don't care."

Adam had taken his spoon to his plate and was mixing the ravioli in with the coleslaw.

"Ooh, yuck," he said. "Snake guts."

Nicky grinned.

"Hey, that's what it does look like," he said. "The tomato sauce is the blood."

Unfortunately, when Nicky said that, he had a full mouth of ravioli himself, and some of it splurted out on the table.

"Yuk!" Adam cried. "Ooh, Nicky! Say it, don't spray it!"

242

Nicky sat there quietly for a moment. Kristy thought he might be about to burst into tears. Instead, he looked at her and said, "May I please be excused? I want to go to the hideout."

Now, there's an example of one of the few rules in the Pike house. Nicky is allowed to go to the hideout only if he tells whoever is in charge where he's going.

"Eat some more ravioli first," said Mallory.

Nicky did, and he was excused.

The hideout that he disappeared to was the secret passage I told you about, the one that's in my house. Nicky goes in through the trap-door in our barn. He usually just sits in there, reads or whatever. It's his special place.

That day, half an hour passed, then forty-five minutes. Lunch was cleared and cleaned up and the kids all went outside together to play in the backyard. Kristy decided she'd go and check on Nicky. He was right where he said he would be, sitting alone at the head of the tunnel. Kristy climbed down the ladder and joined him.

"Hey, Nick," she said.

"Hi."

"Whatcha doin'?"

"Nothin'."

It took Kristy a while to get Nicky talking, but they did talk a bit about how hard it sometimes was to be a younger brother.

"This feels like when Dawn talked to me," Nicky said.

I was the one who first discovered Nicky's hiding place. And when I found him, we had a pretty good heart-to-heart.

"You miss Dawn?" Kristy asked.

Nicky nodded. "Will she be back soon?"

"At the end of the week," Kristy said.

Nicky heaved a big sigh.

"I don't know if I can last," he said.

Kristy laughed and gave him a hug.

"Come on," she said. "We'd better get going."

Back at the Pikes' house, things were as hectic as before. The only difference was, Mrs Pike had come home.

"There's my Nicholas," she smiled.

She gave her son a quick kiss on the cheek and kneaded his slumping shoulders.

"You didn't get a haircut," Kristy noticed.

"No time," said Mrs Pike. "I suppose I'll have to call you again."

She paid Kristy and Mallory and left to check the backyard.

Hearing about the Pikes and reading Kristy's postcard got me thinking about the Babysitters Club and all the other big jobs we take on. "No job too big, no job too crazy" – that should be our motto. A lot of times it even seems the more chaotic, the more fun. In a way, I'm kind of proud of that. Whenever a problem has cropped up, we've pulled a solution from somewhere, out of our hats if we had to.

Listen to me. I sound like a testimonial.

Of course, the PS on Kristy's card helped. So Nicky Pike missed me, huh? Well, what do you know. . . The truth was, I sort of missed him, too.

13th
CHAPTER

Dear Dawn,
　　Miss you so much, honey.
The old house just isn't the
same without you. You'll be
pleased (?) to know that I've
had date after date with Trip.
We've gone to a chamber concert,
and a wine tasting, and I'll
see him again Friday night
before you get home. This
time we're off to a lecture
on humour.
　　Dawn, the very thought of
picking you up at the airport
has me all in smiles. A big
hug and kiss for my
sweet firstborn girl.
　　　　　　Love,
　　　　　　Mom

A lecture on humour? Oh, give me a break. How could Mum be falling for Trip-Man? That was *exactly* the problem with him. He'd be just the type to go to a *lecture* about humour. That's because he has no sense of it himself. Compare him with Dad. Dad is fun and funny. The Trip-Man is a bore.

I got the postcard from Mum on Wednesday, and no, I still hadn't made up my mind what to do. That wasn't the only postcard that came for me in the mail. There was also one from Jessi.

Dear Dawn,

Last night my family and I went back to visit our old neighbourhood. It was fun, but also strange. All the relatives and all the old friends... It was great to see them, but in a way, it made me think -- where is home? I suppose it's Stoneybrook now. This is pretty heavy - I hope you don't mind my writing to you. It's just that I thought you're sort of going through the same thing, too.

See you soon,
Jessi

Well, what a post! You can see why it was hard for me to make up my mind. My mum's postcard got me all agitated, but that got me thinking. I certainly did feel involved in the whole Trip-Man thing. I wanted to run right back to Connecticut so I could keep my eye on the situation. Did I want the Trip-Man marrying my mother? Moving into *our* farmhouse? No way!

Then, of course, Jessi's postcard. . . I never thought of it before, but she and I really *were* in very similar situations. Of course, Jessi went back to a neighbourhood where everyone is black, and I went back to one where everyone is . . . well, blond. I thought of all my friends in the Babysitters Club. We all *were* very different – our backgrounds, the way we look, our interests. There was something very nice about that. Maybe Mary Anne doesn't read all the ghost stories that I happen to like, but what does that matter? And Claudia – she does eat a lot of junk food, all right, but she draws beautifully. I remembered the slumber party they had given me before I left. I pictured Claudia sitting on her sleeping bag, sketching Jessi, whose legs were stretched long, like a real ballerina's. This sounds corny, but the scene was like an advertisement for the UN or something. Different kinds of people with different interests, all getting along beautifully. (Okay, getting along *most* of the time.)

I headed over to Sunny's to spend the afternoon there. I decided to talk about my dilemma.

"Dawn!" she squealed when I told her. "You're going to stay in California!"

"I didn't say that," I said defensively. "I said I was *thinking* about it."

"What's there to think about?" said Sunny. She picked up the California/ Connecticut list that I had brought along with me. "It's all right here on paper. It's decided."

"It's not that simple," I said. "Different things on the list have different weights."

"Okay," she said, looking down the list. "Your dad and Jeff. They balance your mum."

Well, sort of. How could I ever rate something like that?

"And the We ♥ Kids Club balances the Babysitters Club," Sunny went on.

"Maybe not," I said carefully.

"Dawn, you told me yourself that you love how relaxed the club is here."

"Yeah."

That's what I said, but what I thought was the We ♥ Kids Club is not really as busy or as involved or active somehow as the Babysitters Club. Of course, I couldn't say that to Sunny's face. Instead, I just sort of shrugged my shoulders.

"Okay, another item," said Sunny. "Sunny (and others) versus Mary Anne (and others). I suppose that balances, right?" "Right," I said, halfheartedly. Was Sunny really as good a friend now as Mary Anne was? And really, I had five other friends in the Babysitters Club. Six, counting Stacey. I was much closer to all of them than I was to Jill and Maggie. Same with the kids I babysat for. Did Clover and Daffodil balance out all the kids in Stoneybrook? The Pikes, Jamie and Lucy Newton, the Perkins girls, Kristy's brothers and sister. . .

"Okay," said Sunny. "Here we go. The sun. The beach. Healthy foods. An organized household."

One by one she ticked off all the pros for California.

"Dawn, it's obvious. You're a California girl," she said.

"I know."

"And a California girl *belongs* in California."

I felt my face tighten. All of a sudden I didn't feel like discussing the subject any more.

"You know what?" I said. "Let's drop this. I think it's better if I think about this whole thing myself."

"Okay," said Sunny. She looked a little taken aback.

That evening, when I went home for

dinner, Dad was waiting to talk to me.

"Well, Sunshine," he said. "Is the verdict in?"

"Oh, Dad, not yet," I moaned.

Dad wrinkled up his forehead in concern.

"I know it's a big decision," he said, "but you're due to fly back on Saturday. If you're really thinking of staying, I'll have to talk with your mother, well, at the latest by tomorrow. We'll have to cancel the plane reservation, make other arrangements."

"Can I let you know tomorrow?" I asked. "Just one more day?"

Dad paused a long time.

"Oh, Sunshine," he said. "I don't want to influence your decision. You know what I would love, but there are many considerations here. Take the night to decide, but I really do have to know by tomorrow."

"Oh, thanks, Daddy," I said. I gave him the biggest hug ever.

Dad threw his arms around me and we walked into the kitchen to sit down for yet another terrific meal. The sun was streaming in through the skylight and the terracotta tiles were cool and sparkling under our feet. (Mrs Bruen had just given them one of her good moppings.)

After dinner Jeff and I helped with the dishes and then Dad brought a pack of cards out to the back. The three of us sat down at the picnic table for a game of Sevens.

From where I sat I could see Clover and Daffodil next door, running around their yard barefoot, playing tag. I could smell the smoky scent of grilled fish coming from the barbecue of our other neighbours. A soft breeze rustled the skirt of my sundress against my warm, bare legs.

It'd be nice if Mum were here, I found myself thinking. If she were a part of things, playing cards with me, pottering around the patio. And wouldn't it be great if the doorbell rang and it was Mary Anne, just dropping by for a visit. What I wanted was to be able to share all the *things* I loved with all the *people* I loved. I imagined Nicky Pike out here, holing up in a new, California hiding place. Maybe in the crawl space between the bushes. Maybe in the cave down by the creek.

That night, as I lay in bed, I made my decision. I knew what I had to do, where I had to be. I fell asleep hugging my pillow. I slept the whole night soundly, undisturbed.

14th
CHAPTER

Dear Dawn,
   Kristy says you will be
back on Saturday. If you
hear a noise in the secret
passage, don't get scared.
It'll just be me. Lately I
have a lot of ghost-hunting
to do there. It keeps me pretty
busy.
            Your secret tunnel pal,
                  Nicky
P.S. You think maybe Sunday
     we could search the tunnel
     for old coins?

On Thursday I woke up after Dad had already gone to work. I spent the day riding bikes with Jeff and came home to Nicky's funny note. Of course, I knew what I was going to do and by that point I was bursting to tell.

When Dad came home from work I sat him down to prepare him for my decision.

"I've decided to leave California and go back to Connecticut," I said.

Phew! That was a hard thing to get out.

"I like both places," I continued. "I like them a lot. But I've made my home at Mum's now. It's time for me to go back."

Dad's eyes were all misty as I was explaining.

"I know," he said. "I suppose I knew it all along."

Jeff, who had been standing in the doorway, turned around and stamped down the hall. It would take him another day or two to adjust to the disappointment.

"Well," said Dad, "for such a young girl you've had a big decision to make. You've got two homes. Just remember – this is always your home, too. We'll always be in touch, you can always visit. Your room here is reserved. And so is your place in our hearts."

Oh, Dad! He was ace. By the time he finished his speech, my eyes were all misty, too. Okay, they were more than misty. Tears were streaming down my cheeks like rain.

"Dad," I blubbered. "Can I tell Mum?"

"Sure, Sunshine," he said.

He left the room so I could be alone.

I think Mum was surprised to hear my voice all shaken up.

"I was wondering," I asked. "Could you bring Mary Anne along to the airport with you?"

"Of course," said Mum. "I'll call her up as soon as we hang up."

Mum stopped talking. So did I.

"Dawn, honey," she said. "Is everything all right?"

Well, I hadn't meant to tell Mum that I had been thinking about staying in California, but somehow it all came flooding out.

"You know how it is, Mum," I said. "Avocados, the beach. . ."

"Oh, Dawn," she said, "I knew when you went out there you'd start thinking about moving back."

How come everybody seemed to know more about me than I knew? Dad had known I was going to decide to go back to Stoneybrook. Mum knew I was going to think about staying in California in the first place. Parents!

"You know, Dawn," Mum continued, "if you *do* want to stay in California, we could give it some thought. I know it's been difficult for you. I know you love it out there."

"I made my decision," I said. My voice was cracking. "I'm going to come home."

"Dawn," Mum blubbered. "I would've missed you so much."

We certainly were a weepy family that night. Yup, the four of us were a family, even though we were split up in two different houses and separated by thousands of kilometres. And as far as understanding goes, I got a lot of that from my parents. From both of them. My dad might be on one coast and my mum on the other but, parent-wise, I suppose I'm pretty lucky.

Friday, my last full day in California, was a pretty busy day. That morning I babysat one last time for Clover and Daffodil. Daffodil asked if she could write to me. And Clover (always Clover) told me she might come and visit me by space-ship. When Mrs Austin came home, she slipped a thin package into my hand along with my pay.

"What is it?" I asked.

"Open it and see," she smiled.

Inside was a hand-woven purse that Mrs Austin had made and lined in silk. The threads were red and a deep golden colour.

"Like Sunshine," she said. I blushed. Had Dad told her my nickname?

After the job, I ran over to Sunny's house for one last meeting of the We ♥ Kids Club. Actually, it was more like a party, a goodbye party for me. Sunny, Jill and

Maggie had made all kinds of treats – fresh pineapple wedges, carrot cake. They had a big tray of food that they set down in the centre of our circle.

Sunny banged her hand on the floor, like a gavel.

"This party will now come to order," she teased.

Believe me, there was no need to call us to the food.

The party was interrupted only twice by job calls. Maggie took one and Jill took the other.

There really wasn't enough work here to go around, I thought. In a way, it was good I was leaving.

When the "meeting" was adjourned, Sunny pulled two packages out from under the bed.

"Surprise!" she said. "You can't go without your presents."

I *knew* it. I knew Sunny couldn't say goodbye to me without *some* sort of surprise.

One package, the first, was a book, I could feel it. I tore open the wrapping paper. *Kids Can Cook . . . Naturally.*

"Thanks, you girls," I said enthusiastically. "This is great!"

"Open the other," said Sunny.

The other was my very own recipe file. The three of them had made it for me. The file box itself was blue, and they had pasted a picture of a sun on the front. Inside were all their recipes, copied in their three different handwritings.

"You guys!" I cried. "You guys!"

What I was trying to say was, I just loved it.

I said goodbye to everybody. Then it was time for me to head home, for my last dinner with the California branch of the Schafer family.

Dad and I had discussed it, and we'd decided that, for the last night, it would be fun to go out. Dad had suggested a Mexican restaurant, a big favourite of mine and usually a favourite of Jeff's, too. Jeff, though, was still a little upset. He was my last hurdle, the last peace I had left to make. As we drove to the restaurant, Jeff kept a pouty look on his face. He squinted his eyes and puckered his mouth.

"What're you going to order, Jeff?" Dad asked in an effort to draw him out.

"Dunno," said Jeff.

"How about chicken enchiladas? You always like those."

"Yuck," said Jeff.

Dad and I exchanged quick smiles.

When we got to the restaurant, Jeff began twisting his fingers into the hem of the tablecloth.

"Dawn," he said sullenly. "How come you're leaving? Is it because we're boys?"

"No," I laughed. Jeff looked hurt. I tried

to look as solemn as I could. "You thought I was leaving because you and Dad are boys? Not at all. I just have to go back."

"Maybe you can visit Dawn this summer," Dad suggested.

"Maybe she could come back and visit us again *here*," Jeff insisted.

Jeff would always be true to California.

"Anyway, I had a good time with you," he said grudgingly.

"So did I." I smiled back.

"I liked it when I took your picture at Disneyland," he said. "And I liked it when I dropped the crab in your lap at the beach."

The very thought perked Jeff right up. Despite himself, he started to smile.

"Hey, how come you and your friends all wear those bikinis, anyway?" he asked. "Those things are really awful."

I had to laugh. And so did Dad.

When the waiter came, Jeff didn't even bother to look at the menu.

"Chicken enchiladas," he said.

That's our Jeff.

The meals came and we all ate hungrily. Dad ordered coffee before we left.

"You really can come back any time you want, Sunshine," he said. "Anytime during the summer, any holiday."

He took a sip from his cup.

"And hey," he said, suddenly inspired. "Why not bring all those friends of yours?

All your friends in the Babysitters Club. I've certainly heard enough about them."

"Really?" I asked.

"How many would that be?" he calculated. "Six?"

"Six girls!" Jeff choked. "No way!"

"And all of them babysitters," Dad laughed. "Jeff, they'd have you cornered in no time."

The Babysitters Club in California? It was a *great* idea.

"Could I really bring them?" I asked. "When?"

"When?" Dad smiled. "Whenever!"

15th CHAPTER

saturday

Dear Dad and Jeff,

Hello from me (and from John Wayne, too!). I'm curled up in my window seat, watching the West disappear beneath me. Well, as you said, Dad, it's only a plane-ride away. But how come it's such a long plane ride?

Jeff, I hope you write to me. Keep me posted about school, Clover and Daffodil, and, of course, the most important thing -- what Mrs. Bruen makes for dinner! (Just so I can eat my heart out.)

I love you both. I'll miss you a lot. Thanks for a fabu-ful, wonder-ific time.

Dawn

261

Well, it was C-Day again, only this time "C" stood for Connecticut, not California. That morning we had to get up pretty early to get me to my flight – because of the time change, the plane east leaves much earlier than the one going west. The neighbourhood was quiet when we woke up, and the three of us sat groggily at the breakfast table, slowly coming awake.

"Mmm, coffee," Dad said, sipping from his cup.

That's about all the conversation any of us could muster.

When we got to the airport and got me all checked in, Jeff didn't want us to go to the gate.

"Wait! Let me take your picture by the John Wayne statue," he said. "Wait! Don't you want to buy another postcard?"

I think he thought that if he stalled long enough, I would miss my flight and then I would just stay in California forever.

Dad rested his hands on Jeff's shoulders.

"We'd better get your sister to her plane," he said. "Flights don't wait for passengers buying postcards."

By the time we got through the metal detector (we got delayed there – Jeff had a "Super Special" penknife in his pocket) and to the gate, the flight was already boarding. Dad gave me a last hug.

"You take care now, Sunshine," he said.

"And don't go forgetting about your California family."

"Don't worry, Dad," I laughed.

Jeff was shifting from one foot to the other.

"Come on," he said. "The plane's going to leave."

I think now that he knew I was really going to go, he just wanted to get the whole thing over with. But as I got in line and was waiting for the steward to take my ticket, Jeff called after me.

"Hey, Dawn!" he said.

I turned around.

"Smile!" he called. Jeff took my picture one last time, then gave an awkward little wave.

I went through the door and boarded the plane.

Out of one world and back to another. I was a little choked up as I found my way to my seat. I had a window again, this time over the wing. Outside, on the runway, the heat was already shimmering off the asphalt. I wondered what the weather was like in Connecticut.

I dug my hands deep into the pockets of my cotton jacket, just for comfort, I think. Inside one I felt a little slip of paper. I pulled it out.

"*Cat Dancing,*
Romeo in Joliet,
Scheherazade's Tales," it read.

Hmm. What was tha—? Oh, yes, the list of plays that Tom, my seatmate, had written down for me exactly two weeks before.

I found myself wondering whether Tom might be on my same flight back also. It wasn't impossible. Maybe his auditions had taken two full weeks. I glanced around at the other passengers on the plane, looking for Tom's sandy hair and fair complexion. The flight was not very crowded. There were lots of empty seats. I didn't spot Tom, but as I glanced back towards the kitchen in the rear, I spotted. . . Oh, no! That air hostess! I crouched down in my seat and covered my eyes. I bet she was assigned to my area. It was fate! There was no escape!

Sure enough, when it was time for the safety demonstration, there was the Barbie doll, right at the head of my row.

Well, there was only one thing to do. I waited until we had taxied to the runway, had taken off, and were safely in the air. When the "Fasten seat belt" sign clicked off, I gathered up my flight bag and the blanket I had tucked around my legs. I glanced behind me. The stewards were back in the rear, preparing drinks trolleys, or whatever they do back there. I made my way up the aisle and across, to the other side of the plane. Since there were lots of empty seats I plonked myself down at another window. I stowed my bag, tucked the blanket up around me, and started the postcard to Dad and Jeff (I had saved one last John Wayne postcard and decided to use that. I knew it would make Jeff smile.)

When the drinks trolley came around, I had an ordinary, nice air hostess, who even gave me extra orange juice when I asked for it. I threw a glance back at my old row. My old friend was at work, all right. I could see a passenger trying to wave her down. She had passed that person just as, two weeks ago, she had passed me.

Me, I was safe on the other side of the plane. Two weeks older and two weeks wiser. I smiled and went back to my postcard.

As the plane droned on, I got kind of sleepy. I don't think I'd ever really woken up that morning. My eyes started to slip shut and I think I slept through a lot of the flight.

I did wake up for the film, though. It was (can you believe it?) *Adventures in Babysitting*. Hurray! That got me thinking about all my friends waiting for me at home. I couldn't *wait* to see Mary Anne and, of course, Claudia, Kristy, Jessi and Mallory, too. And then there were all the kids I sat for. I wondered if Nicky Pike really would come over on Sunday to explore the tunnel with me. I wondered if Mary Anne might want to come, too.

Going home felt very exciting all of a sudden. It really was home I was going to, too. "One home out of two," as Dad had put it, but I really did have a lot of ties there.

I started thinking about Mum and how glad I would be to see her. I had packed her some avocados in my luggage, the wrinkly, dark green California kind. I'd picked out ones that weren't yet ripe, so she could eat them all next week. A little piece of California for Mum, because I knew she missed it sometimes, too.

I looked at my watch and set it ahead to East Coast time. Right about then Mum would probably be darting around the house, looking for this and that. I hoped she would remember to pick up Mary Anne and bring her along, like she said she would. With Mum, you just never knew.

When we had watched the film and eaten our meals, the pilot came over the loudspeaker and told us about the weather on the East Coast.

"A light rain is falling," he said. "But the sun is apparently trying to peep through."

Exactly, I thought with a smile. That's Connecticut. (The sun, of course, was me.)

As we started our descent, my stomach got butterflies. It always does for arrival. I don't know if it's the descent of the plane, or the anticipation of arriving somewhere, but I always feel it.

When we finally landed, I jumped into the aisle, ready to race out the door. The people in front of me were blocking my way. One was reaching into the overhead luggage compartment and handing each bag – slowly – down to the other. "Come on!" I thought impatiently. I was ready to *burst* off that plane!

"Dawn!" a voice called out to me as I came through the door. It was Mum. She broke through the crowd, ran to me, and threw her arms around me. I was so glad just to see her – that Mum face of hers, that funny smile, and that pretty, light, curly hair.

"Mum," I cried. Again I got choked up.

What was it with my emotions lately? I felt like a crying machine.

Mum picked up my canvas bag and led me through the crowd. It was only then that I noticed the big white banner stretched across the room.

"Welcome home, Dawn!" it said.

Mary Anne was holding up one end of the banner, Claudia was holding up the other, and Kristy, Mallory and Jessi were gathered underneath it. It was the whole club!

"Surprise!" they cried.

In an instant, the banner was dropped and everyone crowded around me, firing questions at me and hugging me hello.

"You're so *tanned*!" Mary Anne cried.

She grabbed my arm and held it up for the others to see.

"Did you have a good time?" asked Claudia.

"Did you miss us?" asked Kristy.

"Tell us about We ♥ Kids," said Mallory.

"What was Disneyland like?" asked Jessi.

Phew! I couldn't answer everything at once, so I just stood there grinning. I dug into my bag and pulled out the five pairs of Mickey Mouse ears I had bought my friends as presents. Everyone grabbed for them and put them on right there in the airport.

We made our way to the baggage claim area, giggling and talking in a tight cluster. I suppose we looked pretty funny. The people walking by smiled at us as they passed.

"We've got you signed up for some jobs," Mary Anne told me. Throughout the chaos, Mary Anne had stuck right by my side. "Hope you don't mind."

"Mind? That's great!" I said. Home just a few minutes and already I was booked. That was the Babysitters Club, all right. Bustling and busy.

When my suitcase came around on the carousel, Mum grabbed it up and the rest of us followed her out of the automatic airport doors. She strode right to the car park, directly to the row where she had left the car.

"Here we are," she smiled, very pleased with herself. "Bet you thought your old mum would forget where she parked. My memory's getting better. Really. I'm making an effort."

We all piled in and I squeezed next to Mum. She steered the car to the ticket window and stopped to pay the charge.

The ticket. Mum fished into the pocket of her blouse. She grabbed her bag off the floor and rummaged through the various compartments. She looked through her purse.

"Dawn," she said. "Will you check the glove compartment?"

No ticket.

"Maybe you stuck it behind the sun visor," I said.

She flipped the visor down. There was the ticket, tucked into the visor's pocket.

Mum handed the attendant his money and we drove out of the airport, on to the highway. As we sped home, I couldn't help smiling. My friends were chattering, my mum was Mum, and I was snug in the middle. I was home, all right. And it felt fantastic!

KRISTY AND THE MOTHER'S DAY SURPRISE

For Amy Berkower

1st CHAPTER

I've been thinking about families lately,
wondering what makes one. Is a family
really a mother, a father and a kid or two?
I hope not, because if that's a family, then
I haven't got one. And neither do a lot of
other people I know. For instance, Nannie,
Mum's mother, lives all by herself. But I
still think of her as a family – a one-person
family. And I think of my own family as a
real family . . . I suppose.

What I mean is, well, my family didn't
start out the way it is now. It started out as
two families that split up and came
together as. . . Uh-oh. I know that's confusing. I'm a little ahead of myself. I'd
better go back and begin at the beginning.

This is the beginning: Hi! I'm Kristy
Thomas. I'm thirteen years old. I'm in
eighth grade. I'm the chairman of the

Babysitters Club (more about that later). I like sports, and I suppose you could say I'm a tomboy. (Well, wouldn't you be one if you had four brothers?) I'm not the neatest person in the world. I don't care much about boys or clothes. I'm famous for coming up with big ideas.

Okay, enough about me. Let me tell you about —

Knock, Knock.

Darn, I thought. Who could that be? It was a Friday evening and I didn't have any plans or even a babysitting job. I was in my bedroom, just messing around, enjoying my free time.

"Who's there?" I called.

"Oswald!" my little sister replied.

Oswald? *Oh.* . . "Oswald who?" I asked.

"Help! Help! Oswald my gum!"

I was laughing as I opened the door and found a very giggly Karen in the hallway.

"Pretty funny," I said, as Karen ran into my room and threw herself on my bed. "Where did you hear that one?"

"In school. Nancy told it to me. What are you doing with the door closed?"

"Just fooling around."

"But this is our first night here."

"I'm sorry, Karen. I didn't mean to shut you out. It's just that I had a rotten week at school and today was especially rotten, so I wanted to be by myself for a while."

You're probably wondering why Karen

said, "But this is our first night here." I think now would be a good time to explain my family to you. You see, Karen isn't exactly my sister. She's my stepsister. Her little brother Andrew is my stepbrother, and her father is my stepfather. Karen and Andrew only live with us part-time. I like it when they come over because then my family consists of Mum, Watson (he's my stepfather), Sam, Charlie and David Michael (they're my brothers), and Karen and Andrew. Oh, and Shannon and Boo-Boo. They're our dog and cat, and they're part of the family too.

How did I get this weird family? Well, you can probably imagine. My mum and dad were divorced. They got divorced soon after David Michael was born. Then, a couple of years ago, Mum met Watson and started going out with him. Watson was divorced, too. And after a while, Mum and Watson got married, and then Mum and my brothers and I moved into Watson's house. That's how I got my big family. The only unusual thing is that Watson is a millionaire. Honestly. That's why we moved into his house. It's a lot bigger than our old one. It's huge. In fact, it's basically a mansion. Living in a mansion here in Stoneybrook, Connecticut, is fun, but sometimes I miss my old house. It's on the other side of town, where all my friends are.

So now I'm part of a six-kid family. My brother Charlie is the oldest kid. He's seventeen, a senior in high school, and thinks he's a big shot. Sam is fifteen. He's in high school too. Then there's me, then David Michael, who's seven, and then Karen and Andrew, who are six and four. Usually, Karen and Andrew only live with us every other weekend and for two weeks during the summer. The rest of the time they live with their mother, who's not too far away – in a different neighbourhood in Stoneybrook. But the night Karen bounced into my room with her knock-knock joke was the beginning of a much longer stay. Karen and Andrew were going to be with us for several weeks while their mother and stepfather went on a business trip.

"Knock, knock," said Karen again.

"Who's there?" I replied.

"Hey, Karen! Come here!" It was David Michael, yelling down the hall.

"What?" Karen yelled back.

"Come and look at this insect!" (David Michael just loves insects.)

Karen was off my bed and out of my room in a flash.

I smiled. I really like my family, especially when Karen and Andrew are here. The bigger, the better. Sometimes I think of my friends as family, too. Is that weird? I don't know. But my friends do feel like family. I suppose I'm mostly talking about my friends in the Babysitters Club. That's a club I started myself. Actually, it's more of a business. My friends and I sit for families in Stoneybrook and we earn a lot of money.

Here's who's in the club: me, Claudia Kishi, Mary Anne Spier, Dawn Schafer, Mallory Pike and Jessi Ramsey. We are six very different people, but we get along really well (most of the time). That's the way it is with families.

For instance, I'm pretty outgoing (some people say I have a big mouth), and as I mentioned before, I like sports and couldn't care less about clothes and boys. My best friend is Mary Anne Spier (she's our club secretary) and we are *so* different. Mary Anne is quiet and shy, hates sports, is becoming interested in clothes, has a boyfriend, and comes from a very small family. She lives with just her dad and her kitten, Tigger. Her mum died a long time ago. Mary Anne and I have always been different and have always been best friends. We lived next door to each other until Mum married Watson, so we practically grew up together. One thing that's the same about us is our looks. We both have brown hair and brown eyes and are short for our age.

The vice-chairman of the Babysitters Club is Claudia Kishi. Claud lives across the street from Mary Anne. There is nothing, and I mean *nothing*, typical or average or ordinary about Claudia. To begin with, she's Japanese-American. Her hair is silky and long and jet-black. Her eyes are dark and almond-shaped and exotic. And her skin, well, I wish it were mine. I'm sure her skin doesn't even know what a spot is. Which is interesting when you consider Claudia's eating habits. Claud is pretty much addicted to junk food. Her parents don't like her to eat much of it, though, so she has to resort to hiding it in her room. Everywhere you look, you find something: a packet of crisps under her bed, a box of Jelly Tots in the cupboard. This makes for a crowded room because Claudia is a hoarder. She has to be. She's an artist and needs to collect things for her work, such as shells, leaves, and interesting pebbles. Also, she has loads of supplies – paper, canvases, paints, pastels, charcoals – and most of them are stored under her bed. Claud likes Nancy Drew mysteries and is a terrible pupil (even though she's bright). She lives with her parents, her grandmother, Mimi, and her older sister, Janine. It's too bad that Claud is such a poor pupil, because Janine is a genius. One last thing about Claudia – her clothes. They are just . . . so cool. Well, I mean Claud is. She's the coolest kid in our grade. Her clothes are amazing. Claud loves trying new things and she has an incredible imagination. She wears hats, weird jewellery (she makes some of it), bright colours – anything she can get away with!

Dawn Schafer is the club's treasurer. Now *she*'s got an interesting family. Dawn used to live in California. She lived there with her parents and Jeff, her younger brother. Then her parents got divorced and Mrs Schafer moved Dawn and Jeff all the way across country to Stoneybrook. The reason why she chose Stoneybrook is that she grew up here, and her parents (Dawn's grandparents) still live here. We got to know Dawn and she joined the Babysitters Club and everything seemed great. Except that Jeff missed his father and California – a lot. Finally, he moved back there. Now Dawn's family is split in half and separated by a continent. Dawn seems to be handling the changes well, though. She's pretty mature. And she's an individual. She solves her own problems, makes her own decisions, and isn't too affected by what other people think of her or tell her. Also, Dawn is neat and organized, which makes her a good treasurer. Although Dawn has been living in Connecticut for over a year now, she still looks sort of Californian. She's got long hair that is the blondest I've ever seen. It's almost white. And her eyes are sparkly and pale blue. In the summer she gets an amazing tan. (The rest of the year she just has freckles.) And her clothes are casual and as individualistic as she is. She likes to wear layers of things – a short tank top over a long tank top, or socks over tights. Dawn is pretty cool.

The two junior members of our club are Jessi Ramsey and Mallory Pike. They're junior members because they're younger than the rest of us. Mal and Jessi are in sixth grade. They haven't been club members as long as we have. Still, they're beginning to feel like family to me.

Mallory used to be someone our club sat *for*. Isn't that weird? Now she's a sitter herself. Mal is the oldest of eight kids. (Talk about big families.) The Babysitters Club still takes care of her younger brothers and sisters pretty often. Anyway, Mal is a great sitter. She's sensible and responsible – good in an emergency. And she's the most practical person I know. Mal is struggling to grow up. Being eleven can be very difficult, and Mal thinks her parents treat her like a baby. However, they're starting to relax. Recently, they allowed Mal to get her ears pierced and her hair cut. (She had to get a brace too, though, and her parents said she's too young for contact lenses.) Mal likes reading (especially books about horses), writing and drawing. She thinks she might want to be an author of children's books when she grows up.

Jessi (short for Jessica) Ramsey is Mal's

best friend. Like Dawn, she's a newcomer to Stoneybrook, Connecticut. In fact, she's a newer newcomer than Dawn is. Her family moved here from New Jersey at the beginning of the school year. They moved because Mr Ramsey changed jobs. In many ways, Jessi and Mal are alike. Jessi also loves to read, she wears glasses (just for reading), and she thinks *her* parents treat her like a baby, although they did let her get her ears pierced when Mal had hers done. But there are some big differences between Jessi and Mal. I suppose the biggest is that Jessi is black and Mal is white. This hasn't made a bit of difference to the girls, but the Ramseys did have some trouble when they first moved here. Not many black families live in Stoneybrook, and some people gave the Ramseys a hard time. Jessi says things are settling down, though. Another difference between Mal and Jessi is that Mal likes to write and Jessi likes to dance. Jessi is a ballerina. She's very talented. I've seen her dance – *on stage*. I was really impressed. The third difference is that Mal's family is huge, while Jessi's is average – Jessi; her parents; her younger sister, Becca; and her baby brother, Squirt.

And that's it. Those are the people in my family. It's a big family, when you add the members of the Babysitters Club. I could add a few more, too, I thought later that night as I lay in bed. There's Nannie. There's Stacey McGill, who used to be a member of the club, but who had to move to New York City. There are Shannon and Logan, whom I'll tell you about later. And there's my real father. . . But, no, he doesn't count. Somebody who never writes, never calls, never remembers your birthday, never says he loves you, doesn't count at all.

I was growing sleepy, and I forgot about my father. Instead, I thought of my gigantic family. I fell asleep smiling.

2nd CHAPTER

As chairman of the Babysitters Club, I get to run the meetings. I adore being in charge. Club meetings are the best times of my week.

"Order! Order, everybody!" I said.

It was Monday afternoon at five-thirty, time for our meeting to begin. Everyone had arrived and was sitting (or sprawling) in her usual place. As chairman, I always sit in the director's chair and wear my visor. I stick a pencil over my ear. That way, I *look* like I'm in charge. Claudia, Dawn, and Mary Anne loll around on the bed, and Jessi and Mal sit on the floor.

We hold our meetings in Claudia's room. She has her own phone.

This is how our club works: Three times a week, on Mondays, Wednesdays and Fridays from five-thirty until six, our club meets in Claudia's bedroom. People who need sitters call us during our meetings. They're practically guaranteed a sitter. With six club members, one of us is bound to be free. So we end up with lots of jobs. Not bad.

The idea for the club was mine. (That's how I got to be the chairman.) It came to me way back at the beginning of seventh grade, before Mum was really thinking about marrying Watson. We still lived in this neighbourhood then. In fact, we lived right across the street from Claudia. Anyway, one day Mum needed a sitter for David Michael, who had just turned six. I wasn't free and neither were Sam or Charlie. So Mum got on the phone and began making call after call, trying to find a sitter. I felt sorry for my mother, and even worse for David Michael, who was watching everything. And that was when I got my great idea. Wouldn't it be wonderful if Mum could make just one call and reach several babysitters at once? She'd find a sitter much faster that way.

So I got together with Mary Anne and Claudia and told them about my idea. We decided to form the Babysitters Club. We also decided we'd need more than three members, so we asked Stacey McGill, a new friend of Claudia's, to join the club, too. Stacey had just moved to Stoneybrook from New York City because her father's job had changed. I could see straight away why she and Claudia had become friends so fast. Stacey amazed Mary Anne and me. She seemed years older than twelve – very sophisticated with trendy clothes, pierced ears and permed hair. But she was also very nice. Furthermore, she'd had plenty of babysitting experience in New York, so we knew she'd be a good addition to the club.

After Stacey agreed to join us, we sent around leaflets and ran an ad in Stoneybrook's newspaper so people would know when to call us – and we were in business! The club was great. By the time Dawn moved to town, we needed another sitter, and later, when Stacey moved back to New York, we were doing so much business that we replaced her with both Jessi and Mal. And somewhere along the line we decided that we'd better have a couple of people lined up whom we could call on in case *none* of us could take a job. So we signed up two associate members, Shannon Kilbourne and Logan Bruno. Shannon lives across the street from me in my new neighbourhood. We're friends, sort of. Logan is a *boy* – and he's Mary Anne's boyfriend! Shannon and Logan don't come to the meetings. We just call them when we need them, so that we don't have to disappoint any of our clients by saying that no sitters are available.

I run our meetings in the most business-like way I can. As chairman, that's my job. Also, I come up with ideas for the club and generally just try to keep things going smoothly.

The job of the vice-chairman is, well. . . To be honest, Claudia Kishi is the vice-chairman because she has her own phone and personal, private phone number. The club uses her phone so we don't have to take over some grown-up's phone three times a week. The only thing is, our clients sometimes forget when our meetings are and call at other times. Claudia has to deal with those job offers, and she handles things really well.

Mary Anne Spier, our secretary, has the biggest job of any of us. Our club has a notebook (I'll tell you about that soon) and a record book. Mary Anne is the one who keeps the record book in order and up-to-date. She writes down our clients' names, addresses and phone numbers, and is responsible for arranging all our sitting jobs on the appointment pages. This is more difficult than it sounds, since she has to keep track of things like Jessi's ballet classes, Claud's art lessons, Mal's orthodontist appointments – you name it. I don't think Mary Anne has ever made a mistake, though.

Our treasurer, Dawn Schafer, collects subs from us every Monday and keeps track of the money that's in our treasury. We use the money for three things. One, to pay Charlie to drive me to and from the meetings, since I live so far from Claudia now. Two, for club parties. Every now and then we like to give ourselves a treat. Three, to buy materials for Kid-Kits. What are Kid-Kits? Well, they're one of my ideas. A Kid-Kit is a box that we fill with our old toys, books and games, and also some new things, like colouring books, crayons, or sticker books. Each of us has her own Kid-Kit, and we need money to replace the things that get used up. The children we sit for love the Kid-Kits. Bringing one along on a job is like bringing a toy shop. It makes the kids happy. And when the kids are happy, their parents are happy. . . And when their parents are happy, they call the Babysitters Club again!

Mallory and Jessi, our junior officers, don't have any special jobs. The junior officers simply aren't allowed to sit at night unless they're sitting for their own brothers and sisters, so when Mary Anne arranges jobs, she tries to give the after-school and weekend jobs to Jessi and Mallory first. That way the rest of us will be free to take the evening jobs.

And that's it. That's how our club — Oh, wait. One more thing. The club note-book. The notebook is different from the record book, but just as important. It's more of a diary than a notebook. Any time one of us goes on a babysitting job, she's responsible for writing up the job in the notebook. Then, once a week, each of us is supposed to read the notebook. This is really very helpful. We learn how our friends solve sitting problems, or if a kid that we're going to be taking care of has a new fear, a new hobby, etc. Some of the girls think that writing in the notebook is a boring chore, but I think it's invaluable.

Okay. That really *is* it. Now you know how our club began and how it runs, so let's get back to business.

After I had said "Order!" for about the third time, everyone settled down. "Any business?" I asked.

"Subs day!" announced Dawn. She bounced off the bed, blonde hair flying. The treasury envelope was in her hands, and she opened it.

"*Oh*," groaned the rest of us. We earn a lot of money babysitting, but we don't like to part with it for subs, even though we know we have to.

"Aw, come on," said Dawn. "It isn't that bad. Besides, think of me. I have to listen to this moaning and complaining every Monday afternoon." Dawn collected the money, then handed some of it to me. "That's for Charlie," she said. "We have to pay him today."

I nodded. "Thanks, Dawn."

My friends settled down. Claudia leaned against one of her pillows and began plaiting her hair. Mary Anne unwrapped a piece of gum. Dawn flipped through the pages of the notebook. On the floor, Mallory doodled in one of Claudia's sketchbooks, and Jessi absent-mindedly lifted the cover of a shoe box labelled PASTILS AND CHARCAOLS (Claudia isn't a great speller), and exclaimed, "Hey, there are M & M's in here!"

"Oh, yeah," replied Claud. "I forgot about those. Hand them around, Jessi, okay?"

"Sure!" said Jessi. She took out the bag of sweets, replaced the lid on the box, opened the bag, and sent it around Claud's bedroom.

Everyone took a handful of M & M's except for Dawn, who mostly eats health food – she won't even eat meat – and can't stand junk food, especially sweets. Claudia remembered this and handed Dawn a packet of wholewheat crackers. Dawn looked really grateful.

This is just one of the things I love about my club family. We really care about each other. We look out for each other and do nice things for each other. Of course, we fight, too – we've had some whoppers – but that's part of being a family.

"Well, any more club business?" I asked.

Nobody answered.

"Okay, then. We'll just wait for the phone to ring." I picked up the record book and began looking at the appointment calendar. "Gosh," I said, "I can't believe it's already April. Where did the school year go? It feels like it was just September."

"I know," agreed Mary Anne. "Two more months and school will be over." She looked pretty pleased.

"Yeah," said Dawn happily. "Summer. Hot weather. I'll get to visit Dad and Jeff in California again."

"Whoa!" I cried. I was still looking at our calendar. "Guess what. I've just realized that Mother's Day is coming up – soon. It's in less than three weeks."

"Oh, brother. Gift time," murmured Mallory. "I *never* know what to get Mum. None of us does. She always ends up with lots of things she doesn't want and doesn't know what to do with. Like every year, Margo" (Margo is Mal's seven-year-old sister) "makes her a handprint in clay and paints it green. What's Mum going to do with all those green hand sculptures? And the triplets" (ten-year-old boys) "always go to the corner shop and get her really ugly plastic earrings or a horrible necklace or something."

"Once," said Jessi, "my sister gave our mother a bag of chocolate drops and then ate them herself."

We began to laugh.

"This year," Claud began, "I am going to give my mother the perfect present."

"What?" I asked.

Claud shrugged. "I don't know yet."

"I never have to think of Mother's Day presents," said Mary Anne softly.

The talking and laughing stopped. How is it that I forget about Mary Anne's problem year after year? I never remember until somebody, usually the art teacher, is saying something like, "All right, let's begin our Mother's Day cards," or "I know your mothers will just love these glass mosaics." Then I watch Mary Anne sink lower and lower in her seat. Why don't the teachers say, "If you want to make a Mother's Day gift, come over here. The rest of you may read." Or something like that. It would be a lot easier on the kids who don't need to make Mother's Day stuff.

Dawn looked at Mary Anne and awkwardly patted her shoulder.

Claud said, "Sorry, Mary Anne."

We feel sorry for her but we don't quite know what to say. Sorry your mother died? Sorry the greeting card people invented Mother's Day and you have to feel bad once a year? Sorry we have mums and you don't?

I was relieved when the telephone rang. (We all were.) It gave us something to do. I answered the phone, and Mary Anne took over the record book.

"Hi, Mrs Newton," I said. "Friday afternoon? . . . Yeah, it is short notice, I suppose, but I'll check. I'll get right back to you." I hung up. "Check Friday after school," I told Mary Anne. "This Friday."

Mary Anne checked. "Claudia's free," she said. "She's the only one."

I glanced at Claud and she nodded.

So I called Mrs Newton back. "Claudia will be there," I told her. We said goodbye and hung up. The Newtons are some of our oldest clients. They have two kids – Jamie, who's four, and Lucy, who's just a baby. We all love sitting at the Newtons', but Claudia loves it especially. I knew she was happy with her job.

The phone rang several more times after that. All job calls. Then, towards the end of the meeting, we began talking about Mother's Day again. We couldn't help it. We knew Mary Anne felt sad, but the rest of us really needed to think about what to give our mums.

"Flowers?" suggested Jessi.

We shook our heads.

"Chocolate-covered cherries?" suggested Claudia.

We shook our heads.

"Oh, well. It's six o'clock," I announced. "Meeting's over. Don't worry – we've got plenty of time to think of presents. See you all in school tomorrow."

3rd
CHAPTER

When I left Claudia's house, Charlie was waiting for me in the Kishis' driveway. He has been really good about remembering to drive me to and from the meetings of the Babysitters Club. We *are* paying him, but still . . . I keep thinking he might get tied up with an after-school activity and forget me sometime.

Moving across town was *so* inconvenient. I'm not near any of my closest friends, and I'm not near my school. Now I have to get lifts all the time and take the bus to school. The other kids in my new neighbourhood go to private schools. But I wanted to stick with my normal school (so did my brothers), so we're the only ones who go to a state school. We really stand out.

Charlie pulled into the drive, and

Watson's huge house (well, *our* huge house) spread before us. I'm amazed every time I see it. We parked, and my brother and I went inside.

We were greeted by Sam. "Kristy, I just don't know how you do it," was the first thing he said.

"Do what?"

"Babysit so much without going crazy."

I grinned. Sam had been watching David Michael, Andrew and Karen, since Mum and Watson were still at work. "Babysitting is easy," I replied. "It's a piece of cake. What happened?"

"What do you mean 'What happened?' Nothing *happened*. They're just kids. I'm worn out. I couldn't give another cannonball ride if my life depended on it."

"That's Charlie's fault for inventing cannonballs," I told Sam.

At that moment, Andrew came barrelling into the front hall, crying, "Sam! Sam! I need a cannonball ride!"

Without pausing, Sam picked Andrew up, Andrew curled himself into a ball, and Sam charged off towards the kitchen, shouting, "Ba-boom-ba-boom-ba-boom."

"I thought he couldn't give another cannonball ride," said Charlie.

"Andrew's hard to resist," I told him.

Dinner that night was noisy. It was one of the few times when everyone was at home.

294

Andrew and Karen usually aren't with us, and when they are, they're almost always here at the weekend – when Charlie's out on a date or Sam is at a game at school, or *some*thing. But that night was different. We ate in the dining room. Watson sat at one end of the table, Mum at the other. David Michael, Karen and I sat along one side of the table; Charlie, Sam and Andrew sat opposite us.

When everyone had been served, Mum said, "Isn't this nice?" She had been a little emotional lately.

"It's terrific," agreed Watson, who sounded *too* enthusiastic.

Mum and Watson get all worked up whenever we're together as a family, and I know why. I like my family and everything. I like us a lot. But sometimes I think we feel more like pieces of a family instead of a whole family. We're a shirt whose seams haven't all been stitched up. I mean, Mum and Watson got married, but I would only go to Mum if I needed to borrow money. And Andrew usually heads for Watson if he's hurt himself or doesn't feel well. *We're* Mum's kids and *they're* Watson's kids. Two teams on the same playing field.

Don't get me wrong. It isn't bad. Really. Our family just needs to grow together – so Mum and Watson make a big thing out of us all sitting down at the dinner table.

Our dinners are usually not very quiet.

That night, David Michael started things off by singing softly, "*They built the ship Titanic to sail the ocean blue. A sadder ship the waters never knew. She was on her maiden trip when an iceboard hit the ship —*"

"Cut it *out!*" cried Karen suddenly. "I hate that song. All the people die. Besides, it's '*iceberg*', not '*iceboard*'."

"I know that," said David Michael. But he didn't. He had said "iceboard" every time he had sung that song.

He stopped singing. He made a rhythm band out of his plate, glass, fork, and spoon.

Andrew joined him.

Chink-a-chink. Chinkety-chink, chink.

Mum beamed. Why did she look so happy? Usually dinnertime rhythm bands gave her a headache.

"Hey, Karen. Your epidermis is showing," said Sam from across the table.

"What? What?" Karen, flustered, began checking her clothes. Finally, she said haughtily, "Sam. I am not wearing a dress. How can my epipotomus be showing?"

We couldn't help it. Watson, Mum, Charlie, Sam, David Michael and I began to laugh. Not rudely, just gently. Well, all right. David Michael laughed rudely – loudly, anyway.

"*What?*" Karen demanded.

"It's 'epidermis', not 'epipotomus'," said David Michael, glad to be able to correct *her*, "and it means 'skin'."

296

Karen looked questioningly at Sam.

"He's right," said Sam. "It does mean 'skin'."

"My *skin* is showing?" said Karen. "Oh, my *skin* is showing! That's funny! I'm going to say that to everybody in my class tomorrow."

"Now let's have a little eating," said Watson. For a few moments, we ate. At her end of the table, Mum put down her fork and looked lovingly at Watson. "We're so lucky," she said.

Watson smiled.

I glanced at Sam and Charlie. Mum had been acting weird lately.

"We've got six beautiful children —"

"I am not beautiful," said David Michael. "I'm a boy."

"We live in a lovely town," continued Mum, "we like our jobs, we have a gorgeous house . . . with plenty of rooms. Do you realize that we have three spare bedrooms?"

My mother was looking at us.

I glanced at Sam and Charlie again. They shrugged.

"It *is* a nice house, Mum," I agreed.

Mum nodded. "Plenty of extra space."

Suddenly Sam said, "Hey, Mum, you're not pregnant, are you?"

(My mother *could* have been pregnant. She's only in her late thirties. She had Charlie right after she graduated from college.)

"No," Mum replied. "I'm not. . . But how would you kids feel about another brother or sister?"

Oh. So she was trying to *become* pregnant.

"Another brother or sister?" David Michael repeated dubiously.

"A *baby*?" squeaked Andrew and Karen.

"Great!" said Sam and Charlie.

"Terrific!" I added honestly. I love babies. Imagine having one in my own house, twenty-four hours a day.

But the little kids just couldn't be enthusiastic.

"Why do you want a baby?" asked Karen bluntly.

"Oh, we didn't say we want a *baby* ——" Watson began.

But before he could finish, Andrew spoke up. "A baby," he said, "would be the youngest person in the family. But that's *me*. *I'm* the youngest. I don't want a baby."

"Babies smell," added Karen.

"They cry," said David Michael. "And burp and get baby food in their hair. And you have to *change their nappies*."

"Kids, kids," exclaimed Watson, holding his hands up. "Elizabeth just asked about another brother or sister, that's all."

Silence.

At last David Michael said, "Well, brothers and sisters start out as babies, don't they?"

And Andrew said, "I think we've got enough kids around here."

"Yeah," agreed Karen and David Michael.

But I couldn't help saying, "Another kid would be great. Really."

Sam and Charlie nodded.

No one seemed to know what to say then, but it didn't matter because Boo-Boo came into the dining room carrying a mouse that he'd caught, and we all jumped out of our chairs. The poor mouse was still alive, so we had to get it away from Boo-Boo and then put it back outside.

That was the end of dinner.

Later that night, I lay in bed, thinking. Sometimes I get in bed early just so I can do that. First I thought about Boo-Boo and the mouse. Charlie and I had caught Boo-Boo and held him. And David Michael had got Boo-Boo to open his mouth, which had caused the mouse to drop out and land in the oven gloves Mum was wearing. Then Mum, Karen, Andrew and David Michael had taken the mouse into the back garden and let it loose in some shrubbery. It had scampered off.

I thought of Mum wanting to have another baby. Even though she's rather old for that, it made sense. I mean, she's married to Watson now, so I supposed that she and Watson wanted a baby of their own. Wow. Mum would have five children and two stepchildren then.

She would need an extra special Mother's Day present. What on earth could I give her? I slid over in bed so I could see the moon out of my window.

The moon was pretty, but it was no help, Jewellery? Nah. Mum likes to choose her own. Stockings? Boring. Sweets or flowers? Let Watson do that. Something for her desk at the office? Maybe. Clothes? If I could afford anything.

I had a feeling I was missing the point, though. I wanted to say thank you to Mum for being such a wonderful mother. (She really is.) So I needed to give her something special, something that would tell her, "You're the best mum. Thanks." But what would say that?

I thought and thought. And then it came to me. It was another one of my ideas. Carrying it off might take some work, but my friends and I could do it.

I couldn't wait until the next meeting of the Babysitters Club.

4th
CHAPTER

I don't know whether to describe myself as
a patient person or not. I mean, when I'm
babysitting, I can sit for fifteen minutes,
waiting for a four-year-old who wants to tie
his own shoelaces. But when I have a big
idea, I want to get on with it right away.
And I had a *huge* idea.

On Wednesday, I begged Charlie to leave
early for the club meeting. I reached
Claudia's at 5:15.

None of my friends was there, not even
Claudia.

"She is babysitting," Mimi told me. "At
Marshalls'. Back at . . . at five, no at thirty-
nine. No, um . . . back for meeting."

Mimi is Claudia's grandmother, and we
all love her. She had a stroke last summer
and it affected her speech. Also, she is getting a little slower, and . . . I don't know.

301

She just seems older. I wish people didn't have to change.

But they do.

"Go on upstairs?" Mimi said to me, as if it were a question.

"Is that okay?" I replied.

Mimi nodded, so I kissed her cheek and ran to Claud's room. I found the notebook and record book and put them on the bed. Then I put on my visor. I stuck a pencil over my ear and sat in the director's chair. I was ready for the meeting. The only thing I needed was all the rest of the club members.

Claudia arrived first. The others trickled in after her. By 5:29, the six of us had gathered. I was so excited that I rushed through our opening business and then exclaimed, "I've got an idea!"

"This sounds like a big one," said Dawn.

"It's pretty big," I agreed.

"Bigger than the Kid-Kits?" Mary Anne wanted to know.

"Much."

"Bigger than the *club*?" asked Mallory, awed.

"Not quite. This is it: I was trying to come up with a Mother's Day present for my mum," I began. (I couldn't look at Mary Anne while I talked about Mother's Day, I just couldn't.) "And I was thinking that her present should be really special. That it should have something to do with

302

saying thank you and with being a mum. And I thought, what would a mum like more than anything else? Then the answer came to me – *not* to be a mum for a while. You know, to have a break. And *then* I thought, maybe we could give this present to a lot of the mums whose kids we sit for."

"Huh?" said Claudia.

"I suppose I'm a little ahead of myself," I replied. (I'm usually a little ahead of myself.)

My friends shifted position and I looked at them as I tried to work out how to explain my great idea. Mallory, with her new short haircut, was sitting on the floor, leaning against Claud's bed. She was wearing jeans with zips up the bottoms of the legs, and a sweat shirt that said STONEYBROOK MIDDLE SCHOOL across the front. In her newly pierced ears were tiny gold hoops.

Jessi was wearing matching hoops (I think she and Mal had gone shopping together), a purple dance leotard and jeans. Over the leotard she was wearing a purple-and-white striped shirt, unbuttoned.

On the bed, in a row, sat Mary Anne, Dawn and Claudia, watching me intently. Mary Anne's hair was pulled back in a ponytail and held in place with a black-and-white checked bow that matched the short skirt she was wearing. Around her neck was a chain and dangling from it were gold letters that spelled out MARY ANNE.

Dawn was wearing a necklace, too, only hers said I'M WONDERFUL. Honestly. Where had she got it? California, probably. And in her *double* pierced ears were hoops of different sizes. See what I mean about Dawn being an individual? Also she was wearing a fairly ordinary dress, but on her feet were tartan trainers.

Then there was Claudia. She was wearing a pretty amazing dress, too – with a red tie! Then, she had on these new, very cool roll socks. When she pushed them down just right, they fell into three rolls. The top roll was red, the middle one was peacock blue, and the bottom one was purple. She looked as if she were wearing ice-cream cones on her feet. In her hair was a plaited band in red, blue, and purple, like her socks. And dangling from her ears were – get this – spiders in webs. Ew. (But they were pretty cool.)

And me? I was wearing what I always wear – jeans, a sweater and trainers. Okay, so I'm not a creative dresser. I don't have pierced ears, either. I'm sorry. That sort of thing just doesn't interest me much.

"My idea," I began, "is to give mothers a break in their routine. I thought that as a present to the mothers whose kids we sit for – you know, Mrs Newton, Mrs Perkins, Mrs Barrett, some of our own mothers –

we could take their kids off their hands for a day. We could do something really fun with the kids so they'd have a good time, and while they were gone, the mothers could enjoy some peace and quiet."

All round me, eyes were lighting up.

"Yeah!" said Claudia slowly.

"That's a great idea," agreed Jessi.

"Brilliant," added Dawn.

Mal and Mary Anne were nodding their heads vigorously.

"Good idea?" I asked unnecessarily.

"The best," said Dawn.

I breathed a sigh of relief. Sometimes I get so carried away with my ideas that I can't tell whether they're good or stupid.

The phone rang then, and we stopped and arranged a sitting job for Jessi.

"I was thinking," I went on as Mary Anne put down the appointment book, "that we could take the kids on some kind of outing. I don't know what kind exactly, but we'll come up with something. And maybe we could do this on the day before Mother's Day. That way, the present will be close to the actual holiday, but we'll still be able to spend Sunday with our own moth—"

I stopped abruptly. How could I be so thoughtless? I glanced at Mary Anne, who was looking down at her hands.

"With – with, um, our families," I finished. I prayed for the phone to ring then, to save my neck and Mary Anne's feelings, but it didn't.

Instead, Jessi said, "If we're asking our little brothers and sisters on the outing, I *know* Becca would like to come. Especially if we invite Charlotte, too." (Charlotte Johanssen, one of our sitting charges, and Becca Ramsey are best friends.) "Becca might be shy, but she always likes a good day-trip."

I smiled gratefully at Jessi. She meant what she'd just said, but I knew she'd only said it to take everyone's attention away from mothers and Mother's Day. Also, she got our discussion going again.

"My brothers and sisters would like a trip, too," spoke up Mal. "Well, most of them would. The triplets and Vanessa might think they're too old for this. But, well, what about money? If this really is a present to mo— to our clients, then I suppose we're going to pay for everything, right?"

"We should talk about that," I replied. "I really haven't worked out all the details."

Ordinarily, I might have come up with some solution and said, "Okay, this is what we're going to do." But I know that I can be bossy. Sometimes it gets me in trouble. Not long ago, it nearly caused our whole club to break up. Well, maybe I'm exaggerating. But it did cause a huge fight.

So all I said was, "I don't think the day

has to be very expensive. Maybe we could use money that's in the treasury. We have quite a bit at the moment, don't we, Dawn?"

Dawn nodded.

"Okay, then, *But* – everyone has to agree to this. This isn't usually how we spend the treasury money."

We were in the middle of taking a vote when the phone rang. And rang and rang. We stopped to arrange a few jobs. Then we returned to the vote. It was unanimous. We agreed to use our treasury money.

"Now," I went on, "what should the outing be? I mean, where should we go? It should be some place that's fun, but easy to get to and cheap."

We all thought. No one came up with a single idea. There isn't a lot to do here in Stoneybrook. Not a lot that's within walking distance anyway.

Claudia cleared her throat and we looked at her expectantly. "I don't have an idea," she said. "I was just thinking that the way we could ask kids to come on the outing would be to send invitations to their mothers. I think the outing would seem more like a gift then. An invitation could say, 'Happy Mother's Day, Mrs Rodowsky. As a special present, the Babysitters Club would like to give you a day to yourself. Therefore, Jackie, Archie and Shea are invited to go' . . . wherever we decide to go. Something like that."

"Ooh, that's great, Claud," said Jessi.

"Yeah," agreed Dawn. "Would you design the invitations, Claud? We'll help you make them, but you do the best artwork."

"Thanks," replied Claudia. "Of course I'll design something."

"Maybe the fathers could be involved," I said slowly. "I'm not sure how to get them to do this, but they should be the ones to drop the kids off and pick them up. Things like that. And of course we can't take babies on the outing. So, for instance, if we take Jamie Newton for the day, Lucy will still be at home. Maybe Mr Newton will agree to watch her while Jamie's with us."

My friends nodded. We talked and talked. We talked until it was after six o'clock. We worked out all the details, but not what our outing would be. Where could we take the kids?

"You know," said Jessi, as we were getting ready to leave Claud's room. "I think our Mother's Day surprise solves a problem for me."

"What?" asked the rest of us.

"I think it can be my present to Mama. It'll get Becca *and* me out of her hair for a whole day. And if Daddy will watch Squirt, then Mama will really have a holiday."

"Same here," said Mal. "The younger kids can come on the trip, and I'm sure I

308

can convince the triplets and Vanessa to stay out of Mum's hair. Or maybe Dad can do something with them."

"And same with me," I added. "Andrew, Karen and David Michael will come with us. Charlie and Sam are hardly ever around on Saturdays anyway. I *think* this will be my gift. I'll just have to see."

"I wish the outing helped me," said Dawn with a sigh, "but it doesn't."

"Me neither," added Claudia. "All I've decided is to *make* Mum's gift, whatever it will be."

"Maybe I'll make mine, too," said Dawn. "Would you help me, Claud?"

"Of course."

We were filing out of Claudia's room, tired but excited.

Mary Anne was being awfully quiet, but just as I was starting to worry about her, she gave me a little smile to let me know that she would handle Mother's Day some-how – just as she had handled it every year before.

5th CHAPTER

Friday

I babbysat for Jamie newton today guess waht. Thanks to jamie I think I discovred the place wher we can take the kids for there outing. Jamie was in the bake garden and he was printinding to be in a circos or something. He was printinding to walk on a thight rope and be a clone.

Then I took him inside for a glas of water and guess waht I saw. It looked like the anser to our probelms.

Claudia's job at the Newtons' on Friday afternoon turned out to be profitable. Not only did she have fun and get paid, but she found something pretty interesting. It was a leaflet stuck on their refrigerator.

Well, once again I'm ahead of myself. I bet you don't have any idea what I'm talking about. (I don't blame you.) Okay. Let me go back to when Claud arrived at the Newtons'.

She turned up on time, of course. (A good sitter is *always* on time.) But she didn't bring her Kid-Kit. It was a sunny afternoon and she knew that all Jamie would want to do was play outside.

Mrs Newton greeted Claudia at the door.

"Hi, honey," she said. "Come on in."

"Thanks." Claudia stepped into the Newtons' hallway.

"How are you? How are the art classes?" asked Mrs Newton. She and Claud are pretty close. Mrs Newton is interested in whatever Claudia does.

"I'm fine. My classes are great. And look what I made." Claudia pulled her hair back to show Mrs Newton the earrings she was wearing. They were painted sunbursts.

"You *made* those?"

"Yup," said Claudia proudly.

Mrs Newton shook her head in amazement.

"Where are the kids?" asked Claud.

"Jamie's out in the garden, and Lucy's upstairs taking a nap. I just put her down, so she should sleep for a while. You can go out with Jamie, but stick your head inside every now and then to listen for the baby."

Claudia nodded. "Okay. Anything else?"

"I don't think so. You know where the emergency numbers are. And I'll be at a meeting at Jamie's school. The number is on the refrigerator."

A few minutes later, Mrs Newton called goodbye to Jamie and left. Claudia joined Jamie in the back garden. She found him tiptoeing around with his arms outstretched. He was singing "Home on the Range", but he was getting a lot of the words wrong.

"*Oh, give me a comb,*" he sang loudly, "*where the buffaloes foam, and the deer and the antinope pay. Where seldom is heard a long-distance bird, and the sky is not crowded all day.*"

Claudia smiled, but she managed not to laugh. "Hiya, Jamie," she said.

"Hi-hi!" Jamie replied happily. He didn't seem to mind having been interrupted at all.

"What are you doing?" Claud wanted to know. (Jamie was still tiptoeing around.)

"I'm a tightrope walker. Now watch this. I'm going to be someone else."

Jamie walked a few steps. He tripped and fell. Then he picked himself up and fell again. When he stood up, he shook himself all over like a puppy dog.

Claudia wasn't sure what was going on, so she was relieved when Jamie began turning somersaults and making silly faces. "You're a clown!" she exclaimed.

"Right!" said Jamie. "And now I'm going to be another person."

He raised his arms in the air and ran back and forth across the yard. "*Oh, he fries food the air,*" he sang, "*with the greatest of vease!*"

"A trapeze artist," said Claud.

"Yup."

The Newtons must have gone to a circus, she thought. And she thought that until she took Jamie inside for a glass of water. His throat was dry from all his singing and running around. Claud went to the refrigerator to get out the bottle of cold water she knew was inside – and her eyes fell on a colourful leaflet posted next to the phone number of Jamie's school.

COME TO SUDSY'S CARNIVAL! it read. GAMES! RIDES! SIDESHOW ATTRACTIONS! REFRESHMENTS!

Carefully, Claudia read every word on the leaflet. The carnival would be in Stoneybrook on Mother's Day weekend. It would be set up in a large car park that was near a playground not far from Claud's house. It would have rides, plenty of food (candyfloss, peanuts, ice-cream, popcorn, lemonade) and even a sideshow. Claudia raised her eyebrows. Were there *really* bearded ladies and people who were half-man, half-woman or who could swallow fire or swords? She wasn't sure. But she didn't care. All she was interested in was finding out more about the carnival.

Jamie saw Claud looking at the leaflet. "The carnival," he said sadly.

"What's wrong?" asked Claud.

"I really really really really really want to go, but I can't. Mummy and Daddy can't take me."

"Too bad, Jamie," said Claudia.

"I know. I want to see that man. That one right there."

Jamie reached up to touch a picture of a clown carrying a bunch of helium balloons.

"The balloon-seller?" Claudia asked.

Jamie nodded. "I would buy a yellow balloon. Maybe after that I would buy a green balloon for Lucy."

"That would be very generous of you."

"And then I would play some games. I would win some prizes, like a whistle and a teddy bear. The bear would be for Lucy, too."

Claudia smiled.

"But," Jamie continued with a sigh, "I can't go. No clowns. No balloons. No prizes."

Claudia gave Jamie a hug, and then poured him his glass of water.

"Thank you," he said politely.

"You're welcome. And Jamie, you never know."

"What?"

"You never know about things. You can't be too sure. I remember once when I was six, a big circus came to Stamford, and Mum and Dad said our whole family could go. Only – a week before we were going to the circus, I got chicken pox."

"Yuck."

"I know. And when circus day came, I was much better but I still had spots, so I wasn't allowed to go. Mimi took care of me while Mum and Dad and Janine went to the circus. Guess what, though. People liked the circus so much that it stayed an extra week, and Mimi and I went to it the next Saturday."

"*Really? Wow.*"

Claudia suddenly realized that she shouldn't get Jamie's hopes up *too* much. After all, the carnival was still not definite. So she said again, "You just never know, Jamie. I'm not saying you will go to the carnival. But it's several weeks away. A lot could happen, right? . . . Right?"

"*Oh, give me a comb. . .*"

Jamie wasn't listening. He and Claudia went back outside. Jamie played carnival again. Every now and then, Claudia tiptoed into the house and stood at the bottom of the stairs, listening for Lucy. The third time she did that, she heard baby sounds. Lucy almost always wakes up happy. She doesn't cry. She just sits in her cot and talks to herself in words only she can understand.

Claudia poked her head out of the back door. "Jamie!" she called. "Come on inside. I have to get Lucy up."

Jamie came in and found *Sesame Street* on the television, while Claudia dashed upstairs. She opened the door to Lucy's room slowly.

"Hiya, Lucy-Goose," she said.

Lucy's face began to crumple.

"I know. I'm not your mummy or daddy. I'm sorry. But it's me, Luce. It's Claudee." (That's what Jamie sometimes calls Claudia.)

Claudia pottered around Lucy's room, not going too near her. She sang "The Eensy Weensy Spider" and "The Wheels on the Bus."

Lucy began to smile. Claudia tickled her and changed her nappy, and she seemed to be okay. So Claud carried her downstairs. She could smell Lucy's baby smell – powder and nappies and soap and milk.

"Jamie, look who's here!" said Claudia.

Jamie turned away from the TV. When he and Lucy saw each other, their faces broke into grins.

What a change from when Lucy first came home from hospital, thought

Claudia. Jamie wanted to send his sister back.

Claudia, Jamie and Lucy played on the floor of the family room until Mrs Newton came home at five-fifteen. Then Claudia raced to her own house for our Friday meeting. She couldn't wait to get there. For once, she would be the one with a big idea, and if everyone liked it, she'd make a lot of people very happy – especially Jamie Newton, who just might get to go to the carnival and see the balloon-seller after all.

6th
CHAPTER

For the second time in a row I arrived at our meeting early. There was a good reason for this. It was because I had begged Charlie to leave early. "Please, please, please take me over now," I'd said. My next step would have been to kneel down and plead, but Charlie agreed to go.

I don't know why I was so eager for the meeting. It wasn't as if I had any news. I just wanted to get on with the plans for our Mother's Day surprise.

Anyway, thanks to Charlie, I reached the Kishis' just before Claudia came running home from the Newtons'. I could hear her calling to me as she dashed along the pavement.

"Hi, Claud!" I replied. I stood on her steps and looked across the street at the house that used to be mine. I'd grown up there. I'd learned to walk and ride a bike and turn cartwheels there. I'd gone off to school and watched my father walk out on us and seen Watson come into our lives. I'd been away from that house for less than a year, but it seemed like a decade.

Time is funny.

Claudia raced up her path and let me into her house. "You're early again," she said. "Do you have news?"

I shook my head.

"Well, I do! But I suppose it'll have to wait until the meeting starts, right?"

"Not necessarily," I replied, since I was dying of curiosity, "but I suppose you might as well. Then you can tell us all at once."

Claudia and I were both a little disappointed, but at least we didn't have long to wait before the meeting started. Mary Anne, Jessi, Dawn and Mallory arrived on time, and I brought us to order immediately.

"The first piece of business," I announced, "is that Claudia has some sort of big news. Claudia?" I said, turning to her.

"My big news," Claudia began, shifting position on the bed, "is that I think I've found a place where we can take the kids on their outing."

Five pairs of eyes widened. The room was absolutely silent.

Then I cried out, "Where, where, *where*?" I couldn't help it.

"To a carnival," Claud began. "You see, I was sitting at the Newtons' this afternoon, and on their refrigerator was a leaflet advertising something called Sudsy's Carnival. It's going to be in Stoneybrook the weekend of Mother's Day. There'll be all sorts of things kids will like – games, rides, even a sideshow. But the best thing is, guess where the carnival will be set up?"

"Where?" the rest of us asked.

"In the car park near Carle Playground."

"Oh, wow!" I exclaimed. "We can walk there easily!"

"Right," said Claud. "And it seems like a nice, small carnival. I mean, it wouldn't be overwhelming for the littlest children, and we'd have an easy time keeping track of everyone."

"I wonder how expensive a carnival would be," said our treasurer. "Any idea what it would cost per child?"

I looked at Claudia.

"It's hard to say," she replied slowly. "The leaflet didn't mention a fee to get in – you know, the way you pay one big price to get into Funland, and then you can go on the rides as often as you want. I suppose one fee wouldn't make sense at a carnival anyway, since so much of it is games that you have to pay for separately." Claud paused. She drew in her breath.

"I'm guessing that the carnival wouldn't be too expensive per child. There's an awful lot just to look at, and if we limit the children to, say, three things each, that wouldn't be too bad."

We asked Claudia a few more questions, but everyone in the room was smiling. We knew we had the solution to our problem, and what a solution it was!

"Jamie is going to *faint!*" exclaimed Claudia. "He's dying to go to Sudsy's."

"I don't think David Michael has ever been to a carnival," I added.

"Becca has," said Jessi, "and when she gets to this one, she'll think she's died and gone to heaven."

"I wonder if the kids will be able to spend all day at a carnival," I said suddenly. "That just occurred to me."

"Hmm," said Mary Anne. "Maybe not. Especially if they can only do a few things each."

"I don't think *I* could spend all day at a carnival," said Dawn. "I was at one recently when I visited Dad and Jeff in California. It was fun, but. . ."

"All day at anything is too long for little kids," I pointed out. "They need to rest. They get bored."

"Maybe," began Mallory, but she was interrupted by the phone.

We arranged several sitting jobs. Then Mallory started again.

"Maybe we should just go to the carnival in the morning when everyone is fresh and awake," she said. "Then we could eat lunch somewhere else, like at the playground, since the children are bringing their lunches anyway, and we'll be right next to the playground. There are tables and benches everywhere at Carle. Our family has been on lots of picnics there."

"That's a good idea," I said. "Really good. Then the kids could play in the park for a while, and then we really should give them a chance to rest before they go home."

"Well," said Claudia, "they *could* come to my house. Remember last summer when we ran the play group in Stacey's back garden? We could do something like that here. It would probably be for just an hour or two. We could read stories and maybe do an art project. The kids could make Mother's Day cards or little gifts or something. It would be a nice way for them to unwind after all the excitement."

"Great!" I exclaimed. "I think we've got our Mother's Day surprise." Then I remembered about being bossy and added, "Everyone who thinks this is a good plan, raise her hand."

Five hands shot up, including mine.

"Dawn? What's wrong? You didn't raise your hand."

Dawn grinned. "I don't think it's a good plan," she said. "I think it's a brilliant one."

322

Everyone laughed, and Claudia threw a pillow at Dawn.

"Okay," I said, when we had quietened down, "I know we don't have much time left today, but I think we should make a list of kids to invite so we can get the invitations out soon. There really isn't *that* much time until Mother's Day."

"I'll take notes," said our secretary. Mary Anne turned to a blank page in the back of the record book. "All right. I'm ready."

"Let's start with our little brothers and sisters," I began. "Karen, Andrew and David Michael will be invited. And Becca Ramsey. And . . . Mal, who in your family?"

"I suppose everyone except the triplets. Claire, Margo, Nicky and Vanessa. I'm really not sure Vanessa will come, though. She's funny about big group things sometimes. She'd rather stay in her room and write poetry."

Mary Anne nodded. "Well, if she comes, that's eight so far."

"Jamie Newton," said Claudia.

"The Barretts," said Dawn. "Buddy and Suzi, anyway. Marnie's too little."

"Myriah and Gabbie Perkins," added Mary Anne, writing furiously. "And, of course, Laura is much too little."

"The Rodowsky boys," spoke up Jessi. "Oh, and the Braddock kids. How could we forget them?"

"I hate to say this," said Mary Anne, "but Jenny Prezzioso. We just *have* to ask her if we ask the Barretts and Mal's brothers and sisters."

"Oh, ew!" I cried. "Ew, *EW*! Jenny is so spoiled." But I knew Mary Anne was right. So Jenny's name was added to the list.

We kept on thinking of kids to invite — Charlotte Johanssen, some kids in my new neighbourhood. When we couldn't come up with another name, I said to Mary Anne, "What's the grand total?"

Mary Anne counted up. "Oh, my goodness! Twenty-nine!"

"Twenty-nine!" exclaimed Claudia. "We're good babysitters, but the six of us can't take twenty-nine kids to a carnival."

There was a moment of silence. Then Jessi said, "Well, they won't *all* be able to come. Mal said Vanessa probably won't want to, and some people are bound to be away that day, or to have plans."

"True. . ." I replied slowly. "Even so. Let's say twenty kids want to go on the outing. There are six of us. Some of us would have to be in charge of four kids all day. That's a lot. And what if we end up with more kids than we think?"

"Well, how about calling our associate members?" suggested Mary Anne, grinning. (You could tell she was just dying to call Logan.)

"Maybe we'd better." I handed the

phone to Mary Anne. She called Logan. His family was going to be out of town that weekend.

Mary Anne handed the phone back to me. I called Shannon Kilbourne. *Her* family would be having weekend guests. Shannon was supposed to stick around and be polite.

"Uh-oh," I said when I'd hung up the phone.

"Wait a second!" cried Claudia. "Oh, my lord! I've got a great idea. Let's call Stacey and invite her to Stoneybrook for the weekend!"

As if you couldn't tell from Claudia's excitement, she and Stacey McGill used to be best friends. (Well, they still are but it's difficult with Claud living in Stoneybrook and Stacey living in New York City.) Anyway, I knew we all wanted to see Stacey, and she's a terrific babysitter.

Claudia made the call. "Stace? It's me," she said. A whole lot of screaming and laughing followed. Then Claudia explained about the Mother's Day surprise. "So could you come?" she asked. "We aren't getting paid or anything. It would just be fun. And you could stay for a while on Sunday before we put you on the train back to the city."

Stacey had to check with her parents, but guess what – she got permission!

"You can come?" shrieked Claudia. She

turned to us. "She's free! She can come! . . . Stace? We'll make the arrangements later. Oh, I'm *so glad*! This will be your first trip back to Stoneybrook."

Well, basically it had been a red-letter club meeting. By the time Claud got off the phone, it was just after six, so we had to leave, but all of us felt as if we were floating instead of walking. We agreed to return to Claudia's the next day, Saturday, to make the invitations.

7th
CHAPTER

The arrangements for the Mother's Day surprise were falling into place. Claudia's parents had spoken to Stacey's parents, and the adults had decided that Stacey would take the train to Stoneybrook on Friday after school. With any luck, she'd reach the Kishis' in time for our club meeting that day! Then she would stay with Claud until Sunday afternoon – and help us out on Saturday, of course.

Also our invitations had been designed, made, and posted out. They were pretty nice, if I do say so myself. Claud had drawn two pictures on them. In the upper left-hand corner was a totally exhausted-looking mum. She was holding a briefcase in one hand and a vacuum cleaner in the other, and a baby was strapped to her chest. Her hair looked frazzled and there were bags under her eyes. In the lower right-hand corner was a rested mum. She was sitting in a deck chair with a book in one hand and a glass of lemonade (or something) in the other. She was smiling, and the bags were gone.

In the middle of the page, we had written: "SURPRISE! Happy Mother's Day! The members of the Babysitters Club would like to give our special mums a special gift."

(I thought that part was corny, but no one agreed with me.)

Then the invitations went on to say who was invited, what we would do, where we would meet, and that sort of thing.

I was at home on the Saturday my own mum received her Mother's Day surprise. It was one of those gorgeous spring days when you look at the sky and think, Could it possibly get any bluer? It was also unusually warm, so David Michael, Andrew, Karen and I were out in our garden with no jackets or sweaters.

"It's summer! It's just like summer!" exclaimed Karen.

We still had a good two months before the holidays, but I didn't say anything.

The kids were doing the outdoor things they missed during the winter, like skipping, tossing a ball around, and turning somersaults. Mum and Watson were inside. They were on the phone. They'd been making an awful lot of phone calls lately. And Sam and Charlie, as usual, were off with their friends.

Sometimes I feel . . . I don't know . . . left out of my own family. I love everybody, but I'm too young to hang around with Sam and Charlie, and too old for Andrew, David Michael and Karen. They're fun, but they *are* just kids.

Anyway, David Michael's game of catch with Andrew was beginning to get out of hand.

"David Michael," I said, "you don't have to throw it so hard. Andrew's not that far away from you."

"But he keeps missing the balls."

"Maybe he's afraid of them. They're coming at him like freight trains."

"I'm not afraid!" protested Andrew.

I sighed. Since I wasn't babysitting, I didn't feel like getting involved in this argument. "I think I'll take Shannon for a walk," I said.

Shannon was playing in the garden, but I knew she'd want to take a walk. Any change of scenery was fine with her. I clipped her lead to her collar and we set off. I chose one particular direction. It was the direction in which Bart Taylor's house lies.

Bart Taylor is nice. Oh, okay, he's gorgeous and wonderful and clever and athletic. We sort of like each other, even though we don't go to the same school.

Bart coaches a softball team called Bart's Bashers, and I coach one called Kristy's Krushers. So Bart is my rival, too. We try not to think of that. But we hardly ever see each other anyway.

Which is why I walked Shannon past his house that day. I tried to glance at it casually every few steps, but I couldn't see a thing that way. So finally I just stared. The front door was closed, the curtains were drawn, the garage door was pulled down.

No one was at home.

I walked Shannon sadly back to my house, feeling lonely and a little depressed. But the warm weather and the thought of the weekend stretching before me cheered me up again.

"Hey, you lot!" I called when I reached our garden. "How about some batting practice? The Krushers have another game coming up!"

Andrew, David Michael and Karen are in my softball team. That ought to give you some idea of what the team is like. It's a group of kids who are either too young for Little League or even T-ball, or who are too embarrassed to belong to one of those teams – but who really want to learn to play better. The first time the Krushers played Bart's Bashers we almost beat them. That's how much spirit we have.

"Batting practice?" echoed Karen. "Okay. Let's go."

We found several bats and two softballs.

"I'll be the pitcher," I said. "We're going to work on your technique. David Michael, show me your batting stance, okay?"

My brother demonstrated.

"Good!" I cried. "That's really terrific." No doubt about it, my brother had improved since I'd started coaching him. I don't mean to sound conceited, but it was true.

I tossed the ball – underhand, easy.

David Michael missed it by a mile.

I take it back. Maybe he was still clumsy.

"Karen?" I called. "Your turn."

Karen was testing the weights of the bats when Mum dashed into the back garden, waving a piece of paper in her hand.

Oh, *darn*, I thought. Which one of us messed up? What was she waving? A maths test with an E on the top? A report with the words "See me" in red ink? (I swear, those are the worst words teachers ever invented.)

"Kristy!" Mum called.

Yikes! It was *me*! I had messed up!

"Honey, thank you," said my mother breathlessly as she reached me.

Thank you? Well, I couldn't have done anything too bad. I dared to look at the piece of paper. It was the Mother's Day surprise. *Whew.*

"You're welcome," I replied, smiling.

Mum put her arms around me.

"It's your Mother's Day surprise," I said unnecessarily.

Immediately, Mum began to cry. It wasn't that sobbing, unhappy crying that mothers do when they're watching something like *Love Story* or *Brian's Song* on TV. It was that teary kind of crying where the voice just goes all wavery. "Wha-at a lo-ovely invitation," she managed to squeak out. She wiped at her eyes. Then she found a tissue stuffed up her sleeve, so she blew her nose.

(Well, I knew the invitations were nice, but I hadn't expected this. I would have to call Jessi and Mallory to find out if their mothers had freaked out too.)

"Um, Mum," I began, gathering my nerve to ask the question that so far only Sam had dared to ask, "are you pregnant?"

My mother shook her head. She blew her nose again. "No."

"Are you positive?"

"Positive. . . But if you were to have a new brother or sister, how —"

"Well, you know how I feel about kids, Mum," I said. "It would be fine."

But suddenly it didn't seem quite as fine as it had seemed in the past. I love babies. I really do. But what would it be like if Mum and Watson had a baby of their own? That would be different from Mrs Newton or Mrs Perkins having a baby. It might draw Mum and Watson closer together – and shut us out, just when we needed to be drawn closer to everyone in the family. Why hadn't I thought about that before? But all I said was, "Fine, fine."

Mum smiled. The two of us sat down on the grass. "So tell me more about this invitation," said my mother. "Who planned the surprise?"

"Everyone in the Babysitters Club," I answered, "only, the basic idea was sort of mine. Well, it was all mine."

"I'm sure it was. You always did have big ideas."

"Remember when we lived in the old house, and I worked out the torch code so Mary Anne and I could talk to each other from our bedroom windows at night?"

"Of course. And your big idea to marry me to the postman?"

"David Michael wanted a father," I reminded her. "I was only ten then."

Mum and I laughed. We watched Andrew, Karen and David Michael practise their pitching and catching.

"Well, anyway," I said, "we sent out invitations to twenty-nine kids."

"Twenty-nine!" squawked Mum.

"Don't worry. They won't all be able to come. Besides, Stacey is going to be in town that weekend. She's going to help us. So there'll be seven sitters. If we end up with, let's say, twenty kids, that's only about three kids per sitter. We can handle that."

"And you're taking the children to a carnival?"

"Yes. It's called Sudsy's. It's just a little one. It'll be set up in that big car park near Carle Playground. We'll spend the morning at Sudsy's, go to the playground for lunch and some exercise, then walk back to Claudia's house for stories and stuff, so the kids can rest. We reckon we'll have the kids from about nine until four. That'll be a nice rest for you, won't it, Mum?"

"A wonderful one."

The phone rang then. We could hear it through the open kitchen window. A moment later, Watson called, "Elizabeth? This is an important one."

My mother leaped to her feet like an Olympic athlete and dashed inside.

I went back to my sister and brothers.

"How are you lot getting on?" I asked. I asked it before I saw the scowls on the kids' faces.

"He is so clumsy," said David Michael with clenched teeth, pointing to Andrew.

"I am not."

"You are too, you little wimp. And you're Watson's favourite."

"No, he isn't," cried Karen indignantly. "Daddy loves us both the same."

"What about *me*?" David Michael threw his bat angrily to the ground.

Karen and Andrew did the same thing. Softballs, too.

"Well, I suppose it stands to reason," my brother went on. "Of course he loves you two more than me. He's your real father. he's just my step."

"Your mum loves you more than us," spoke up Andrew, to my surprise. "She's *our* step."

"*Hey, hey, HEY*! What is this talk?" I cried. "Everybody loves everybody around here."

"No," said David Michael. "Sometimes Thomases love Thomases more, and Brewers love Brewers more."

Karen sighed. "I'm tired of this. Let's play ball again."

The kids picked up their bats. They forgot their argument for a while.

But I didn't.

8th
CHAPTER

"Well, it's finally happened!" I announced. "What?" asked Claudia, Jessi, Dawn, Mary Anne and Mallory.

We were holding a meeting of the Babysitters Club, and the last of the RSVPs for the Mother's Day surprise had just been phoned in. I gave the news to my friends.

"We can get a total count now," I said. "That was Mrs Barrett. Buddy and Suzi can come on the outing. They were the last kids we needed to hear about. Mary Anne?"

Mary Anne had opened the record book to a page on which she was listing the kids who'd be coming to Sudsy's with us. "Ready for the total?" she asked.

The rest of us nodded nervously.

"Okay, just a sec." Mary Anne's pen

moved down the page. Then, "It's twenty-one," she announced.

"Twenty-one! That's perfect!" I cried. "Seven sitters including Stacey, so three kids each. We can manage that."

"Of course we can," said Dawn.

"We can help each other out," added Claudia.

"Read us the list, Mary Anne," I said. "Let's see exactly what we're dealing with here."

"Okay." Mary Anne began reading, running her finger along the list. "Claire, Margo, Nicky and Vanessa Pike." (Vanessa had surprised everyone by immediately agreeing to come.) "Becca Ramsey; David Michael Thomas; Karen and Andrew Brewer; Jamie Newton; Jackie, Shea and Archie Rodowsky; Jenny Prezzioso." (I tried not to choke.) "Myriah and Gabbie Perkins; Matt and Haley Braddock; Charlotte Johanssen; Nina Marshall; and Buddy and Suzi Barrett."

"And who couldn't come?" I asked.

"Let's see," said Mary Anne, turning to another page in the record book, "the Arnold twins, Betsy Sobak, the Papadakises and the Delaneys."

I nodded. "Okay. I was just curious."

Ring, ring.

Dawn reached for the phone. "Hello, Babysitters Club," she said. "Yes, hi, Mrs Arnold. . . Oh, we're sorry, too. The twins

337

would probably love Sudsy's. . . Yeah. . . Yeah. . . Okay, on Tuesday? I'll check. I'll call you right back."

We arranged for Mal to sit for Marilyn and Carolyn Arnold (can you believe their names?) on Tuesday afternoon. Then we went back to our work.

"I suppose we should make up groups of kids for the outing," said Claudia. "That worked well before."

Once, our club had sat for fourteen kids for a whole week. We kept the kids in groups according to their ages. It was really helpful, and we had done the same thing when Mary Anne, Dawn, Claudia and I had visited Stacey in New York and taken a big group of kids to a museum and to Central Park.

"The only thing is," said Mary Anne, "that I'm not sure we should group the kids by age. I think we should group them, but, well, Matt and Haley will have to be in the same group, even though Matt is seven and Haley's almost ten now. Haley understands Matt's signing better than anybody." (Matt is deaf and communicates using sign language.)

"And," I added, "I think Karen and Andrew should be in the same group, and David Michael should be in a different one. Andrew is really dependent on Karen, and lately the two of them have been having some problems with David Michael."

"And Charlotte and Becca *have* to be together," added Jessi. "Becca won't come

338

if she can't be with Charlotte."

"Hmm," I said. "Anything else?"

"Keep Jenny away from the Braddocks," said Dawn.

"And Nicky away from Claire," added Mallory.

"Boy, is this complicated," commented Claudia.

"I know," I agreed. "But we can do it. Let's try to draw up some lists. Let's just see how far we get. Everyone, make up seven lists and then we'll compare them."

Mary Anne passed around paper and we set to work. We were interrupted four times by the telephone, but at last everyone said they had done the best they could.

I collected the papers. I looked over the groups my friends had come up with. I said things like, "No, that one won't work. Matt and Haley aren't together." Or, "Oh, that's good, that's good, that's — Nope. We've got Claire and Nicky together."

"I've got an idea," said Dawn after a while. "Why don't you cut out all the groups, all forty-two of them, sort through them, and try to find the seven best?"

"Okay," I agreed. Claudia handed me a pair of scissors. "But I think I'll need some help."

Every single club member got down on her hands and knees. We spread the lists on the floor, examined them, and shuffled them around.

"This is a good one," said Jessi.

"This is a good one," said Claud.

Finally we had chosen seven good lists. We counted the kids. Twenty-one. We checked the kids against Mary Anne's list. Nina Marshall turned up twice; Shea Rodowsky was missing.

"*Darn* it!" I cried.

We started again. Finally, finally, finally we had seven lists that worked:

Kristy

Karen Brewer
Andrew Brewer
Shea Rodowsky

Claudia

Myriah Perkins
Gabbie Perkins
Jamie Newton

Mary Anne

Jenny Prezzioso
Claire Pike
Margo Pike

Dawn

Suzi Barrett
Nina Marshall
Archie Rodowsky

Jessi

Matt Braddock
Haley Braddock
Nicky Pike

Mallory

Buddy Barrett
D. M. Thomas
Jackie Rodowsky

Stacey

Charlotte Johanssen
Becca Ramsey
Vanessa Pike

"Well," I said, "we've got all the necessary

combinations – Matt and his sister are together, so are Charlotte and Becca, Jenny is separated from the Braddocks, and that sort of thing. There are some good combinations here, too. Like, Jamie and the Perkins girls are together, and they're friends. And I think Jenny will work out okay with Claire and Margo, don't you, Mal?"

"Yeah, that should be all right."

"But," I went on, "there are some odd combinations here, too. Not bad, just odd. For instance, Shea Rodowsky is with Karen and Andrew. Shea is nine. He's a lot older than they are. But where else could we put him?"

The six of us leaned over to examine the lists.

"I don't really see anywhere," said Dawn after a moment. "Claudia's group, Mary Anne's, and mine are too young. Stacey's is all girls. Jessi's is perfect the way it is. Mallory's would be good because the kids are all boys, but they're younger than Shea, too. Besides, I wouldn't mind separating Shea and Jackie."

"Here's another odd list," said Claudia. "I'm not sure what Archie Rodowsky will think of Suzi and Nina. At least the three of them are about the same age."

"I think we've made good choices about the babysitter in charge of each group," Mary Anne pointed out. "Kristy, Andrew would want to be with you."

341

I nodded. "I know."

"And Claud, you're a good choice for Jamie and the Perkins girls. I think I'm the only one who will handle Jenny. Dawn knows Suzi Barrett really well. Jessi *has* to stick with Matt and Haley since she's the only one of us who knows sign language really well. Mallory will be good with the boys, and Charlotte Johanssen will just *die* to have her old sitter back. Remember how much she loved Stacey?"

"Boy, do I!" I said. I looked at the lists a few moments longer. "Okay," I said at last. "We know the groups are going to get all mixed up anyway, but they *will* be helpful. And I think these are the best we're going to do. Do you all agree?"

"Yes!" It was unanimous.

"Gosh, this is so exciting!" cried Mary Anne.

"Yeah!" agreed Jessi. "It's the first big Babysitters Club project I've been part of."

"Me, too," said Mal.

"And I'll finally get to meet Stacey," Jessi went on. "It's so funny to think that I live in her old house – that I *sleep* in her old *bedroom* – and I've never even met her."

"Well, it won't be long now," said Claudia.

"How many of these big – I mean, really big – projects has the club worked on?" Mal wondered.

"Three, I think. Right, Kristy?" answered Dawn. "There was the week before your mum and Watson got married when we took care of the fourteen kids, and there was the play group in Stacey's back garden, and then there was New Yor —"

Ring, ring.

Mary Anne answered the phone while Dawn kept talking. But after about a minute we realized we were listening to Mary Anne instead of Dawn.

"You won't *believe* this!" Mary Anne was saying. (I guessed the caller was not a client.) "We were just talking about New York. Dawn was going to tell about when we took the kids to the museum."

"Is that Stacey?" Claudia cried suddenly. She scrambled off the bed.

I could feel excitement mounting. Stacey! Our old club member! Soon the club would be together again. Actually, when I thought about it, I realized the club would be together again for the first time – because the seven of us had never worked together. Jessi and Mal had joined the club after Stacey had left.

Claudia and Stacey talked to each other.

Then I got on the phone with Stace. "Hi! How *are* you? I can't wait till you get here. We are going to have such a great day. You won't believe how some of the kids have changed. Andrew is so much taller!

Oh, and you can meet Matt and Haley Braddock and Becca Ramsey. And Jessi, of course."

"Same old Kristy," said Stacey, and I could tell she was smiling. "I'm fine. Mum and Dad have been arguing, arguing, arguing, but it's just a phase, I think. At least they aren't arguing about *me*."

Stacey has diabetes and her parents sometimes don't agree about the way Stacey manages her disease, even when she's following doctor's orders.

"What are they arguing about?" I asked.

"Oh, who cares? I can't wait to get back to Stoneybrook. Mum wishes she could come with me. She loves Connecticut. What's up with you?"

"Get this. *My* mum wants to have a baby."

"No!"

"Yeah. She and Watson want a baby. Can you imagine? I think they're too old," I said, which I knew wasn't true at all.

I changed the subject quickly, and Stacey and I talked a little longer. I told her about the day we'd planned, and about the groups we'd lined up. By the time we got off the phone, I was just as excited as Claudia about seeing our blonde-haired, blue-eyed, super-sophisticated former treasurer.

9th CHAPTER

"Aughh!"

"I don't believe it!"

"Oh, my gosh. She's here!"

"IT'S STACEY, EVERYBODY!"

It was 5:25 on the day before the Mother's Day surprise. Mary Anne, Dawn and I had just entered Claudia's room for a club meeting – and found Claudia and Stacey there. Stacey was sitting on Claud's bed, as if she'd never left Stoneybrook. Claud was the one who'd shouted, "IT'S STACEY, EVERYBODY!"

Stacey leaped up, and she and I and Mary Anne and Dawn began hugging and jumping up and down – a group hug. And then we all began talking at once.

"You're here in time for the meeting!" I exclaimed.

345

"When did you get here?" Mary Anne wanted to know.

"Just a little while ago," replied Stace. "I caught an early train."

"You cut your hair!" Dawn cried.

"Yeah, a little. Do you like it? I went to this really punk place and told the guy not to make it too punk."

"We love it!" said Mary Anne, speaking for all of us.

We were finding places and settling down. I sat in the director's chair, of course. Dawn and Mary Anne squeezed on to the bed with Claudia and Stacey. We left room on the floor for Mal and Jessi.

"This is just so incredible," said Stacey. "Here I am, sitting in on a meeting of the Babysitters Club. A *real* meeting, not like the ones we had when you all came to visit in New York. I feel like I never left here."

"I wish you never had," said Claud wistfully.

Stacey leaned over suddenly and put her arms around Claudia. Claud is not a big crier, but that hug was all it took for the tears to start to fall.

"I miss you so much," she said to Stace. And I knew what she *wasn't* saying: that Stacey was Claud's first and only best friend. And that she hadn't made a new best friend since Stacey had left.

It was while this was going on that I glanced up and saw Jessi and Mallory hovering uncertainly in the doorway to club headquarters. Jessi looked confused, and Mallory looked bewildered.

"Come on in, you two," I said loudly to our two junior officers. "This isn't going to be a crying session . . . is it, Claud?"

Claudia pulled herself together. She wiped her tears with a tissue and sat up as straight as she could.

And Stacey slid off the bed. "Mal!" she exclaimed. "I am *so* glad to see you! Congratulations on becoming a club member."

"Thanks, Stacey. Babysitting really is more fun this way. It's nice to be official."

Stacey turned to Jessi. "I suppose you're Jessi Ramsey," she said.

This comment was a little unnecessary. For one thing, Stacey knows that Jessi is black. I'm sorry to be so blunt, but that's the truth, and anyway I'm always blunt. Besides, who else would Jessi be? We don't bring guests to meetings.

"Yes," said Jessi. "Hi. I moved into your bedroom."

We laughed at that.

"Jessi is a terrific sitter," I said, as Stacey returned to the bed, and Jessi and Mal dropped to the floor. "She even learned sign language so she could communicate with a deaf boy."

"Matt Braddock," added Jessi, looking a little embarrassed by the attention she was getting. "You'll meet him tomorrow. And his sister, Haley."

"Great," replied Stacey. "I can't wait. I can't wait to see the other kids, either. I bet they've really changed."

I was about to say that she might not even recognize some of the youngest ones, when I realized that it was 5:35. "Oh! Order!" I cried. "Order! I cannot believe I forgot to bring the meeting to order, and we're five minutes late!"

"Kristy," said Claudia, "it isn't going to kill you."

I knew Claud sounded annoyed because she was still upset, but even so, I replied testily, "Well, I know that. But let's get going here. Hmm. No subs to collect. Any club business?"

To my surprise, Stacey said, "Can I ask a question?"

"Of course."

Ring, ring.

"Oops, the phone. Hold on just a sec, Stace."

I was reaching for the phone (so were Mary Anne and Jessi), when Stacey leapt up. "Can I answer it, please? It's been months and months since I've taken a –" (*Ring, ring.*) "– job call here with you lot."

"Sure," the rest of us replied at once.

Stace reached for the phone. "Hello, Babysitters Club," she said, sounding like she might either laugh or cry.

(This meeting was emotional for everyone.)

"Doctor Johanssen!" Stacey suddenly exclaimed. "Doctor Johanssen, it's me, Stacey! . . . No, you called Stoneybrook. I'm visiting. I'm here for the weekend. I'm going on the Mother's Day outing tomorrow." (Dr Johanssen is Charlotte Johanssen's mother, and in case you can't tell, she and Stacey are pretty close. Stacey helped Charlotte through some rough times, and Dr Johannsen helped Stacey through some rough times.) "Oh, don't tell Charlotte I'm here, okay?" Stacey was saying. "I'll surprise her when she gets to Claudia's tomorrow. . . Yes. . . Right. . . Oh, a sitter for next Saturday? Boy, I wish it could be me. . . No, I'm leaving the day after tomorrow. But we'll get you a sitter. I'll call right back, okay? . . . Okay. 'Bye."

Stacey's face went from excited to disappointed and back to excited while Mary Anne looked at our appointment pages. The Johanssen job was for the evening, and we signed Dawn up for it.

Stacey called Charlotte's mother back. While she did, Claud began searching the bedroom.

"What are you looking for?" asked Mal, as if we didn't know. (It must have been junk food.)

"Junk food," Claud replied. "I bought a

bag of those liquorice strings. I thought we could make jewellery out of them before we ate them. Oh, and Dawn and Stacey, I've got pretzels for you. I know that's not very interesting, but at least the pretzels look like little goldfish."

Claud handed around our snacks.

Then Stacey said, "Um, I had a question. . . ?"

"Oh, right!" I exclaimed. "Sorry, Stace."

"Well, I was just wondering. Could we run through tomorrow's schedule and all the details? I mean, like, who exactly is coming, and if we should expect any problems. I don't even know some of these kids. And you've talked about a carnival, but. . ."

"Oh, of course we'll run through everything," spoke up Mary Anne, who was playing with a liquorice bracelet. "We didn't mean to leave you out. It's just that *we've* been making plans for so long."

"Anyway, it'll probably help *us* to run through the schedule," added Jessi.

I jumped right in. "I'll start," I said. I try hard not to be bossy, but after all, I *am* the chairman.

"The kids will come here at eight-thirty," I began. (I was trying to make liquorice earrings.) "The fathers have been really co-operative, and they're doing all the stuff like dropping the kids off and picking them up. They're making the lunches, too, and watching any brothers and sisters who are too little —"

"Or too big," added Dawn.

"— to come on the outing. So the mums will really have a day off tomorrow."

"One exception," interrupted Mallory, as she plaited together three strings of liquorice. "The Barretts."

"Oh, yeah," said Stacey. "No Mr Barrett."

"Right. So guess what?"

"What, Mal?"

"My dad is going to be Mr Barrett for the day. He's going to bring Buddy and Suzi with my brother and sisters in the morning and pick them up at the end of the day. He's going to make their lunches, and he's even going to babysit for Marnie all day."

"You are kidding!" cried Stacey.

"Nope. Dad loves little kids. Why do you think there are eight of us?"

We laughed, and I added, "Marnie ought to spend the day with my mother. It would be like a dream come true for Mum."

At that point we almost got off the subject, but I went ahead and outlined the day for Stacey (in between a few job calls).

We were just finishing when Mimi wandered into Claudia's room, and I mean *wandered* in. She looked like someone who had gone for a walk without any destination in mind. She just sauntered in – and then she seemed surprised to find us there.

"Oh . . . oh, my," said Mimi vaguely.

Claudia leaped to her feet. "What are you looking for, Mimi?"

"The . . . cow."

The cow? My friends and I glanced at each other. But not one of us was tempted to laugh. This was not funny.

Claudia took her grandmother by the arm and led her gently towards the doorway. On the way, Mimi seemed to "wake up".

"Dinner is almost ready, my Claudia," she said. "To please help salad with me after meeting." (That was normal for Mimi.)

"Sure," agreed Claudia. "Just a few more minutes. Then Stacey and I will come and help you."

Mimi left. An awkward silence followed. Jessi tried to make conversation. "I really like your bedroom, Stacey," she began. "You should come over and see it, if you want. The wallpaper is so pretty that we left it up, and my furniture looks great. . ." She trailed off.

Claudia had tears in her eyes again.

Stacey said, "I decided I like it better than my room in New York."

Another awkward silence. Both Mallory and Jessi looked awfully uncomfortable. I wondered if they felt like the new kids in the street all over again.

"I wonder," I said, as if it were the only thing on my mind, "what my mum will look like when she's pregnant."

"Like she's going to tip over," replied Dawn, and we all cracked up. We became ourselves again. In the last few moments of the meeting we giggled and laughed and told school gossip to Stacey. Then the meeting was over. We left Claudia and Stacey, calling to each other, "'Bye!" and "See you at eight!" and "Remember your lunches!"

That night, I could barely get to sleep. I was so, so excited about the Mother's Day surprise.

10th CHAPTER

Saturday

I can't believe it. I am actually writing in the Babysitters Club notebook! I wasn't sure if this would ever happen again. Mum and Dad made all sorts of promises about letting me come back to Stoneybrook to visit but, well -- a club event is almost too good to be true.

Anyway, the morning of the Mother's Day surprise got off to a shaky start. It reminded me of the first day we took care of those fourteen kids at Kristy's. Even though the kids in today's group know each other (mostly) and know us, there are just some children who never like to be left in a new situation. And they let you know by crying....

Well, we did have some tears, but Stacey was right. The morning got off to a shaky start – but not a bad one.

However, the kids' tears came later in the morning. *Stacey* began her day much earlier, waking up on the mattress that had been placed in Claudia's room. She yawned and stretched. She looked over at Claudia. Claudia was dead to the world. She could sleep through a tornado. No, a tornado and a hurricane. No, a tornado, a hurricane, a major earthquake and a dust cart. Luckily, when Claudia *does* wake up, she gets up fairly easily.

But Stacey didn't need to wake her up straight away, which was fine because Stacey wanted to lie in bed and daydream. Actually, what she wanted to do was "rememberize", which was an old word of hers meaning "to remember something really well."

She rememberized the first time she ever met Claudia. It was the beginning of seventh grade – I think it might even have been the first day of school – and they ran into each other in the hallway. I mean, ran *right* into each other. Each of them was a bit angry because the other was dressed in such cool clothes – and each wanted to be *the* coolest. But they calmed down and became very close friends.

Then Stacey rememberized the first time she babysat for Charlotte Johanssen. After that, she was about to begin a good day-dream about Cam Geary, the gorgeous star, when she realized she really ought to wake up Claudia.

So she did. She leaned across Claud's bed and tapped her on the arm.

"Claud. Hey, Claud!"

"Mmm?"

"Time to get up."

"Why?"

"Mother's Day surprise. The kids'll be here in just a couple of hours."

"Oh!"

Claudia was up in a flash, and she and Stacey got dressed.

Now, here's a big difference between them and me. That morning, I dressed in my jeans and running shoes, a T-shirt with a picture of Beaver Cleaver on it, and my collie dog baseball cap. Then I added my SHS (Stoneybrook High School) sweat shirt that used to belong to Sam, since the weather would probably be chilly in the morning.

Stacey, however, put on a tight-fitting pink jumpsuit over a white T-shirt, lacy white socks and those plastic shoes. What are they called – jellies? And Claudia wore a pale blue baggy shirt over black-and-blue leopard-spotted trousers that tied in neat knots at her ankles. On her feet she wore purple trainers. And they both wore loads of jewellery and accessories, like big,

big earrings, and headbands with rosettes on them, and nail polish. Claudia even wore her snake bracelet. Honestly, what did they think we were going to do? Enter a fashion show?

Oh, okay, I'll admit it. They looked great And I was a teeny bit jealous. I wouldn't even know *how* to dress the way they do.

Anyway, Stacey and Claudia ate a quick breakfast – they were both rather nervous – and then waited for the rest of us to turn up.

"You girls eat like hawks," said Mimi, while they waited.

"She means 'birds'," Claudia whispered to Stacey.

Stacey nodded.

"What happen today?" Mimi wanted to know.

Claud and the rest of the Kishis had only explained this to Mimi about a million times already, but Claudia tried again.

She was half-finished when the bell rang. Stacey ran for the door. She opened it and found – me!

"Hi!" I cried.

"Hi!" replied Stacey. (We were both a little *too* excited.) "You're the first one . . . oh, but here come Jessi and Mallory."

We all arrived before eight o'clock.

"What needs to be done?" asked Stacey nervously.

"Divide up the group tags," I answered.

357

We had decided that we would colour-code our groups. My group was red, Mary Anne's was yellow, Jessi's was green, and so on. It would help the kids to know who they were supposed to be with. It isn't a very good idea to let kids go out in public places wearing name tags, but we decided that if, for instance, I was wearing a red tag around my neck, and so were Karen, Andrew and Shea, at least they'd know the four of us were supposed to stick together.

So at our Wednesday club meeting that week, we'd cut twenty-eight circles out of cardboard and strung them on wool. They looked like large necklaces. Now we each put one on.

Stacey and I looked at ourselves in a bathroom mirror.

"Ravishing," said Stacey.

I giggled.

"Kristy?" Mal called. "Claud wants you."

"Okay!" I replied.

Stacey and I ran downstairs and found the rest of the club members in the kitchen with Mr Kishi and Mimi.

"Could you just tell Dad about the lunches again?" Claudia asked me.

"Oh, sure," I said. "All the kids are bringing packed lunches. We're going to leave the lunches here – if it's still okay with you – and then, if you don't mind, could you drive them to Carle Playground at twelve-thirty? We'll meet you there. That way, we won't have to carry the lunches around the carnival all morning. Is that okay with you? We'd really appreciate it."

Mr Kishi smiled. "It's still just fine. Mimi is going to help me."

But all Mimi said then was, "I've got to get that box over to the planet." She was gazing out of the window.

Ordinarily, one of us might have burst into tears then. We were frustrated by not understanding how Mimi's mind was working these days. We wanted badly to understand.

But the doorbell rang.

"Someone's here!" cried Stacey, leaping to her feet. "The first kid is here!"

All seven of us raced for the Kishis' front door.

Not one but six kids were crowded on to the doorstep with their fathers: Jackie, Shea and Archie with Mr Rodowsky, Myriah and Gabbie with Mr Perkins, and Jamie with Mr Newton.

"Hi, you lot!" we greeted them.

We babysitters stepped outside with the colour tags, and the fathers left after kisses and hugs and goodbyes. We thought the kids would feel more comfortable in the garden, where they could run around.

I was about to explain the tags to them when Jamie shrieked, "Stacey!" He ran to her and threw his arms around her legs. "You came back!"

"Just for a visit," she told him. "Boy, am I glad to see you! I think you've grown another foot."

Jamie looked down. "No. I've still got just two," he replied, but he was smiling.

"Okay," I said loudly, clapping my hands. "I have something special for each of you to wear today." I handed out the tags (Shea Rodowsky said he felt like a *gi-rl*) and then – Becca Ramsey and Charlotte Johanssen arrived.

They were wearing plastic charm bracelets and were so busy comparing the charms that Charlotte didn't see Stacey.

Finally, as Mr Ramsey was leaving, Stacey stepped up behind Char and tapped her on the shoulder. "Excuse me," she said. "Can you tell me where I could find a Charlotte Johanssen?"

"I'm —" Charlotte started to say. She turned around. She looked up. Her eyes began to widen. They grew and grew and grew. "Stacey!" she managed to say, gasping.

Becca grinned. She was in on the surprise.

"I'm back for the weekend," said Stacey in a wavery voice. Then she knelt down, held her arms open, and Charlotte practically dived into them. Stacey held Charlotte for a long time.

360

"Yuck," said David Michael, who was watching. He and Karen and Andrew had just arrived.

"Okay, kiddo," I heard Watson say to Andrew. "See you this afternoon. Have a great time at the carnival. I know you'll have fun with Kristy and Karen and David Michael."

Well, even with me there, Andrew was the first of our criers. The next crier was Suzi Barrett. She looked pretty confused as Mr Pike dropped her off along with her brother and four of the Pike kids. Then Jenny Prezzioso began to wail. And finally Archie Rodowsky joined in, even though he'd been fine before.

"Oh, boy," said Stacey.

Two of us took the criers aside and tried to quieten them. They had just calmed down (after all, they knew who we were, where they were, and where they were going), when Mr Braddock brought Matt and Haley along.

Silly old Jenny Prezzioso let out a squeal. "Is *he* coming?" she exclaimed, pointing to Matt.

Mr Braddock was leaving – so Haley made a beeline for Jenny.

"Do you want to make something of it?" she asked fiercely. "You've got a problem with that?" (Haley is a *really* nice kid, but she is super-protective of her brother.)

"No," said Jenny in a small voice. To

361

her credit, she did not start to cry again.

"Kristy," said Stacey, "introduce me to Haley and Matt, okay? Oh, and to Becca. I don't know Jessi's sister."

I nodded. Then I spoke to Jessi. Jessi and Haley introduced Matt to Stacey, using sign language. Then Jessi introduced Becca to her.

"I think," I said, "that you know everyone else, Stacey. It's pretty much the same crowd."

"Just older," she replied. She smiled ruefully.

"Well, let's get this show on the road!" I said brightly. "Are you kids ready for the carnival?"

"Yes!"

"Are you wearing your tags?"

"Yes!"

"Have you been to the bathroom?"

"Yes." . . . "No." . . . "I have to go again." . . . "Me too." . . . "I went at home." . . . "I don't *want* to go."

It took nearly half an hour for everyone to use the bathroom. When we were ready, we set out for Sudsy's Carnival.

11th CHAPTER

"We're really, really going to the carnival!" exclaimed Jamie Newton, as my friends and I led the twenty-one kids along the pavements of Stoneybrook. "Oh, *give me a comb*," he sang.

I looked around and smiled. The groups were staying together. (So far.) And oddly enough, my funny little group was working out nicely. Because Andrew had cried earlier, Shea was very protective of him. And Karen seemed to have a crush on Shea. She hung on to every word he said, and gazed at him as if he were a superhero. Shea was playing the part of their big brother.

From the other children around me came excited comments:

"I'm going to ride on the big wheel!"

"Oh, I hope there's a roller coaster!"

363

"I'm going to win a teddy bear for my sister." (That was Jamie.)

"I wonder what a sideshow is."

"Is there *really* such a thing as a bearded lady?"

"My daddy told me there used to be a circus man named P.T. Barnum, who said there's a sucker born every minute."

"What's that mean?"

A shrug. "Don't know. . . I hope there's candyfloss."

At that point, Stacey turned to me and said, "How are we going to pay for all this? The kids want rides and food and tickets to the sideshow. I don't blame them. I would, too, if I were their age, but . . . this morning is going to be expensive."

"Don't worry," I told her. "First of all, we decided no food at the carnival. We want the kids to eat their own lunches later. Second, we found out how much most of the rides and attractions at Sudsy's will cost and realized that we have enough money for each kid to do three things. And third," (I grinned) "every single kid came with extra money – either part of his pocket money, or a little something from one of his parents, so we don't have to —"

"THERE IT IS!"

The shriek came from Jamie, who was at the head of the line with Claudia and the Perkins girls. We had rounded a comer, and in the huge car park behind Carle

Playground was Sudsy's Carnival. It spread out before us, a wonderful, confusing mess of rides and booths, colours and smells, people and even a few animals.

The kids looked overwhelmed, so we walked in slowly, trying to see everything at once. There was a big wheel, a merry-go-round, waltzer, a train, a funhouse and a haunted house. At the railings were a penny pitch, a hoopla, a horserace game, a shooting gallery and a fish pond for the littlest kids. The sideshow tent was set up at one end of the car park, and wandering among the crowds were a man selling oranges with fizzle sticks in them, an organ-grinder with a monkey, and – Jamie's precious clown selling balloons.

"Oh, my goodness," whispered Shea Rodowsky, taking it all in.

Even he was impressed. I took that as a good sign.

Impressive as it was, though, the carnival wasn't all *that* big. I mean, it was just set up in a car park. Still, there was plenty to see and do. We sitters wondered where to start.

The kids solved the problem for us. Karen had spotted the haunted house.

"Please, please, please can we go into that haunted house?" she begged.

I hesitated. Would it be too scary? I glanced at my friends and they just shrugged.

So what? I thought. How bad could it be?

Sixteen of the kids wanted to walk through the haunted house. (Andrew, Archie Rodowsky, Suzi Barrett and Gabbie Perkins were too young, and prissy Jenny announced that the house would probably be filthy dirty.) So Mary Anne stayed outside with them (she looked relieved), and the rest of us paid for our tickets and filed into the house.

"Where are the cars?" asked Karen. "What do we ride in?"

Not long ago, we had been to Disney World in Florida. We went on this incredible ride through a haunted mansion.

But that was Disney World, this was Sudsy's.

"You just walk through this house, Karen," I told her.

Karen looked disappointed, until we turned the first dark corner – and a ghost suddenly lit up before us. Shea, Buddy Barrett, Nicky Pike and David Michael burst out laughing. A few kids gasped. Karen shrieked.

"It's all right," I told her, taking her hand.

We passed through the Death Chamber. "Cobwebs" swept over our faces. "Thunder" roared overhead. And a very realistic-looking bolt of lightning zigzagged to the floor with a crackle and a crash.

"Let me out!" cried Karen, as a headless ghost floated by. "Let me out!"

"Karen, I can't. We're in the middle of the spook house. We have to keep going. There's no other way out."

"Oh, yes there is," said an eerie voice.

I almost screamed myself before I realized that the voice sounded weird because it was coming from behind a mask.

"I work here," said a person dressed as a mummy. "There are exits all over the place. I can let you out if you want."

"Karen?" I asked.

"Yes, please," she replied, shivering.

I tapped Claudia, who happened to be standing right behind me, and told her that Karen and I were leaving. "The rest of you will have to watch the kids. Karen and I will meet you at that bench near Mary Anne."

"No problem," replied Claudia.

The groups were all mixed up, but it didn't seem to matter.

The mummy discreetly opened a door in a pitch-black wall, and Karen and I followed him into the bright sunshine.

"Whew," said Karen.

The mummy removed his mask. He was a she.

"Thank you so much," I said. "I suppose we were a little panicky." I was trying not to lay all the blame on Karen.

Karen looked at her feet in embarrassment anyway.

The mummy smiled. "My name's Barbara," she said. "And don't feel bad. At least once a day, someone needs to use one of the special exit doors." She knelt in front of Karen. "I'll tell you some secrets," she said.

Tell Karen secrets? That was like telling secrets to the National Broadcasting Company.

"I'll tell you how they do the special effects," Barbara went on, "but you have to promise never to reveal the secrets."

Oh, brother, I thought. All of Stoneybrook would know within a week.

By the time we reached Mary Anne, the other kids were emerging from the haunted house. They were excited, and so was Karen, who was bursting with her precious knowledge.

"Rides! Rides! Let's go on rides!" chanted Vanessa Pike.

The chant was taken up by the other kids, so we set out across the car park. Before we were halfway there we were stopped by —

"The balloon-seller!" exclaimed Jamie.

Only he turned out to be a balloon-giver. The clown handed a free Sudsy's Carnival helium balloon to each kid. Then he walked away.

"What a nice man," said Suzi Barrett.

We sitters began tying the balloons to the kids' wrists and our own. Just before

Mallory could tackle Jackie Rodowsky's, it slipped out of his hand and floated away.

"Oh, Jackie," cried Mallory in dismay, even though he *is* our walking disaster. We know to expect these things.

But Jackie didn't look the least bit upset. "My balloon is on its way to the moon, you know," he said. "That's where these things go." He pointed to the colourful garden of helium balloons around him.

"They go to the moon?" repeated Nina Marshall.

In a flash, the kids were slipping the balloons off their wrists.

"My balloon is going to the moon, too," said Claire Pike.

"Yeah," agreed Myriah Perkins.

"Not mine," said Jamie firmly. "Mine is for Lucy." He held out his wrist so Claudia could tie his balloon to it securely.

Balloonless (or almost balloonless) we reached the rides. Suddenly, my friends and I could hear nothing but, "I'm going on the waltzer," or, "I hope we get stuck at the top of the big wheel," or, "Look, Gabbie, a train."

I smiled. I kept smiling until I heard a voice say, "*Please* let me go on the waltzer with you, Nicky."

"No way," he replied.

"No way is right, Margo." I looked around for Mallory. "Mal," I said urgently, running over to her and her purple group, "Margo wants to go on the waltzer."

"No. Oh, no."

Margo is famous for her motion sickness. She gets airsick, carsick, seasick, you name it. So you can see why the waltzer was not a good idea.

Mallory ran to her sister. "Margo," she said in a no-nonsense voice, "you can't go on any rides."

Margo's face puckered up. "But everyone else is going on something. Even the little kids are going to ride on the train."

The train was pretty boring. All it did was travel slowly around a track in a circle. The kids sat in the cars and rang bells.

"Hey," said Mallory, "you could go on the train, Margo. That wouldn't make you sick. At least, I don't think so."

"The train is for babies!" cried Margo, looking offended.

Mallory and her sister watched the rest of us line up for rides we'd chosen. At last Mal said, "We-ell . . . maybe you could ride on the merry-go-round, Margo. You can sit on one of those fancy benches. I don't want you on a horse that goes up and down."

"All right," agreed Margo, brightening. Mallory accompanied her sister on the roundabout. They sat on a red-and-gold bench. The music started. The ride began. It went faster and faster until —

"Mallory," said Margo suddenly, "I'm dizzy. I don't feel very well."

The words were barely out of her mouth before Margo's breakfast was all over the floor of the merry-go-round.

The Sudsy's people were not too happy. Neither was Stacey, who had seen the whole thing and started to feel sick herself.

It was time for quieter activities. We left the rides. Some of the kids played games and won prizes. Jamie tried desperately to win a teddy bear for Lucy, but all he could get was a water pistol.

The younger kids had their faces made up.

Mallory and Margo sat in the first-aid tent.

Jessi's group peeped into the sideshow tent and decided it looked like a rip-off.

By 12:15, half the kids were begging for candyfloss and popcorn, so we left Sudsy's. It was on to Carle Playground for lunch.

12th
CHAPTER

"But . . . but . . . box is not at planet. No, I mean is at planet, but where are my forks? And TV people. I try to watch *Wheel of Fortune*, and TV people are bother me. Will not leave alone."

I glanced at Claudia. My friends and I and the children had just reached Carle Playground, and there were Mr Kishi, Mimi and our lunches.

And as you must have guessed by now, Mimi was having some trouble again. I think it was because she wasn't quite sure why she was at a playground with her son-in-law, her granddaughter, her granddaughter's friends, twenty-one children and twenty-eight lunches. It could confuse anybody.

I gave Mimi a kiss and told her not to worry about the TV people.

Mimi flashed me an odd look. "TV people? What TV people? We have lunch to hand out. Better begin. Big job. Where is Claudia?"

Mimi fades in and out.

I found Claudia. Then Mr Kishi, Mimi and my friends and I handed out the lunches. Very reluctantly, I put Margo's in her hands.

"How are you feeling?" I asked her, as she climbed onto a bench between her sisters.

"Hungry!" she replied, as if she didn't expect me to believe her.

"Really?"

"Really."

"Okay," I said doubtfully. "But eat very, very slowly."

Margo nodded seriously. "I will."

Mr Kishi and Mimi slid into the car then and drove back to their house.

The twenty-eight of us sat down and began eating right away. (We were starving.) We took up three entire picnic tables. I looked at my red group. Andrew, with a purple juice moustache, was munching away at his tuna-fish sandwich. Shea, a doughnut in one hand and an apple in the other, was watching Andrew fondly.

"I bet you're going to eat that whole sandwich, aren't you?" he said to Andrew. "That's really great. If you do, you might get muscles as big as Popeye's."

And Karen was just gazing adoringly at Shea. At one point she said, "You know how they —" but she clapped her hand over her mouth. I knew she had almost given away one of the secrets she learned at the haunted house. I'm sure she thought it would be a really terrific "gift" for Shea.

Up and down my table and even at the other tables, I could hear various comments and see various kinds of eating going on. For example:

Jenny Prezzioso is a slow, picky eater. She ate almost everything that was in her bag, but she did it in her own way. First she nibbled the crusts off her sandwiches. "Okay. All tidy," she said to herself. Then she ate the insides of the sandwiches in rows. When she had two strips left, one from each sandwich half, she began playing with them. (I think she was getting full.) She played with them until they were dirty and had to be thrown out.

Jackie Rodowsky, our lovable walking disaster, dropped everything at least once. He was like a cartoon character. Accidentally (it's *always* an accident with Jackie), he flipped his fork to the ground. As he picked it up, he knocked his orange off the paper plate it was resting on. He returned the orange, knocked the fork off again, picked it up, spilled his Coke, and while trying to mop up the Coke in his lap, knocked his fork to the ground again.

374

Mary Anne, sitting opposite him, nearly turned purple trying not to laugh.

Another kid I liked to watch was Buddy Barrett. He was the last person on earth I would have expected to be picky – but he was picky. He examined nearly every bite before putting it in his mouth.

"This has," he said, frowning. "a black speck. Look, right there." He leaned across the table to show it to Nicky Pike.

"So pick it off," said Nicky, who would probably eat something that had been rolling around in a mud puddle.

Buddy picked it off and gingerly ate the rest of the bite of sandwich.

Then there were Myriah and Gabbie, who were nibbling their sandwiches into shapes – a bunny, a cat face, a snowman and a dinosaur.

Shea ate everything practically without chewing it. He just wolfed things down – an apple, a sandwich, a bag of crisps. He finished his entire lunch before Margo Pike ate a quarter of her sandwich.

"Margo?" asked Mallory. "Are you feeling okay?"

Margo nodded. "I'm just eating slowly. Kristy said to."

I glanced at Mallory and shrugged. I hadn't meant Margo to eat like a snail, but I thought it couldn't hurt an upset stomach.

Fwwwt. Nicky Pike blew a straw paper at

Matt Braddock. Matt grinned, grabbed a straw from his sister, blew the paper at Nicky, then returned the opened straw to Haley.

Haley signed, "Very funny," to Matt.

Matt signed back, "I know."

Suddenly from the end of one table, I heard the beginnings of a song that I knew could lead to trouble – the hysterical kind of trouble in which a kid may laugh so hard that he won't be able to finish his lunch. Or worse, he'll lose his lunch.

Shea Rodowsky choked on his crisp, then laughed. And Haley Braddock laughed so hard she sprayed apple juice out of her nose.

"Oh, lord," said Claudia, looking at Haley. "What a mess."

We cleaned up Haley and her apple juice. Then we cleaned up straw papers and napkins and plastic forks.

"If you lot are finished," I announced to the kids, "please put your flasks and things back in your bags or lunch boxes. Anyone who's finished can go and play. *Quietly*, since you've just eaten."

A sea of kids rose from the picnic tables. The only one left was Margo Pike. She was now eating the second quarter of her sandwich.

Stacey looked at her oddly. But before she could say a word, Margo said, "I'm eating slowly, *okay*?" She acted as if she'd

376

been asked that question seventy-five times.

So while Margo ate, the rest of the kids explored the playground.

"Look! Horsies!" Nina Marshall called to Gabbie Perkins and Jamie Newton. She had found three of those horses on springs. They were painted like the horses we'd seen on the merry-go-round at the carnival.

"Go easy!" Claudia called to them:

The older boys found a much better activity. Shea started it. Our groups were completely mixed up again (which was okay, since everyone seemed to be getting along) and Shea, Jackie, David Michael, Buddy, Nicky and Matt were gathered around two water fountains that were facing each other.

"Hey!" said Shea. "Look!" He turned the water on, then held his thumb over the stream of water which sent it in an arc to the other fountain.

"Cool!" cried Nicky. He tried the trick with the second fountain and sent the water to the first one.

"Oh, I am so thirsty," signed Buddy to Matt. He stood by one fountain, opened his mouth, and Matt, catching on, sent a stream of water from the other fountain right into Buddy's mouth.

"Whoa, I have an idea," said Nicky. "But I have to go and get Claire. I'll be right back." Nicky went in search of his youngest sister.

He found Margo at the picnic table. "What are you doing?" he asked her.

"Still eating," she replied with clenched teeth. She took a tiny bite out of a plum.

"Well, where's Claire?"

Margo pointed to the slide, where Claire was whooshing down headfirst on her tummy. She stopped at the end and leapt to her feet like a gymnast.

"Hey, Claire! Come here!" called Nicky.

"Why?" asked Claire warily.

"Just come."

Claire followed him reluctantly to the water fountains.

"Stand here," Nicky directed her.

Claire stood between the fountains.

Nicky poised himself at one fountain. Buddy was at the other.

"Now!" cried Nicky.

Claire was hit by streams of cold water on both sides of her face.

Jessi went running to the water fountains. "Nicky! Buddy!" she began.

But before she could get any further, Claire burst out laughing. Water soaked her hair and dripped down her face, but she giggled and exclaimed, "Do it again!"

The boys, sure they were in trouble, looked at Jessi.

"Once," said Jessi. "You may do it once more. Then leave the water fountains alone."

The boys sprayed Claire, and she

practically fainted from laughter. Jessi smiled but ushered everyone away.

Margo sat at the table, putting crumb-sized bites of cracker in her mouth.

Nina, Gabbie and Jamie rocked on the horses.

By the swings, a small group of kids was gathering. Karen was at the centre of them. They were very quiet – except for Karen. I glanced at Dawn. "I'd better see what Karen's up to," I said.

I crept towards the group until I could hear Karen say, "And they use masks to make the awful —"

Karen looked up and saw me. I raised my eyebrows at her.

"To – to, um, make the. . . Oh, it isn't impor — My goodness, look at that!" she exclaimed.

Eight faces turned to see a robin sitting in an ash tree.

"Big deal," said David Michael.

"I've seen a thousand robins," added Haley Braddock.

"Yeah!" called Margo, still at the picnic table. She took a tiny bite out of her plum, most of which was still uneaten.

"Boy, are you a slowcoach," said Jenny, running to Margo.

"She is not!" cried Claire, rushing to defend her sister. "She was sick."

"She's still slow."

"No she's not!"

"Is too!"

Claire rushed at Jenny, but Mary Anne ran between them, just in time to ward off a fight.

At that moment, Andrew tripped, fell, and grazed both knees. He burst into tears.

"You lot!" I said to the other sitters. "I think it's time to go to Claudia's. We all need a rest."

13th CHAPTER

Saturday

Well, I think today went pretty well. Really. I mean, so there were a few scrapes and arguments. We were taking care of twenty-one children. What did we expect? (With seven brothers and sisters, you learn to "go with the flow" as my mum would say.) I think one upset stomach, one set of grazed knees, one argument, and a practical joke are pretty good.

Anyway, after Andrew fell, and Jenny and Claire had been separated, we left the playground. My group -- Buddy, David Michael, and Jackie -- was in fine shape. They'd had a great day so far. They'd been to the carnival, walked through a haunted house, flown balloons to the moon, ridden the waltzer, won some prizes, and discovered the greatest water fountains of all time.

A few other kids weren't quite so happy, though.

381

That's true. Mallory's group was in fine shape, while a few others weren't, but it wasn't any great problem. Everything was under control.

We babysitters helped the kids collect their things – lunch boxes and flasks, plus souvenirs from the carnival. Jamie tucked his water pistol into his lunch box. Suzi was wearing a hat that made her look like the Statue of Liberty. Myriah was wearing a plastic necklace, and Gabbie was wearing a red bracelet that said *Sudsy's* on it.

"WAHHH!" cried Andrew as we walked away from the playground. We'd washed his knees at the water fountain, using clean napkins, but they did look a little painful.

"We can get some plasters at Claudia's," Mallory said to me.

Andrew wasn't the only one crying.

"WAHHH!" wailed Jenny and Claire.

"Keep them apart," Mallory whispered to Mary Anne. "I'm not kidding. They get along okay most of the time, but when they're angry, well. . ."

I almost expected Mal to say, "It's not a pretty sight."

Anyway, poor Mary Anne had her hands full between trying to separate Claire and Jenny, and keeping her eye on Margo and her touchy stomach.

Mallory saved the day, though. We'd just reached the edge of the playground and our criers were still crying. Jamie was starting to get upset about not having won a teddy bear for Lucy (even though he had a balloon for her), and Nicky and Buddy were walking behind Vanessa, trying to see if they could touch her hair without her noticing.

Trouble was brewing.

So suddenly Mallory let loose with, "*The ants go marching one by one —*"

"*Hurrah! Hurrah!*" chimed in Nicky and Mal's sisters.

"*The ants go marching one by one—*"

"*Hurrah! Hurrah!*"

"*The ants go marching one by one,*" sang Mal, "*the little one stops to suck his thumb, and they all go marching down . . . beneath . . . the earth.*"

Most of the kids were looking at the Pikes with interest. The criers had stopped crying. The complainers had stopped complaining. The teasers had stopped teasing.

So the song continued. The kids didn't know it, but they chimed in when they could. They always had to stop singing to find out what the little one did, though. (Two by two, he has to stop to tie his shoe. Three by three, he falls and cuts his knee.) The song occupied the kids all the way to Claudia's house, by which time we were pretty glad to hear it end. Mallory knew only twelve verses, and we heard each of them a number of times.

"Just be glad it wasn't 'Ninety-Nine

Green Bottles Hanging on the Wall'," said Stacey, looking pale.

"Shh!" I hissed. "One of the kids might hear you."

At Claudia's we sitters went into action.

I took Andrew into the Kishis' bathroom, washed his knees again, put some first aid cream on them, and then applied a fat plaster to each one. Andrew liked the plasters a lot.

"I feel better already!" he announced.

By the time we were outside again, things were going so smoothly I was amazed. The kids – all of them – were gathered under a tree with Mallory, Stacey and Jessi, who were singing with them while the rest of us got organized.

I kept hearing snatches of song, most of them sung by Mallory.

I heard: "*I've got sixpence, jolly, jolly sixpence. I've got sixpence to last me all my life. . .*"

Then I heard: "*Oh, we ain't got a barrel of money. Maybe we're ragged and funny. . .*"

And then: "*Won't you come home, Bill Bailey? Won't you come home?*"

(Where does Mal learn all this stuff?)

Finally I heard Jessi and Stacey teach the kids a round: "*Heigh-ho, nobody at home. Meat nor drink nor money have I none. Yet will I be me-e-e-e-erry. Heigh-ho, nobody at home.*"

The round sort of got lost because the

kids were saying things like, "*Heigh-ho, no one's at my house.*" But you could get the gist of it.

Anyway, while the kids were singing, Dawn, the world's most organized person, took their bags, flasks, lunch boxes, prizes and extra sweaters, and organized them under a tree. When the fathers arrived to pick up the kids, nothing would be missing or hard to locate. Meanwhile, Claudia had found her art materials and was setting them out on the Kishis' picnic tables. And Mary Anne had found the stack of books we'd borrowed from the library.

"Okay!" I called as another round of "Heigh-Ho" came to an end. "Who wants to make a Mother's Day card?"

"Me!" cried all twenty-one kids.

"Great," I replied. "Everyone will get a turn, but half of you will read stories with Mallory and Jessi and me first. Then we'll switch."

Well, *that* was not the way to present things, because all the kids wanted to go first, but at last we got the problem sorted out. Live and learn.

Mal and I read *Where the Wild Things Are* and *One Morning in Maine* and *The Cat in the Hat* to the younger children, while Jessi read *If I Ran the Circus* and a chapter from a Paddington book to the older kids.

Then it was time for the children to swap places. The ones who had just made cards brought them over to Mal and Jessi and me. They were very proud of them.

"Look," said Claire. "Look at my card."

I looked. It said, "HAPPY MOTH'S DAY LOVE CLAIRE."

Shea held his out shyly. On the front was written, "Dear Mum, you are. . ." and inside was written:

$$
\begin{aligned}
&\mathcal{M}\text{arvellous}\\
&\mathcal{O}\text{utstanding}\\
&\mathcal{T}\text{ops}\\
&\mathcal{H}\text{onoured}\\
&\mathcal{E}\text{xcellent}\\
&\mathcal{R}\text{enowned}
\end{aligned}
$$

Jackie's was covered with smudges and drops of glue, with splotches and mistakes. It read: "Dear Mum, I love you. Love, Your sun, Jackie Rodowsky."

"Beautiful, Jackie," I told him, and he beamed.

The stories began again. The card-making began again. And before we knew it, Myriah Perkins was calling, "Hey, there's Daddy!"

And there he was. He was followed by Mr Pike and Mr Prezzioso. The kids started to gather their things. The littlest ones ran to their fathers and threw their arms around them.

Our day was over. The Mother's Day surprise was over. I felt sort of sad. But glad, too, because it had gone so well. I listened to the kids chattering away: "Daddy! I went on a ride. Let's tell Mummy!" said Jenny. And, "I have to tell Mummy about the balloon man," said Jamie. And, "We found the best water fountains," exclaimed Nicky. And, "Daddy, I threw up on the merry-go-round," said you-know-who.

"Oh," replied Mr Pike, "Mummy will love to hear that."

14th
CHAPTER

"Well?" I said.

"Well what?" replied Claudia.

The children were gone. Except for Andrew, Karen and David Michael. They and I were at the Kishis' waiting for Charlie to pick us up and take us home. The rest of the sitters were still at Claud's, too. We had cleaned up every last crayon and shred of paper, but we just couldn't bear to part. So while my little sister and brothers sat under the tree and looked at the library books, the members of the Babysitters Club lolled around on the Kishis' porch.

"Well what?" said Claudia again.

"Well, what did everyone decide about Mother's Day presents?" I asked, not daring even to glance at Mary Anne. "Was the Mother's Day surprise good enough?"

"I'll say," said Mal. "It turned out better

than I'd hoped. I bet it was the best Mother's Day present Mum ever got. Especially when Dad pitched in."

"Ditto," said Jessi.

"Ditto," I said. "Mum got to spend the day alone with Watson, since Sam and Charlie went to school to help at a car wash to raise money for the football team."

"And our homemade presents are finished," announced Dawn.

"Well, they are, except for mine," said Stacey. "But Claudia's helping me, so I'll be done tonight."

"What did you make?" I asked.

Claudia, Stacey and Dawn exchanged grins.

"Personalized badges," replied Claud. "My idea," she added proudly.

"They're more like brooches, though," said Stace.

"What do you mean, personalized badges?" asked Jessi.

"You see," said Claud, "we went to the gift shop and bought things that are appropriate for our mothers. . . Well, I had to get Stacey's things for her since she wasn't here."

"Yeah," agreed Stacey, "and she did a good job. My mum can sew, and she likes to travel and read, and she likes dogs even though we don't have one. So Claudia bought a tiny aeroplane, book, thimble, pair of scissors and dog."

"And then," Dawn continued, "we mixed up the little charms with glass beads and coloured flowers, and we glued everything to a metal piece with a pin attached —"

"You can get those things at the craft shop," added Claudia.

"— and, ta-dah! A brooch. Each one different. Just for our mothers."

"Great idea!" I exclaimed.

"I, um, made a decision. I mean about Mother's Day," said Mary Anne.

Six heads swivelled towards her.

"I'm giving my father a Mother's Day present. He's been a good father and a good mother to me, or at least he's tried to be, and I want to let him know it."

"Mary Anne! That's great!" I cried. "We never thought of giving your *dad* a *Mother's* Day present."

The others were smiling, so Mary Anne began to smile, too. "You don't think it's silly?" she asked.

"No way!" exclaimed Mallory.

"What did you get him?" asked Jessi.

"A book. It's not very original, but it's hard to know what to get men. And I have to give him stuff on his birthday and Christmas and of course Father's Day, too. So I can't always be original. Anyway, I know he wants this book."

Beep, beep!

Charlie had pulled into the Kishis' driveway. Sam was next to him in the front seat. The car was sparkling clean. It looked as though they'd taken it through the car wash. Mum and Watson would be happy. The money had gone to a good cause, *and* the car was clean.

"Come on, all of you!" I called to Andrew, David Michael and Karen.

I said goodbye to my friends. Then my sister and brothers and I squashed into the backseat, and Charlie drove home.

The six of us entered our house (okay, our mansion), bursting with news and stories. But we stopped in our tracks when we reached the living room. No kidding. We came to a dead halt.

There were Mum and Watson standing next to each other, very formally, their arms linked. They looked nervous, happy, and surprised all at the same time.

Karen and my brothers and I glanced from our parents to each other, then back to our parents. Not one of us said a word.

After a few moments, Watson cleared his throat. Then Mum cleared *her* throat. Mum was the one who finally spoke.

"Watson and I have some wonderful news," she said. "We just heard it this afternoon. Let's sit down."

So we did. I sat on the floor, leaning against a couch. Andrew sat in my lap. Karen sat beside me, her head resting on my shoulder. My brothers lined up on the couch behind us. We knew this was good news – but not like we'd just bought another video recorder or something. This sounded like life-changing news.

(I was pretty sure Mum was finally pregnant.)

"Hey, Mum, are you pregnant?" asked Sam for the four-thousandth time.

"No," she replied, "but we've adopted a child."

Adopted a child! Well, that was a different story!

"You've *what*?" cried Charlie.

"We've adopted a little girl," said Watson. "She's two years old, she's Vietnamese, and her name will be Emily Michelle Thomas Brewer."

"We'll pick her up at the airport tomorrow," added Mum. "And then she'll be ours."

"We wanted to tell you about this before," said Watson. "It's been in the pipeline for so long. But we didn't want to say a word until we knew something for sure. Things kept falling through. This is definite, though."

Andrew stirred in my lap, and I knew he didn't really understand what was happening.

"So," said my mother nervously, "what does everybody think?"

What did we think? What did I think?

"I think. . ." I said, "I think this is totally fantastic!"

Suddenly I was so excited I could barely contain myself. A baby (sort of). But it wasn't Mum's and Watson's. Furthermore, I was getting another sister! I'd always thought there weren't enough girls in my family. Before Mum married Watson, it was me against three brothers. After the wedding, it was Karen and me against four brothers. Emily Michelle Thomas Brewer would almost even things up.

But it was more than that, of course. Even more than the stuff about Mum and Watson. I love kids. And we were adopting a two-year-old girl. She would be somebody to dress and play with. She would be somebody to teach things to. Things like, a family is just a group of people who love each other, whether they're brothers and sisters and parents, or stepbrothers and stepsisters and step-parents. Or adopted kids.

Sam and Charlie were as excited as I was.

"This," said Sam, "is really cool." He grinned.

"I can't wait to teach her how to play baseball," added Charlie.

"Hey, that'll be my job!" I cried.

David Michael seemed less certain. "Do two-year-olds wear nappies?" he wanted to know.

"Some of them do," answered Mum.

"Well, I'm not touching those things.

Dirty or clean. But I suppose a little sister will be okay. I mean, I've already got one," he said, poking Karen's back with his toe. "And she hasn't killed me yet."

Karen turned around and stuck her tongue out at David Michael.

"Karen?" said Watson. "What about you?"

"What about me?" Karen knew what her father meant, but she was being difficult. After a pause she sighed and said, "I thought *I* was your little girl."

Watson looked thoughtful. "You're one of them. Kristy's my little girl, too."

I didn't complain about being called a little girl. I knew that Watson was trying to make a point.

"Think of it, Karen," I said. "She's only two. Practically a baby. You can help her with things. You'll be her big sister. You can show her how to play with toys, you can teach her to colour, and you can dress her up. It'll be fun!"

Karen smiled, despite herself. "Yeah. . ." she said slowly.

"Andrew?" said Watson. "What do you think?"

"*Whose* baby is she?" asked Andrew. "Why is she coming to our house? Did her mummy and daddy give her away?"

Oops. I suppose we had some explaining to do.

Watson took care of the explaining while

Mum and the rest of us did other things.

Boy, was there a lot to do. "We have to get a room ready for Emily," said Mum. And suddenly I remembered my mother talking about our spare bedrooms.

"A room!" I said. "What about clothes? What about toys?"

"I think we have plenty of toys here for now," said Mum. "We can buy some things for a younger child later."

"Well, we don't have any clothes for two-year-olds," I pointed out.

"She'll have a few things of her own, darling," Mum said patiently. "I'll buy her more on Monday. I think the room is the most important project to tackle now. She needs a place of her own from the beginning."

"Wait a sec," I said. "You'll buy her clothes on Monday? On Monday you'll be at work. So will Watson. The rest of us will be in school. What are we going to do with Emily all day?"

Mum was bustling upstairs and I followed her. "Watson and I are taking some time off from our jobs to be with Emily," she said. "We're going to find a nanny while we're at it."

A nanny? Like Mary Poppins? Boy, were things changing. I wondered if a nanny would make my bed for me.

We started on Emily's room, all eight of us. We chose a room that was near Mum and Watson's. Some furniture was in it already, but it looked like an old lady's room. We got toys and a cot out of the attic, and put some pictures on the wall. The room began to improve. A rocking chair helped. So did a white bookshelf and an old Mother Goose lamp.

"Not bad," I said. I still couldn't believe that the next day I would have a new sister.

Andrew looked up at me. We were alone in the room while everyone else was in the basement, searching for a particular chest of drawers. I was supposed to be arranging some of David Michael's old picture books on the shelf.

"It's awful," wailed Andrew, and he began to cry. His cry wasn't one of those Kristy-I-grazed-my-knees-and-want-plasters-the-size-of-dinosaurs cries. It was a Kristy-I'm-very-confused-and-a-little-afraid cry.

I knelt down and drew him to me. "Whatever happens, you know," I told him, "you're still going to be our Andrew."

That night, I called every single member of the Babysitters Club to tell them the news. I was so excited, I didn't know how I was going to wait until the next day for Emily to arrive. But making five phone calls helped pass the time. I would say to each of my friends, "I'm going to have a new sister!"

396

And whoever I was talking to would say, "Oh, your mum's going to have a baby! That's great!"

And then I would tell my news. Each time I did, the person on the other end would have to shriek and scream for a few seconds. Then she would ask lots of questions. I was glad of that, because by the time I got into bed, I was exhausted and knew I would be able to sleep.

15th
CHAPTER

I slept okay that night, but I was up at six o'clock the next morning. I don't know the last time I voluntarily got up at that hour at the weekend. But who can sleep on the day her adopted sister is arriving? Not me.

I tiptoed downstairs and found that I wasn't the first one awake. Mum and Watson were sitting at the kitchen table, sipping coffee. A high chair had been placed at one end of the table.

"Morning, Watson," I said. Then, "Hi, Mum. Happy Mother's Day!" I kissed her cheek.

"Thanks, darling."

"I wish I had a present for you, but you got your gift yesterday."

"Oh, I know," replied Mum enthusiastically. "And it was great."

"Funny," I said. "We called yesterday's

outing the Mother's Day surprise. But I think Emily is the *real* Mother's Day surprise. At least she is to me."

"In a way she is to us, too," spoke up Watson, as I slid into my chair with a glass of orange juice. "We've been trying to adopt for quite a while. It takes time. We feel lucky to have Emily at last."

"Mum? Watson?" I asked. "Why have you adopted? You could have had a kid of your own, couldn't you?"

"Yes," said my mother, "we could have. But I've already given birth to four children."

"And I've got two," added Watson.

"So we decided not to create a seventh. We decided to find a child who's already here but who needs a home. And when we went looking, we finally found Emily."

I nodded. "I like that . . . it's weird to see all this baby stuff." The high chair was at the table, a buggy was parked by the back door, and a car seat was waiting to be taken into the garage.

Mum and Watson smiled, looking like proud new parents.

They left for the airport around noon.

When Sam, Charlie, and I told them we weren't going to leave the house – we wanted to be here for the very first glimpse of Emily – we kids were left in charge of each other.

As soon as Watson's car left the garage, I looked at my sister and brothers. "What are we going to do now?" I asked them.

We made about a thousand suggestions – and turned them down. At last I said, "I know what we're going to do. Well, I know what *I'm* going to do."

"What?" asked Sam and Charlie:

"Invite the Babysitters Club over." That would be great. Even Stacey could come. She wasn't leaving for New York until much later in the afternoon.

"Oh, no, no. Please, no!" moaned Sam.

"All those *girls*?" added David Michael.

I made a face at him. "You know all those girls. You spent yesterday with them."

"*I* didn't," said Sam. "I don't want them here."

"I thought you liked girls."

"I like girls in my class. If you invite your friends over, it's going to be like a pyjama party here."

"Oh, it is not," I replied, reaching for the phone.

"Besides, what's wrong with girls?" asked Karen.

My friends turned up within an hour. Each time the doorbell rang, Sam and David Michael pretended to faint. But I have to admit that Sam was pretty impressed when Stacey immediately suggested a good project for the afternoon.

400

"We should welcome Emily," she said. "We should bake her a cake or something."

"Make a sign," added Sam, brightening.

"How about cookies instead of a cake?" said Mal. "She's only two. She might like cookies better."

"Okay," I agreed.

"From scratch, or those packet-mix things?" asked Charlie.

"Scratch," I replied immediately. "That'll take longer, and we want to fill up the whole afternoon. If we need any ingredients, you can run to the shop."

"Oh, thanks," said Charlie, but I could tell he didn't really mind, as long as he was here when Emily came home.

"Why don't I get cookies?" asked Andrew, clinging to my legs. "Did anyone bake cookies for me when I was born?"

"I don't know," I replied honestly. What I did know was that Andrew didn't really want answers to his questions. He wanted a hug. So I gave him one.

It turned out that we had all the ingredients for chocolate chip cookies. We also had paper, scissors, string and crayons for making a WELCOME EMILY sign. We divided up the jobs. Stacey, Claudia, Mary Anne, Jessi, Sam and David Michael covered the dining room table with newspaper and went to work on the sign. The rest of us began making a triple batch of cookies.

Except for Andrew. He wandered back and forth between the projects, occasionally whining. He couldn't seem to settle down.

I stood at the table next to Dawn, who was stirring the cookie batter. She was humming a vaguely familiar song under her breath.

"What is that song?" asked Charlie.

"It's — You know, it goes, '*Lucy in the sky-y with di-i-amonds*'."

"Oh," said Charlie. "That old one."

Dawn nodded. She continued singing it softly. ". . . *the girl with colitis goes by.*"

"What?" I said.

"*What?*" cried Sam. He let out a guffaw. Dawn looked puzzled.

"It's '*the girl with kaleidoscope eyes*'," he informed her.

Dawn and I glanced at each other and shrugged.

"Either way it's a weird song," I said.

We finished our cookies. The signmakers finished their sign.

"Did someone make me a sign when I was born?" asked Andrew.

I hugged him again. Then I sat down and pulled him onto my lap. "I will always love you," I whispered into his ear. "No matter what. Even if we adopt sixteen more kids, I will always love you because you're Andrew. And so will Karen and your daddy and my mum and David Michael and Sam and Charlie and everyone else."

Andrew smiled a tiny smile. He looked relieved.

"Where should we put the sign?" asked Claudia.

We ended up stringing it across the kitchen. (We were pretty sure Mum and Watson would bring Emily in through the door from the garage to the kitchen.)

Then we piled the cookies into a neat mound on a plate and put the plate on the kitchen table.

"Well, now what?" asked Sam.

"Now," I began. I paused. "They're here! They're *here*!" I screeched. "I heard the car pull into the garage! I swear I did!"

"Oh, lord!" cried Claudia.

"What should we do? What should we *do*?" Mary Anne was wringing her hands.

"Let's stand under the sign," I suggested, "next to the cookies."

We posed ourselves – the six Thomas and Brewer kids in the front, and my friends in the back, even though Mary Anne didn't show up because she's short and was standing behind Charlie.

We were ready. Emily's first sight when she came into her new home, would be of her special sign, her welcome-home cookies, and her brothers and sisters and friends.

The door opened. Mum came in first. Watson was behind her. He was carrying

Emily Michelle Thomas Brewer in his arms.

She was fast asleep.

Mum looked at the sign and the cookies and then at Emily. I could tell she felt sorry for us. But *we* didn't feel *too* bad. Emily would see everything later.

Mum put her finger to her lips, and we all crowded silently around Emily. I knew we wanted to say things like, "Ooh, look!" Or, "She's so *cute!*" Or, "I can't believe she's my sister!" But we just stared.

Emily's hair is dark and shiny. It falls across her forehead in a fringe. Her skin is smooth, and her mouth and nose are tiny, like any two-year-old's. I wished I could see her eyes. You can tell a lot about a person by looking at her eyes.

Emily Michelle. She's my sister, and David Michael's and Sam's and Charlie's. She's Andrew's and Karen's. She's the one person in our family who isn't a Brewer or a Thomas. Her mother is Mum and her father is Watson, but she isn't *their* baby; if you know what I mean.

She's just *ours*. She belongs to Watson and Andrew and Karen, and she belongs to Mum and my brothers and me. She would bring us together. She would unite us. That was what Mum and Watson's wedding was supposed to have done. But it hadn't exactly worked. Emily just might do the trick.

Mum made motions to let us know that she and Watson were going to take Emily upstairs to her cot. I nodded. Charlie and I followed. The others stayed behind. They could see Emily later.

Charlie and I stood in the doorway to Emily's room. We watched Watson lay our new sister in her cot. We watched Mum take Emily's shoes off, then cover her with a blanket. Emily stirred and made a soft, sleepy noise but didn't wake up.

When Mum and Watson left, so did Charlie, but I tiptoed over to Emily's cot and looked down at her.

Hello, there, I thought. You are a very special little girl. I suppose you are lucky, too. You found a family. And we are lucky. We found you. Do you know how much we want you? No? Well, you will when you're older, because we will tell you.

You have a lot of brothers, by the way. You have two sisters, as well. And a mum and a dad and a cat and a dog. Someday you'll know all this.

I tiptoed out of Emily's room – my new sister's room. Emily, I decided, was the best Mother's Day present ever.

The Babysitters Club

Need a babysitter? Then call the Babysitters Club. Kristy Thomas and her friends are all experienced sitters. They can tackle any job from rampaging toddlers to a pandemonium of pets. To find out all about them, read on!